MW00834196

ERADICATION

ALSO BY JAMIE THORNTON

Feast of Weeds Book 4

ERADICATION

Jamie Thornton

IGNEOUS
BOOKS

 IGNEOUS BOOKS
PO Box 159
Roseville, CA 95678

This novel is a work of fiction. Names, characters, places, and incidents either are the product of the author's imagination or are used fictitiously. Any resemblance to actual persons, living or dead, events, or locales is entirely coincidental.

Copyright © 2015 by Jamie Thornton
Cover Art by Deranged Doctor Design
Copyedited by Melanie Lytle

All rights reserved. No part of this book may be reproduced or transmitted in any form or by any means, electronic or mechanical, including photocopying, recording, or by any information storage and retrieval system, without the written permission of the author, except in the case of brief quotations embodied in critical articles and reviews. For information please write: Igneous Books, PO Box 159, Roseville, CA 95678.

ISBN-10: 069260796X
ISBN-13: 978-0692607961

TO THE READERS WHO TRY TO DO THE RIGHT THING
THOUGH IT BRINGS THE SKY CRASHING DOWN

CONTENTS

July - Two Years After Infection

CHAPTER 1

"WE WILL RUN AND WE'LL LOSE THEM in the orchards." I looked both parents in the eyes as I said it.

We stood outside the shadow of a long, unused warehouse. Me and the Garcia family. I had helped the four of them escape this far—to the part of the landfill so hazardous the guards rarely spent time here.

The guards would pursue. We needed only to keep our head start.

The winter sun felt warm on my afflicted skin. Smells of rot and astringent chemicals floated on the breeze. My stomach grumbled for more food because breakfast had been the refugee special: weak coffee and bread that had cut my tongue.

"How do you know this will work?" the woman, the mother, said. "There is nothing to hide us. You are so young for this."

She reminded me of my own mother, or, well, pictures I had seen of my mother. Soft brown hair, oval face, and warm brown eyes.

"How can you tell?" I joked.

No one laughed.

"Mamí," the daughter said, a warning note in her voice.

I was only a few years older than the girl. Fifteen compared to her eleven years, but age no longer mattered. Well, age mattered more now than ever before. The uninfected killed the Vs and the Faints—anyone too far gone from infection—but rounded up Feebs like us into their work camps. Feebs were people infected with both the virus and bacteria, people with aged skin beyond their years, people with memories that came back as ghosts and fevers and hallucinations.

"She's a rustler," the father said. "It doesn't matter how old she is. Gabbi said she was the best."

The parents looked at each other, at me, at the bare hills that had once been green but were now yellow, the dead grasses chewed to stubs by ranging cattle and a dry winter. Not a tree or a bush or a telephone poll to hide us.

"The bare hills are a problem," I said. "The fence is two stories tall, but we're going under it and then we only need to get across the hill." And across the abandoned freeway and then into the orchards, but I decided not to point out those facts.

When my uncle had cared for me at the beginning, when I had been like a wounded animal, we spent hours together on black-and-white crosswords, jigsaw puzzles with beautiful landscapes, interlocking blocks the size of his hand that needed to separate in a certain way. This escape was a puzzle. I was good at puzzles.

"And full sun to highlight our infected skin," the mother said. "And not a single cloud or anything moving out on the valley floor to hide us and—"

"I've done it a dozen times before," I interrupted, "in other places, for others like you. I thought Gabbi told you?"

"She did," the boy piped in.

At her brother's high-pitched voice, the girl looked up. Her hazel eyes, sunk deep in wrinkled and bruised skin, stared at me like I was some kind of hero. And maybe I was when it came to smuggling Feebs out of prisons and experiments and hangings, but it made me uncomfortable.

"Okay, then you know. I never lose anyone." I said it matter-of-factly because it was the truth. In the two years since Gabbi and I had been freeing Feebs with Alden's help, I hadn't failed once. "The way we do it this time is get outside the fence and hide in the orchards."

I pointed to the trees. They were a few hundred yards on the other side of a freeway that hadn't seen traffic in years. Green leaves and fermenting fruit hung heavy from the trees, creating a dense canopy. From winters spent on my uncle's orchard ranch, I knew underneath that canopy we'd find room to run and places to hide and the rotting fruit would cover our scent from the dogs. The slight breeze would work in our favor, creating enough noise as it rustled the organic matter to allow us a decent pace without revealing our location.

But the citrus orchard was a familiar place and sometimes familiar places triggered the zombie in me. Others didn't like calling it that, but it's the only thing that made sense. I knew about three of my triggers: a slap to the face, jingling bracelets, and the smell of my uncle's sandalwood cologne.

A hand tugged at the hem of my shirt. I looked down, into the brown eyes of the boy. His plump cheeks held hints of tiredness, wrinkles, bruising—normal for our kind. An ache started in my stomach. I did not understand how eyes could look so happy outside this building of broken windows, rodent droppings, dust that tracked every shoe print.

"Don't get lost in the memory-rush. Jump up and down if you need to. Exercise helps."

I smiled. A kid reminding me what every Feeb knew. Exercise held back the memories. No one knew why, but it worked.

"Thanks." I tousled his hair.

His eyes lost focus, caught in his own memory-rush. I shook his shoulder. He flapped his arms up and down. I held back a laugh, afraid it would offend him.

His eyes cleared.

"Come on," I said.

The mother didn't move but held my gaze for a long moment. Her cheeks were lined and gaunt, aged beyond what the double infection had done. I wondered what she had endured to keep this family alive and together. My eyelids twitched, but I knew if I turned away she would not trust me. She looked at me like adults do when they are deciding whether to treat you like a kid or like one of their own. She looked at me like my aunt used to do when she was getting ready to tell me off. But then something changed. She rested a hand on her daughter's shoulder. "We must go, mamita."

The daughter brushed off her worn pants and shirt. She held out her hand. It dangled in the air until I understood and shook it. She nodded solemnly. "Thank you for taking us through the fence."

I made them cover their clothing with dirt to blend in with the yellow hillside. We dusted our hair, our skin, every inch of our clothes. The mother and father helped the little one. I helped the girl. I inspected twice, fussing about missed spots and clothing edges.

Once they camouflaged themselves to my satisfaction, we crawled to the next abandoned building. The landfill covered hundreds of acres. The work camp never used this side because of the rectangular pond and the general disrepair of the buildings here that had been used for processing hazardous waste. The uninfected ran the camp from the offices on the other side. The refugees lived in Cell Four, in makeshift tents and wooden barracks, with newspaper for insulation. Alden didn't know what this camp did even though he was part of the uninfected side of camp—and Sergeant Bennings' son.

All Gabbi and I knew was this camp didn't grow food like the other camps. Everything was barren except for the orchard—and that was left unpicked.

There had been at least six camps once. Now there were three. The other camps had fallen to the Vs—people infected with the virus that made them relive and reenact every horrible moment of their lives.

Alden had told us we needed to get this family out. He didn't share any details beyond that, but it was enough. When the rest of the runaways and I had been imprisoned at Camp Eagle, Alden and I became friends in spite of everything. He'd been helping us get Feebs out of the camps for two years. I knew I could trust him.

We hid now in Cell Three. The boy was tucked under his father's arm. The girl pressed into her mother's side. I was behind them. I was apart from them. They were so perfect.

Acidic fumes rolled off the neon green water of the pond

nearby. A headache formed behind my eyes. I forced tears away and blamed it on the chemicals. These four people, the Garcia family, were alive and together. It was my job to keep them that away. They saw me as some kind of savior, superhero, saint, and maybe I was a little of all those things. Out of all of us who helped other Feebs escape, I had helped save the most. Others like Gabbi and Ano would get V bites along the way and fall into fevers, but I was able to dodge and anticipate and escape tight spots that had gotten others killed. I would not lose any of them. People I had been tasked to save—I saved them.

"The guards patrol the fence," I said to no one in particular, except that I had to talk. "Between us and the valley floor are abandoned cattle ranches, abandoned distribution centers, abandoned vineyards, abandoned orchards, abandoned mining operations, get it?" I didn't wait for a response. The fumes made my head dizzy. "The guards wear gas masks in this section, which messes with their sight. The pond will make your eyes water, and then you'll start sneezing, and then after the sneezing, the trembling begins—"

The daughter narrowed her eyebrows and grimaced.

"—but we'll be gone before that," I finished, feeling lame. Gabbi wanted me to grow into a hard, silent type like her. Corrina didn't think it was possible. I suspected Corrina was right.

I motioned for the family to press themselves against the exterior cement wall of the last building. Maybe fifty feet stood between us and the small depression of dirt I'd hidden at the base of a pole along the fence line. Push the dirt aside and the space uncomfortably fit one large adult. We only had to get through it before anyone noticed the family of four had gone missing.

A mechanical noise filtered through the silence and froze my group. I motioned for them to hug the ground and keep their faces turned to the dirt while I did the same. The soil felt cool and gritty against my bare palms. It even smelled like chemicals, though less so than the breeze. The landfill had been closed for a number of years before the V virus had swept everything away, but chemicals always leached and containment measures always failed. That's why we were going to win.

The noise grew louder, turned into an engine. I balanced my chin in the dirt, daring to look. A deep urge to blurt out something, anything, grew inside me. A jeep with two men and guns and spotlights appeared on the outside of the fence. The vehicle kicked up rocks into the metal links, throwing sparks. I held my breath and waited for them to stop.

They disappeared around the hill's base. The engine noise faded into a silence broken only by the rustle of wind in the scrub grass.

I whispered around the grit on my tongue for the group to crawl out of the building's shadow and run for the fence.

The shuffle of our shoes coupled with our hard breathing seemed fatally loud.

I dug into my dip of dirt and pushed the pile away from the fence in deliberate strokes to the right and left, minimizing the dust cloud that might bring back the patrol. I forced back a sneeze. My eyes watered.

First the father went under the fence. The waist of his pants caught on the metal links, shaking the entire section, sending pins of reflected light that could probably be seen for miles. Blood pounded in my ears. I unhooked where his pants had caught and used my feet to push him the rest of the way.

Without waiting for him to get up, I pushed the boy through. He did not make a peep and laid himself flat on the dirt. Next came the mother. She smiled at me. I helped her through, and she squeaked when the edge of the fence scratched at her neck.

"Shh," I said. I turned for the girl.

She stood several feet away, looking back the way we'd come, looking back at the building's deep shadow.

The stillness was no longer still.

Two men with rifles and gas masks broke the edge of the shadow. One held up an object with an antenna and spoke into it.

The faint noise of an engine reappeared.

"Come on, come on!" I yelled, not caring now about quiet. Guilt tore into me. I hadn't asked for their names. They were the Garcia family. That was all I knew. We had been so silent, and then I had rambled on about the plan. I had never asked for their names. There was nothing I could call out to help her out of the memory-rush that locked up her muscles.

The mother screamed. She threw herself against the metal fence and the entire wall of it shimmered in the sun.

I ran to the girl and tackled her to the ground. I turned her face to me, her brown hair and eyes and nose a perfect match to her mother. Her hair was wrapped around her head like a crown, sprinkled thick with dust. I shook her thin shoulders.

Her head whipped around. She blinked, but did not come out.

I wondered what she relived and whether the memory-rush created a nightmare, or people she did not want to leave, or a ghost I could not see.

The littlest one shouted for his sister in Spanish.

I would not let him lose his sister. Not like this.

My hand snaked out like it had a mind of its own. I realized what I did a second too late. I slapped her sharp and hard across the cheek.

The shouts and the engine noise stopped. The men with gas masks disappeared.

I looked back at her on the ground, but we were no longer on the ground and a different woman had taken her place.

We stood in a carpeted room that had always smelled of dried-up roses, a cloying scent that reminded me of dead things ready to crumble at the slightest hint of shame. My aunt opened her eyes and gripped my wrist like she did every time she slapped me for being born a daughter instead of a son. Her long, proud nose was pointed like a hawk, her brown eyes were like beads, her grip was like a clamp.

"You are a disgrace!" She pulled her long robe closed with her other hand. "You should have died with your mother."

Tears streamed down my face. "I am sorry," I said for the millionth time, the words catching in my throat like a ball.

Her hand snaked out. The slap came as a sound first. Sharp, echoing, like the wap-wap of shoes on new linoleum. The sting came next, burning, like a million needle pricks. The heat moved from my cheek outward like a flow of lava from my head to the rest of my body until my feet burned and I could not stand still. I had to run. I had to run. I had to run.

The room disintegrated. I pounded down the hallway and out the front door, but my aunt's face remained.

I released her thin, dusty wrist. I was back on the hillside, with the girl on the ground, lost in a memory-rush. Men with masks shouted, but it was my aunt's face that moved me.

I ran away. I left the girl behind.

My brain screamed at me to go back, go back, go back. I dived under the chain-link fence instead. I sprinted by the father and mother on their hands and knees who screamed out of mouths that no longer smiled.

Wind pumped into my lungs. Gunshots sounded. The mother's screams cut off. My feet stumbled when they hit the freeway pavement. More shots and all their screams went silent. I hoped for the burn of a bullet next. I had heard the shots. One must be meant for me. Next would come the pain and I would welcome it because I deserved it, because I had abandoned them. Please, please, please. The girl had not moved and I had slapped her like a fool.

But the burning did not come and I lost myself in the orchards.

June - Three Years After Infection

CHAPTER 2

THE BOWL OF OATMEAL CONGEALED into wavy lines and then became solid on the kitchen counter. I forced my eyes to stay open because sometimes the Garcia family memory-rush faded away and then came right back.

I gripped the edge of the counter top, willing the oatmeal to stay steady. My stomach roiled and I threw up saliva in the sink. I did not curse the memory of that family and the heat that day and the way I had failed them. I had killed the girl with her crown of braids. I had killed her entire family because of my mistakes. The least I could do was remember.

My brain told itself to calm down. The girl had died almost a year ago now but that didn't matter to the bacteria and virus fighting for territory inside me. The memory-rush was a terrible side effect that kept me from an even more terrible fate: not being able to control the zombie I'd become three years ago when they'd killed my uncle.

The acid burned my throat and I spit. There was a shuffling of sheets behind me, then a low groan.

Molly.

I turned. Her right hand twitched underneath the bedsheets. That meant she was about to start up. I hurried back to the oatmeal. Once she got going, Freanz would too, and then the twins would be close behind. They were the Faints I had made it my job to take care of. There was only one of me and I needed to stop the self-pity. Everyone dealt with the memories. Mine weren't any more traumatic than Gabbi's or Ricker's or anyone else's.

"Come on, Molly," I said. "Just a little longer."

She lay on the bed, except for that hand—it hung off, as if discarded by the rest of her body. I set the teapot to boil on the little propane stove and the wooden floorboards creaked under my steps. The room smelled stuffy from old wood, old paint. The former hotel had been built in the 1850s, Corrina had said.

Molly's foot slipped out from under the bedcovers. Pale brown skin, wrinkled, dirty. She needed to be washed today, I decided.

I finished preparing our late breakfast—if the sun was any indication outside, this meal was more like a brunch. Scrambled eggs and peanut butter and crushed vitamin pills all got mixed into the oatmeal with a large spoonful of honey on top. Ano said it was what the best athletes used to eat—it contained a good balance of protein, fat, and complex carbohydrates, and the mush was easy to spoon-feed down their throats, but it was the grossest thing I could think of—to mix it all together as a gruel.

I crushed up the *galantamine* pill and spread it over their oatmeal. Someone we'd rescued from the camps last year had brought the drugs with him. He said it had been used on Alzheimer's patients. The pills worked to make some Faints wake up enough to get them to eat and go to the bathroom, and sometimes, for brief seconds, seem like they were back. The medicine brought Feebs out of the memory-fevers a lot faster too, though it didn't help with any of the other symptoms.

I wanted to banish the remains of the memory-rush, so I began chatting about plans for the day, the oncoming foot bathing, the breakfast, a possible snack for later, the book I was planning to finish. The twins usually worked themselves into an afternoon replay of a walk in the park. Today I told them if they decided to march around the room smelling imaginary roses I'd throw open the windows and let in the summer breeze.

"The oatmeal deserves a little cinnamon," I said to no one in particular, but maybe they heard me and maybe they didn't.

No one knew for sure what got through to Faints—those who'd only been infected by the bacteria.

Catch the virus and turn into a V, like something out of *28 Days Later*, or somehow catch just the bacteria and turn into something like out of *Night of the Living Dead*, but mixed with some Batman Smilex. Combine the two at the same time, like had happened with us Feebs, and you got a high-functioning zombie—that's what we were, no matter what Corrina and Gabbi wanted to believe.

A yearning inside threatened to spill tears from my eyes. My uncle had believed me. My uncle was the one who had watched all the movies with me. But the Vs got him before we could escape and now he was gone.

There was a tap at the door. It shocked me back into the room. I set the bowl and spoon on the side table and picked up a knife. The town was safe—sentries, patrols, and people looked out for each other—but still.

"Who is it?"

"It's Ricker. Come on, Maibe, open up."

I set down the knife and flung the door open, beaming a smile at him. He smiled back. Even with his shoulders hunched I barely reached his chin. His dishwater blond hair swept across his forehead, too long. His skin was red, like he'd gotten too much sun. "Have you been wearing sunscreen?"

His smile faded and he looked sideways. "Uhhh…well, we're almost out and I thought someone else might need it."

"You are the whitest person in town," I said. "No one needs it more than you!" He might have been several years older than me and streetwise on top of it, but he sure did act stupid sometimes.

"It's not that big of a deal, Maibe."

"It's not that big of a deal—for me." I held out my olive skin. To the annoyance of my aunt, I had always darkened fast. Of course, the skin was riddled with lines and wrinkles and a weird, almost ashy layer that no amount of lotion lessened, but that was normal for a Feeb. "For you—it really matters."

Ricker squinted as if faced with the sudden brightness of the sun. "You know, you sound just like Gabbi." Then he smiled. "Are you going to let me in or what?"

He wiggled his eyebrows ridiculously and I smiled. I couldn't help it. Jimmy always made me feel protective, Ano always made me feel safe, but Ricker always made me laugh. I closed the door behind him and was about to make some witty remark of my own when I saw the angry, rooster red that was the wrinkled skin on his neck.

"Oh, Ricker."

"Yes, my love?" He kept his back turned.

I walked up and poked him in the neck with my index finger. The skin turned a shocking white before it flushed again.

"Owww!" He jumped and whirled around, hand over his neck, though not daring to touch it. The look on his face, a mixture of surprise and shock, almost made me laugh out loud.

"Take it back."

"Take what back?" he said, all innocence now written on his face—his eyes wide, his eyebrows high, his other hand extended palm out.

"You have a serious handicap at the moment." I raised my finger and waved it at him in a threatening manner.

"Okay, okay." He lowered his hands, but the half-grin stayed on his lips. "You're not my love, only someone I love—"

I waved my finger close to his sunburned arm.

"Hey, okay…only someone I love and care about as I would for any true friend."

"As only friends."

He stood straight and snapped his feet together and saluted. "Yes, ma'am. Only friends."

Freanz took that moment to shout about his garbage man, and how he kept tipping the can over, and couldn't he use his damn truck pinchers to set it down right for once?

I sighed, grabbed one of the bowls, and shoved it into Ricker's empty hands. "Get some food into him quick or he'll go on about it for hours."

"I thought Faints are only supposed to relive good memories," Ricker said.

I shuddered. "Yeah, well, this IS a good memory for Freanz.

Can't you tell he's enjoying this?"

Ricker rolled his eyes and sat on the footstool. He arranged the bed pillows so that Freanz was upright. Halfway through a sentence about utility bills, the first spoonful hit Freanz's mouth. He licked his lips involuntarily and took the food without further complaint.

I sat next to Molly and mirrored Ricker, then we both fed the twins. These two ladies, Sera and Lesa, were old and gray and wispy, and they were the fun ones who liked to relive some really wild times.

"You missed morning exercises again," Ricker said.

That startled me. I remember having gone just yesterday. I thought it had been yesterday. I must have gone outside for supplies, or fresh air, or something, right? But I wasn't sure. I hadn't been sure for weeks now and mostly it didn't matter to me anymore.

Ricker stared at me, waiting for answer. I didn't want to admit I couldn't remember. "So you didn't come here just to visit?"

"Maibe, that's not what I meant."

"You can tell whoever sent you that I'm fine. I do exercises on my own. It's not like I don't know the deal."

"No one sent me."

"Just because—"

"Why do you lock yourself in here?" Ricker interrupted while feeding Sera another round.

"I'm not locking myself up." I rushed on when I saw he was about to protest. "Faints need taking care of too and I like it up here. It's peaceful." Lesa took my spoonful of food as if it were the daintiest of tea party sandwiches and then took an imaginary napkin from her lap to pat the corners of her mouth. "I can't abandon them and I can't handle watching Gabbi pick a fight with everyone in town. Especially the mayor."

"She's not the mayor."

"We all voted. There was a meeting and everything."

"I didn't vote for her."

"You didn't vote at all."

"Because power corrupts and just the fact that she wanted the job says she shouldn't have it!" He ran a hand through his hair. "I'm not saying don't take care of them. I'm saying take a break sometimes. I'm saying get back out there. Corrina and Dylan have a whole setup going for the Faints to give them care around the clock. People take shifts, you don't have to do it all yourself."

I stirred the gruel around the bottom of the bowl. "I can't do that," I said softly.

"Why not?"

I couldn't be trusted outside, not when peoples' lives were at stake, not when I'd gotten people killed, not when I froze and practically went unconscious every time I had tried to go back to rustling. "You know why."

Ricker didn't speak for a long moment. "Then it's still happening." It wasn't a question.

Ricker had been there when I'd gone back out again—to help another Feeb escape the camps a few weeks after I'd lost the Garcia family. He watched me fall to pieces even before I could step out of the van. I had ruined that whole mission and four more after it and then I had stopped trying. My Faints needed me. I could be of use with them at least. I could hide away and lose myself in their dreams and needs and the hours of the day that passed by like seconds now.

"We need you."

I shook my head and set the bowl down. Lesa also set her napkin down as if she knew breakfast was over, though I couldn't see how. "You know I can't and if you came up here just to try to talk me down—"

"I came up here because you're my friend and I wanted to spend some time with you, and Maibe…everything keeps changing. You don't know what it's like now. You're never there. People are going nuts. You're not there to talk any sense and it's not like Gabbi listens to anyone else."

A piece of oatmeal dotted Freanz's lips, but Ricker made no move to fix it. I got up and wiped Freanz's mouth. I brushed Ricker's shirt and he turned and wrapped his arms around my waist and buried his head in my hip.

He felt warm and I wanted to wrap my arms around him. Instead, I pushed down on his shoulder but he didn't let go. "Ricker."

"They're going to get themselves killed this time. It's just getting worse and worse. Gabbi's going V and Ano isn't far behind." His words were hot and muffled by my clothing.

I froze, the napkin still in my hand. "What?"

Ricker looked up. His face was blotchy and his eyes darkened. "The double infection isn't working the same anymore. Haven't you felt it?"

I remembered the smell of that chemical pool, the hazel eyes of the girl, the way her braid had crowned her head. The bacteria was supposed to keep the virus in check. If anything, my memory-rushes had been happening less, even though it was always the same awful one. Days of peace and stillness filled my life now as long as I stayed inside with my Faints.

He turned away and picked up the bowl again. The loss of his arms left a cold ache.

"They're planning a raid," he said.

"Gabbi and Ano can't just go out on a raid like they're the Terminator and everything's going to turn out all right just because they say so—"

"They're desperate for some different drugs the healer thinks will help."

"The healer?"

"The guy who brought the *galantamine* with him."

"He calls himself a healer now?"

"Gabbi and Ano think maybe he knows what he's talking about. It doesn't even matter if he's right. They're going crazy and they have to do something."

Panic closed up my throat. "I'm right here. I thought they would—I don't know, come see me or something before—"

Molly mewled and swung her legs off the bed and onto the ground. She stood up and then tumbled onto her knees as if she had forgotten how to use her muscles.

"Molly, wait!"

She crawled across the floor, faster than I would have ever given her credit. Straight for the window, not caring that glass was in her way, not even seeing it, not really. She punched at the glass as if she expected it to be soft like a pillow.

The single pane shattered and rang like a million tiny bells as the shards flowed onto her and the floor, but she didn't stop. Blood streaked her arms and face. She gripped the window ledge and pulled herself upright and then Ricker was there, holding onto her elbow. She struggled, but he picked her up so she wouldn't walk barefoot on the floor and moved her past the massacre of glass.

We made her stand still while we picked the glass out of her hair and clothes and skin. She kept that crazy Faint smile on her face the entire time. I used a clean bucket of water to rinse her wounds and then swabbed the cuts with ointment Corrina had made from her garden.

We laid her back out in bed and Ricker swept up the glass.

I didn't look at him.

I couldn't even take care of my Faints right.

"Maibe," he said, bent over the dustpan. "We need you."

"You need somebody you can count on." Which wasn't me, not by a long shot. I'd proven that months ago and I couldn't risk failing them again. But if I wanted to be really honest with Ricker, I would tell him I was scared to leave this room and the little bits of peace I could sometimes cobble together while inside of it.

"They're going on a raid and I can't stop them, but maybe you can."

"Gabbi used to listen to me, but not for a long time," I said. "Not for months."

He set a knee down and turned to me, dustpan full of glass. "Not for the six months you've been hiding in here, turning yourself into one of your Faints."

I had lost the girl who had trusted and worshiped me almost a year ago. I had tried for almost half a year to get over it, but I couldn't, my infection wouldn't let me. He knew that. He knew I had spent the last six months spending more and more time in this room because it was the only way left to me that I could help. I was still helping, wasn't I? I was doing the best I could.

I stepped over to his kneeling form. I wanted to tell him his words weren't fair, I wanted him to undo the shame he had triggered, I wanted his words to not be true.

I didn't say anything.

"Jimmy's been talking about a cure again," he said.

The shame deepened and flushed my skin. I should have been there to stop Jimmy that first time he'd found a supposed cure two months ago, but I'd already gone into hiding with my Faints. He'd turned comatose for three days. When he'd woken up I told him he was an idiot for taking the drugs on the word of someone who fancied himself a potion maker. Then I had hugged him and cried, but I had retreated to this room again.

"You know this cure isn't real," I said finally. "How many times have we tried to find it? Dr. Ferrad was the only one who knew anything about it and we never found her. It'll turn out to be nothing. Except Jimmy's going to get himself hurt again."

He set down the dustpan, stood up, and brushed the knuckles of his hand across his mouth. "I know."

My lips tingled. I held his gaze and lost myself for a moment and became all mixed up. I could hardly handle being friends and he wasn't looking at me like a friend. I breathed out and stepped back. Suddenly I couldn't be in the room anymore, not with him here.

"I'll go," I said. "But promise to watch my Faints for me, okay?"

ALDEN

He was strapped to the hospital bed. It must be a hospital bed because his back was upright, but his legs were fully extended and his hands were tied to the rails.

Something smelled bad, like body odor, and he figured it must be him.

He'd been so stupid, but Maibe needed the cure. He couldn't pass up the chance the cure really existed this time. He couldn't stand picturing her as a Feeb. Mottled, wrinkled, ashy, aged. Just looking at her made him swear he could see the virus particles infecting every cell of her body. His skin crawled when she got that blank look in her eyes.

"Why are you here?" a voice said.

Alden turned his head, searching for the body attached to such a voice. A voice that spoke in such a neutral tone he couldn't tell if it was a man, woman, or child.

He was in a room. Faint light came from somewhere above

*and behind him, barely lighting the space around his bed. He
looked gray, Feeb-gray. Adrenaline shot through his veins and
his heartbeat raced.*

  Was he a Feeb now?

  He leaned over and examined his skin.

  Clear, smooth, unwrinkled, untainted.

  A new thought came to mind. Did the Feeb-haters have him?

  *"You are not sick," the voice said again. This time it sounded
like a male voice.*

  *Alden swiveled his neck, but that was a mistake because his
head began to pound. One spot on the back of his head throbbed
like a volcano about to erupt.*

  *There, in the corner. A little rectangular speaker mounted
near the ceiling. Metal rings were attached into the cement on
the floor and low on the walls in regular intervals.*

  "Why am I tied up?" he croaked.

  *"We don't have any sort of cages in this section. Not for people,
at least." This time the voice sounded female.*

  "But why—"

  "This is a secret facility. How did you find us?"

  *A man's voice, he decided. It had just a hint of depth. He imag-
ined a skinny guy, basically hairless, thoughtless, full of nerdiness.*

  *"I'm searching for the cure," Alden said. "I'm searching for the
Feeb cure. Do you have it?"*

  *"But you don't need it." Whoever spoke now was someone
different. More childlike. Almost plaintive. It made his head
hurt. Was he talking to one person or three people? Was one of
them a child?*

  "I...It's for a friend," Alden said.

  "I'm sorry to tell you this, friend," the male voice said, "but

there is no cure. Not yet at least."

Alden flexed his hands into fists and tested the straps until they bit so deep that his skin began to turn purple.

"Stop that! Make him stop that!" The childlike voice. There was a murmured conversation, like the male voice was shushing the child. He couldn't understand what they were saying, but he could tell their were three voices. Three different people.

He looked again at the speaker but couldn't see a camera.

"Stop hurting yourself and I'll tell you how we can see you." The child's voice again.

He relaxed, mostly because his wrists hurt and the straps hadn't budged. He wasn't strong enough for this. He was never strong enough.

"Above you," the child said.

He looked up and there it was, a tiny black circle attached to the ceiling, a glint of light on the lens. Next to it there was a type of vent, like for heat, but it was so cold in there he thought it must be broken. "If I'm your friend, why am I tied up?"

"We were trying to be nice," the child said. "He didn't really mean it."

"Who are you? How did I get here?" Alden said, thinking now maybe he had been talking to a child the whole time because why would the adults let a child talk at all? He tried to remember—he had been scouting a research facility in the old manufacturing district of a small town. There had been rumors of a cure. Or at least, rumors of drugs that could help. He remembered a cave of sorts. Dogs and coyotes and fresh Vs had him on high alert. There had been people. Uninfected like him. He'd run into Gabbi, Ricker and the others out on some raid. They were after some drugs to help with the Feeb symptoms, but he'd been after a bigger

prize. A full cure. The next thing he knew he'd woken up here.

Silence on the speaker's end.

"*Do you know Sergeant Bennings?*" *Alden said, desperate to hear the voice, any voice again. He hadn't wanted to use his father's name. He hadn't wanted anything to do with his father for a long time. No matter how many times he tried to tell Maibe that, she never quite believed him. Watching how his father had controlled the camps and treated the Feebs, he knew it had been wrong, all of it was so wrong. His mother would have thought so too, but she was a Faint. She had been Faint since almost the beginning.*

He had helped Maibe get out as many Feebs as they could until Maibe had gotten too sick to do it anymore. That had almost broken him—watching her disappear into herself. And here he was, throwing his father's name around in the hope that it might save him now.

Maibe had been right all along. He wasn't built right to survive in this new world, but he couldn't bear the thought of being alone in that room with the speaker box, camera lens, and vent as his only cold company. "*Are you working with Sergeant Bennings and the council? I'm his son. I came from his camp. If you just get in contact with him—*"

"*I do not work with the council anymore,*" *the female voice said finally, and this time he sort of recognized it. He knew he should be able to place her. It made his head spin, trying to keep track of the voices without seeing their faces.*

"*I do know Sergeant Bennings,*" *she said.*

Alden didn't know what to say. What to do. "*What do you want?*"

"*The cure, of course.*"

CHAPTER 3

THE STREETS OF THIS LITTLE MOUNTAIN TOWN were dusty and full of people. Pine trees scented the air and cast stark shadows across the buildings and street. I realized it was later than I thought, more like afternoon. It had become easy to lose track of time over the last few months. What would seem like the passing of a few minutes would turn out to be hours. But I didn't mind so much because mostly that meant I wasn't thinking of the bad times, but instead reliving puzzles with my uncle.

I stepped off the wooden porch. The way to Gabbi was uphill, a short block lined with Victorians, deer fences, rusted tin roofs, planked footbridges over the creek, a dish satellite no one had bothered to remove. People noticed me. Of course they looked—they knew who I was. They were people I had helped escape. They also knew I had stopped helping.

Gabbi shared a house with Ano, Jimmy, and Ricker on this street. Brown nets covered the porch and a set of double bunks because it was too hot to sleep inside at night. A cat curled on a wooden rocking chair as if it were just another day. We'd all stayed in a nicer place at first, but then when we'd begun freeing others and bringing more of them back, the mayor kept moving us. For the good of the other survivors. Corrina was furious, Ano said it was to be expected, and we all waited for Gabbi to explode, but she kept a lid on it and stayed outside of town more and more often.

The cat ignored me as I let the screen door slam. Gabbi was going to get a piece of my mind for keeping this raid from me.

Gabbi looked up from the kitchen island and the maps she was pouring over. Her hair was cut short, almost shaved. Corrina stood next to her, brown hair long and frizzy and falling around her shoulders in waves. My hair was flat in the heat and fell in a weird curve so I kept it in a ponytail, which made it easy for Freanz to yank.

Dylan stood next to Corrina, his hand resting lightly on her hip. It had been three years since the virus first stormed our neighborhood, killed my uncle, and threw all of us together. Even without a memory-rush, I remembered Jane's blonde hair and the ugly words she spoke in the store before Corrina and I had been infected. But Dylan and Corrina were solid now.

"Well, well. The deserter returns," Gabbi said.

"Gabbi," Corrina said.

Gabbi snapped her head around and a wild look entered her eyes. Her shoulders locked up and her jaw clenched. She often lost her temper. That was the way she WAS, but this was different. I tensed. That spark of compassion she always carried in her eyes—no matter how much she tried to cover it up with anger and insults and attitude—it winked out for a second. She was going V right then and there.

Jimmy walked in from the back room. He was fourteen now. Still short—shorter than me. His dark hair hung in corkscrews, framing his face. He always had this earnest please-don't-step-on-me look. Gabbi locked onto his movement. I swore her head swiveled on her neck like something out of *Poltergeist.*

"Gabbi!" I yelled.

Jimmy finally noticed what was happening. Papers fluttered out of his hands and onto the floor.

Corrina got into Gabbi's face, only inches away, so that they were breathing the same air. Dylan reached out as if to stop her. Gabbi's expression looked mean. Corrina's expression was peaceful. She held Gabbi's gaze even though you couldn't be sure Gabbi even saw her.

"Gabriela," Corrina whispered. "You are here with your friends. You would never hurt your friends. Gabriela, you are safe. You are safe."

Long seconds of silence. Dylan rocked onto the balls of his feet. Ano moved into a sitting position on the couch, ready to jump in.

Gabbi blinked and the light came back into her eyes. "Don't call me Gabriela."

Corrina smiled, almost devilish. "It worked, didn't it?"

This was the game the two of them played. They showed they cared by doing everything they could to annoy the other one.

Gabbi rolled her eyes and looked away. Sweat dripped down her neck. She mumbled some words that sounded like a mix between an apology and calling Corrina a dumb-ass.

Corrina laughed and grabbed a bunch of papers from the ground to fan herself with them. Dylan dropped his arms to his sides. Ano laid back down onto the flower-print couch and returned a wet towel to his forehead. He never did like the heat.

"What's going on?" I said. The tension in the room was fading but I felt frantic. The puzzle pieces weren't fitting together. What was happening? Why hadn't they told me about this?

"The symptoms are getting worse," Ano said, not taking the towel off his face. "The longer someone's been a Feeb, the more episodes they're having."

"If you'd been around, you would have known," Gabbi said in a harsh voice.

"It's good to see you, Maibe," Jimmy said. His smile dimpled his cheek and light shined in his eyes. He came up and grabbed my hands. I squeezed and smiled back. I could always count on Jimmy to make me feel better.

"It IS good to see you," Corrina said. "How are your people?"

I looked down at the carpet dingy with dirt. Just that motion was enough to smell a hint of smoke still buried deep in the fabrics from who knew how many cigarettes the previous owner had once smoked inside these walls. Corrina cared about the Faints as much as I did. She was the one who had gotten us started on taking care of them.

"Good, I guess. Except Molly broke a window today."

"Is she all right?" Dylan asked.

"A few cuts, but she'll be okay. Ricker's with them right now. He said he'd watch them for me."

"Let me know if you need any help," Corrina said. "We can bring them into the main part of the church and take shifts—"

"No, thank you, I'm fine." A little upwelling of panic choked my throat. If I didn't have Molly, Freanz, Sera, and Lesa to take care of I didn't know what I would do.

"Can we get back to work now? We're leaving in the morning," Gabbi said.

"To where?"

Gabbi still wouldn't look me in the eyes as I approached the kitchen island. Well, I could deal with her anger. I wasn't a thirteen-year-old kid in awe of her anymore. Well, I was still a little bit in awe of her, but I knew how to hide it better.

She pointed to a spot on the map where several swirly black lines merged. "There's a clinic here, near one of the abandoned camps. The healer says it might have more powerful drugs than the ones we've got."

I placed my hands on the cold tile next to the map. "Since when did we start shopping for him?" I arched an eyebrow in disbelief.

"Since Gabbi went into V-mode last week and almost killed a newcomer," Ano said.

"He was teasing one of the Faints!" Gabbi said, but even she looked a little pale at the memory.

Ano set his lips in a grim line. "I've come close a few times too."

"I just go Faint," Jimmy offered. "It keeps happening more and more. Just this morning, I lost it and almost walked in front of a horse. I thought I was eating an ice cream cone on the beach." His face looked wistful. "It wasn't so bad really. I didn't mind it."

The pieces clicked into place. My stomach hollowed out at this new realization—something I had known for awhile, something I hadn't wanted to admit.

I was turning Faint.

I opened my mouth to speak but stopped when I surveyed

their faces. They knew I had been going Faint. Of course they knew it. That's why Gabbi was being so harsh with me. That's why Corrina handled me like fragile glass and why Ricker kept visiting. That's why Jimmy was looking at me now with that shining, earnest face.

"It's not only for the healer," Corrina said quietly. "The *galantamine* doesn't work on the memory-fevers anymore. We need to try something else."

"But...I don't understand," I said. I felt the sweat pooling in my armpits. The entire house smelled musty with the hot air, with our sweating bodies, with the way the infection was still surprising us with new horrors. "Is it happening to the whole town?"

Ano shook his head. "We were some of the earliest. Me and Gabbi, Jimmy, and Ricker."

"And Mary and Leaf and Spencer," Gabbi said, low but fierce.

Jimmy rubbed the scars on his arm.

I touched my own skin. I only had Leaf and Spencer carved there. Gabbi and Ano had many more names. "But what about me? Why is it already so bad for me? I wasn't one of the first."

Gabbi looked away. I waited for someone to speak but the silence stretched out. Finally Corrina said, "There were other factors in your case."

She didn't have to say the Garcia name out loud for all of us to hear it anyway. I couldn't bear that she looked at me like I was already broken. If she kept looking at me like that I really would break into a million pieces. I pushed the hair out of my eyes and wiped the sweat off my forehead.

"It showed up with us first," Ano said. "But it's affecting the whole town now."

"It's not just any old memory like before," Gabbi said. "It's either the worst ones or the best ones." She hunched her shoulders. "We need the *memantine*."

"We could use you on this, Maibe," Ano said underneath his towel, not having moved yet in spite of the tension in the air. He was always like that—too cool, except for him it wasn't an act. "You haven't been as sick as long," Ano continued. "You're still one of the best."

The ghost-memory of the girl with the crown of braids appeared at his words. She looked at me with such awe, with such faith. She stood now next to Ano, smiling, adoring. Her pigtails draped over her shoulders. "No, I can't." The words choked my throat and I held up my hands on instinct to stop him from talking even though he couldn't see me.

"She doesn't have to go," Corrina said. "You can't force her."

"Then who else can go with us? The hospital needs you here," Gabbi said. "I'm like a cripple. Ano and Ricker aren't much better off. Sorry Jimmy, but you need more practice before I let you out there—"

"Hey!" Jimmy said, an embarrassed look flushing his cheeks.

"If we don't get those drugs—"

"What about Kern and Tabitha..." My voice faded into silence at the look on Gabbi's face. Tabitha was Kern's mother. Gabbi and Kern had a thing between them, or could have, if Tabitha hadn't been crazy. Tabitha was a Feeb and she'd suckered us all into believing she cared about what happened to us when we were trapped in the camps. Then she'd betrayed that when she'd turned all the uninfected at the camp into Feebs against their will. Kern hadn't wanted to go along with his mother, but he'd stayed with her.

"We don't know where they are," Ricker said.

"We don't care where they are," Gabbi said, too quickly. There was a pause in the room as everyone acknowledged silently that she clearly did still care about Kern. Of course no one dared say this out loud.

"Okay," I said, "What about Alden? He's helped us plenty of times. Didn't he just get us those antibiotics?"

"That was two months ago," Gabbi said. "After the last of the camps fell. We don't even know where Alden is. He's not going to help. Feebs disgust him after all, notwithstanding his crush on you, of course."

I clenched my teeth. She might be trying to get me back for bringing up Kern, but it still felt like a low blow. Whatever Alden felt for me, it wasn't a crush. He cringed every time I got within a foot of him. "That's not fair. Alden's helped us a million times over." Gabbi's words finally registered. "What do you mean the camps fell? What do you mean you don't know where Alden is?"

Corrina and Gabbi exchanged a look.

"I told you we should have told her," Gabbi said.

"She hasn't been herself." Corrina turned to me, not quite looking at me. "You hardly come out of that hotel room now. I thought if you—I thought you needed more time."

My frustration rose even as a sick feeling entered my stomach. "Just tell me."

"Last time we checked," Gabbi said. "The camps are gone."

"Gone where?"

"Just gone," Gabbi said. "They've been overrun or abandoned. Some of the people must have escaped because the supplies were missing. All the Feebs are gone too, thanks for asking after them."

I cringed but plowed forward. "Why didn't you tell me? You should have told me. I would have—"

"—finally stopped acting like a coward?" Gabbi yelled.

"I'm not a coward!" I yelled back. "I'm protecting all of you. I'm useless. I might get you killed, I might—"

"I didn't say you were a coward, dumb-ass," Gabbi said.

I opened my mouth to protest. She held up her hand and the dangerous look in her eyes shut me up.

"I said you were ACTING like a coward. We've all gotten people killed. That's how this works. Even Jimmy's still walking around, Faint or not. What I want to know is—" Gabbi locked her brown eyes on me "—are you coming or what?"

I opened my throat and told myself to say, yes, I'll come. You need me, I'll come.

I whirled around and slammed through the screen door. The cat jumped out of the rocking chair as if struck by lightning. I fell down the steps and ran.

CHAPTER 4

THE STREET WAS EMPTY. The temperature was only in the upper eighties but the sun beat into you if you dared stand in it.

Laughter filtered from Betty's, the convenience store across the street—it acted as an informal hangout and supply center. I rarely went there. Too many Feebs who thought they knew me and wanted to thank me for rescuing them.

Freanz and Molly and the twins were waiting for me. I pictured climbing the wooden stairs, my weight making the planks creak. The door hinge would squeak while opening. I would smell egg and oatmeal because Ricker wouldn't have remembered to clean up.

Ricker.

He would ask how the meeting went. He would wait and listen and not say anything to make me feel bad, but it would be all over his face. He would try to swallow the disappointment. He would try to smile. But it would be in his eyes because he never could hide anything from me, especially when he was really trying to hide it.

My shoes went past the hotel without stopping.

Not quite yet. I could not face him quite yet. Even the stares I might get in Betty's would be better.

The front of Betty's was a mix of different cement structures from different decades. Slanted stairs on one side, a cracked handicap access ramp on the other. The rail painted with flaked red and green and silver. The windows were single pane and unbroken except for one that Betty had boarded over. I stepped across the threshold—just a piece of wood wide enough to hold the door in place. Signs proclaimed the store's historical significance as a trading hole and post office in centuries past. Inside, the place smelled sour, like overripe fruit.

Those first few months in town, when we'd all gotten back together and were pretty much the only ones around except for the few Faints in town, this place had smelled like a freezer gone really bad, which was exactly what had happened. The electricity was off and half the store was fouled. The smell still lingered, even though Betty had given the place a strong dose of bleach and elbow grease when she moved in.

Betty stood behind the old counter, a waist-level thing of peeling Formica. It wrapped around her in a blocky U. Alcohol and cigarettes lined the shelves behind her, like convenience stores of old—but she only took barter.

Five Feebs sat at a little card table pushed near the back wall. They had mugs of coffee and a deck of cards out. One was lost in a memory-rush and the others waited patiently, chatting, lounging, looking around. I recognized most of them, seeing as I'd had a hand in each of their rescues. I couldn't remember their names except for two of them, Bernice and Nindal—rescued at the same time from under Sergeant Bennings' nose, with Alden's help. I wondered where he was now, if he was safe, if he was infected. My heart ached. Alden had been missing for months and I hadn't even known.

A woman and small child wandered the two meager aisles of supplies Betty got through salvage or trade. The woman nudged her daughter. The child then turned to me with wide eyes and stuck a finger in her mouth. The woman grabbed her hand and toddled her over to me. I waited, knowing what was coming.

"Thank you," the woman said. "You rescued us from Camp Eagle."

I pressed my lips together and forced a smile.

She waited as if hoping I would say something and I would have said more, except if I started talking I wouldn't stop until I told her that she shouldn't be thanking me because I got people killed, and then I would launch into the story and describe the family of four and it would bring them back and it was too much to deal with. I looked at something just past her shoulder.

She frowned slightly. The little girl rocked on her heels, little green socks covering her feet, and then pulled on her mother's arm. They wandered over to Betty's counter and the woman whispered something to Betty, but Betty only shook her head. The pair left and Betty turned her hazel eyes onto me. She wore a royal blue shirt, buttoned, spotless. Black shorts. Her hair domed her head like a gray helmet. She smiled, as if I were just another Feeb. A little part of me relaxed. Betty knew all about my stories. She knew all of our stories. She ran the alcohol headquarters after all.

I sat on one of the bright green bar stools.

"What can I get for ya', darling?" Betty asked.

"I don't have anything to trade," I said. "I just need to sit for a minute if that's okay."

She nodded and turned away. I scratched at the counter with my fingernails and stopped when I starting flaking up bits of the laminate. The next part would be hard—facing Ricker—but once he was gone I could pour everything out to my Faints and they would be the best listeners and then we could pretend that nothing had changed.

Betty set an empty glass down in front of me. In one hand she held a liquor bottle halfway full of brown liquid. The other held a coffee pot full of black liquid.

"I don't—"

"I know." She filled the glass with half of each. "This one's on the house. You look like you need it. It's the least we can do after all you've done."

Before I could protest she went to check on the card players. I stared at the glass. Nobody cared about age anymore when it came to drinking. Not with the whole world fallen apart and everyone having to grow up fast. Still it saddened me that it was so normal not to care about how things used to be. I was only sixteen after all.

I took a small sip of the drink and forced it down even as my nose felt lit on fire. She might as well have dumped rubbing alcohol into the coffee. But this was Betty and I couldn't bear to offend her. I kept drinking it, even as the coffee turned bitter and a buzzing noise rose in my brain. Ano and Gabbi sometimes obliterated themselves with this stuff when they wanted to forget. Maybe what was good enough for them was good enough for me this afternoon.

Steps shuffled in the back. I set the drink down and turned. The players were helping the Feeb coming out of his memory-rush to get on his feet.

"Walk it off," Bernice said.

The group made him do several circuits around the aisles. Once the light came back into his eyes and he seemed able to see things in the present again, the players led him to the counter. They took up the stools around me and suddenly the room seemed overfull.

I decided I didn't want to finish the drink after all. I began to get up.

"You heard the rumors?" Nindal said in my direction.

Betty scowled at him while returning to her side of the counter. "Don't talk about that here. No sense in stirring things up for a bunch of made-up hooey."

"But the camps have been working on a cure since this all got started," Bernice said, his shoulders hunched under Betty's short harangue.

"So, what does that have to do with anything?" Betty said.

"It is possibly the truth," Nindal said. The other Feebs took their turns chiming in.

"Dead is dead," I said and the whole room stopped talking. Corrina's ghost-memory appeared on the bar side next to Betty, looking exactly like she had when Anthony had said those words three years ago in the surplus store—when we'd been running scared and not yet infected.

"What you talking about?" Bernice said.

"We've been turned and there's no going back. There's never been a movie that had a way to go back once you've been turned." I wanted to use the word zombie. It was on the tip of my tongue

and I could see it in the air between us and it was so obvious I
didn't understand how they could be blind to it, but they were,
and if I said it, they'd stop listening altogether.

"You do not know," Nindal said. His dark slashes of eyebrows
drew down and almost met between his eyes. "You cannot say
one way or the other if there is this cure. You cannot."

"There's no going back," I said. "There's no undoing it."

The door squeaked open and boots stamped the floor. "It's
real enough. I met a Feeb who's been cured."

All heads swiveled to the door, even Betty's. I couldn't help
but look myself. A Feeb, no doubt, with his telltale lines and ash
and a light bruising around the neck. Not one I recognized. Not
someone I had helped rescue. Someone who had been rescued
after I'd locked myself away.

"Who are you?" I demanded.

"That's Leon," Betty said. "You just get back? You found
something?"

He nodded. He was tall and lean and was maybe in his forties
before the Feeb-skin took over. He wore jeans, cowboy boots,
a plaid shirt, all he needed was a cowboy hat. As if on cue he
brought out a dingy beige one from behind his back and held
it down at his side.

"Did you ride in on a horse or something?" I said, and felt
shocked at my words. It was something Gabbi would say, not me.

But the words were out there and he squinted a smile at me
and said, "If you know where I can get one, I will next time."

Everyone laughed. I flushed.

Betty wiped down an empty spot at the counter and poured
a drink. "Your usual."

"Thank you, Betty." He sat on the stool next to me, set out a can of creamed corn in trade, then examined the drink before throwing it down his throat.

Bernice held up his hands. "Now, now. Don't keep us waiting. You can't drop a bomb like that and not speak another word."

If I had been Corrina, I probably would have pressed him with my own questions. Gabbi would have probably started a fight over his lies. But I was neither one of them so I just waited with the rest for his answer.

Leon took his time. His arm was covered in coarse hair that obscured the worst aspects of the infection. He twisted his wrist this way and that, examining the dregs in the glass. There was a heat in the air that wasn't there before. A certain tension like a string pulled taut. If he didn't say something fast I didn't know what that would set off.

He peered at them over the rim of the empty glass.

"Fill it for him, Betty." Bernice plunked down three cigarettes.

We waited, holding our breath, as Betty poured the drink and swiped the cigarettes off the counter. Leon tilted the glass back and finished it in one go. "I said, I met someone cured of being a Feeb but he ran off. I can track him, but I need help. I'm going to find him again and make him tell me where to get a cure of my own. So who's gonna help me?"

The store roared to life like he was a magician who'd done his final reveal. They surrounded Leon, pushing me aside like I'd become invisible—but that trick wasn't what they wanted to see. Nindal ran out of the store, yelling over his shoulder that he was getting others to come along. Another one said they should let the whole town know and form a search party with supplies. Bernice wanted to leave right then, because who knew where the cured Feeb was headed or if he was in danger and they better get started. Their voices raised in pitch and intensity. Leon too, there was a shine in his eyes that spoke of a conviction that scared me more than a little bit. It was the kind of light I'd seen often enough in my aunt's eyes before she worked herself up into the righteous indignation that came before a beating.

Their voices got louder. Two of them had now fallen into a memory-rush, but it was as if no one cared all of a sudden. They wandered the store, knocking over supplies and glass jars and then one of them punched the other. It was as if they'd turned invisible too because what mattered all of a sudden was the cure and finding it and everything else could go to hell.

I backed away until my shoulders hit a shelf of cans. I jumped, shock making mt heart pound. Betty glanced my way and I saw the half-crazed look on her face and a certain slack to her jaw, but then she said, "You going?" And I knew that she was still barely all right, but I didn't know for how much longer.

I shook my head. No, not in a million years. Never.

Dead was dead.

CHAPTER 5

I WAS OUTSIDE. The street was dark.

How had the street gotten dark?

I crept along the edge of the building. The space in front of Betty's had turned into this pool of figures with Leon at the head. They almost looked like a bunch of Vs moving around.

This was why I didn't leave my hotel room anymore.

Dozens of them were outside Betty's and it was almost dark. The shouts, the slap of running feet, a sense that people were looking for trouble. I didn't understand. It was summer, the days were long, I had gone into Betty's during the late afternoon.

A panicked feeling climbed into my throat. I had lost time again. I had been—

No. I told myself to stop. My Faints needed me. Ricker would be wondering where I was.

Instead of dreading the stairs and the door and his face, I was eager for it now. I would rise above this terrible energy. I would climb three stories and the crowd's shouts would fade until they stopped altogether, and even if Molly rolled out of her bed on purpose, tonight it would be okay, I would gladly put her back again.

I hurried down the street, away from the crowd. They were fools, going after the cure because someone claimed he heard someone else claim he had struck gold. A small voice in my head wondered if maybe there could be a real cure after all. I shut that thought down. We'd saved so many people and they didn't listen to us anymore. They didn't care what a bunch of kids had to say about things, even if we had rescued them.

I stopped at the edge of the sidewalk, at the part where I was supposed to cross over to the hotel. The chorus of shouts continued on one end, faint, but like a humming that threatened to grow and consume everything in its way. There was quiet on the other side, except for a lone cricket. The darkness would only deepen. I could smell smoke from someone's wood stove. Since the sun was gone so was the heat. Temperatures dropped fast this high in the foothills. My skin prickled into goosebumps.

There was a rustling noise, opposite from the crowd. I snapped my attention to it knowing even as I did that the darkness would keep me from seeing anything. The town always posted sentries and there were only two ways in and out, both guarded. But that didn't keep my skin from crawling like someone watched me. I had felt that way often in my aunt's house, before she had died and I had been sent to live with my uncle here in America. Her breath had always smelled like sardines because she loved them, claiming they made her glow and kept her skin young. She was old, but still beautiful, so maybe she was right about that.

I shook my head like a dog shaking off water. Stop it.

I hopped from one foot to the other and started talking out loud, anything to push my aunt to where she belonged, somewhere far back in my brain where she couldn't come out again. "This is ridiculous. Don't just stand around here hallucinating. Cross the stupid street and go home." The memories began to disintegrate. "There, see? You DO know better."

I crossed the road, the starlight just bright enough for me to avoid the potholes and mounds of weeds that cracked the asphalt. I jumped onto the boarded sidewalk and reached for the stair railing.

A hand came out of the darkness and covered mine, pinching it to the railing.

"Ow," I said and tried to pull it away. The darkness didn't reveal much, other than the shadow was taller than me. The hand was rough but small. "What do you want?" Had a Faint escaped? Had a V gotten inside after all?

A hint of honey hit my nose. Jen Huey liked honey. After we'd rescued her, I helped her go through every empty house in town. She'd taken their honey bears and lined them all up on a counter. At first Gabbi had thought she'd gone crazy, but then Jen explained—Faints responded to sweet things better than to anything else. Plus, she liked a dab of it on her breakfast every morning. She thought it made more of her memory-rushes into good ones.

She'd come from Camp Pacific and they'd done something to her. It had addled her brain just a little more than most of us other Feebs. Still, it had been in a sweet way, like the honey.

"Jen, is that you?"

The hand twitched at the name.

"Jen, how's it going at the hospital? Corrina always says you're the best with all the Faints. They just seem to calm down and listen when you're around."

"You had no right to do that, you know. No right at all." Her voice dripped with venom, stinging, harsh, cutting me through the chest. It was Jen, even though it barely sounded like her. My skin burned as she twisted my hand in her grip.

"Jen, whatever you're remembering…it's me, it's Maibe. I saved you, remember? I helped you collect honey from all the houses and we lined them all up together and—"

She stepped closer and the sugar smell became stronger. Something shined on her cheek, like she had wiped honey on her face. Her eyes were black pits. Her upper body seemed almost detached from the arm and hand that trapped mine.

"Jen, you need to move around and snap yourself out of this." Whatever was happening to Jen, it couldn't be a memory-rush, those mostly stopped you in your tracks while you relived the memory. She must have gotten bitten by a V somehow and sent back into the memory-fevers. The fevers were dangerous, you reenacted things, which was why we always tied each other down when we went through them. It protected everyone else from you.

But if she'd been injured by a V, that meant a V had gotten into town.

Her arm began to shake, making mine tremble. I thought it might mean she was coming back to her senses and I tried to pull away again. Her other arm sprang out of the darkness and wrapped itself in my hair.

I was pulled to my knees. My scalp burned and tears sprang into my eyes from the pain.

"Jen," I gasped. "Jen Huey. Please stop. I saved you, remember?" But she didn't listen and a part of me was almost glad. It was painful and maybe I deserved the pain because I had saved her but I hadn't saved the girl and her family. I couldn't save myself.

"I know better now," she said. "I didn't know then, but now I know and I won't let you hurt anyone else. I won't…no, just try to call the police. Just you try—" She released my hand, but then a slap slammed across my cheek, jerking my head back, pulling my hair out.

I began sobbing. "Please stop. Please." I balled my hand into a fist and tried to force back the vision of my aunt. I would not. I would not let her do this again.

She let go of my hair and I dropped to my knees. Blood dripped cold along my scalp. Hands closed around my throat.

"You will never touch anyone again," she said.

My aunt's face swam across my vision.

"I made that promise to myself," she said.

My throat closed. I tried to scream, but nothing got past Jen's iron grip. She held me up by my neck. Light began to flash in front of my eyes. My aunt's face swirled, flattened, swirled back. I reached out and scratched and found her eye sockets and began to press. The burning in my lungs grew unstoppable, mountainous, all consuming. I pressed with all my remaining strength, not sure how much strength I really had left, not sorry that I would make my aunt pay, but sorry that I would die on the sidewalk and Jen would find me and never forgive herself.

Something popped under my right thumb, gushing wetness and heat.

She screamed and screamed and dropped her hands and I

tumbled and suddenly my aunt's face became Jen's face again. I jumped to her side and caught her before she fell.

"Jen! Jen!" I pulled her back down the street. She was screaming. My muscles shook with her weight and my hands slipped along the slime that coated both of us. Corrina's makeshift hospital was down this block, wasn't it? I worked from memory because there was nothing to light the way except shadows.

"We'll get you help, okay?" I gasped. "It's going to be okay." But I knew it wasn't going to be okay.

My mind replayed how her eye popped under my thumb and how she had been my aunt for a split second. I had been both glad and sickened by what I'd done—the choking, the burning in my scalp, the stream of liquid. Her screams. Jen's horrible, terrible, haunting screams.

What had happened to her? What was happening to all of us?

CHAPTER 6

CORRINA CLEANED AND WRAPPED JEN'S EYE. When she was finished, Jen still hadn't come back to herself, not completely. She whimpered and thrashed about, so we tied her at the hands and ankles to the bed frame. I didn't speak a word while we worked. I couldn't.

We searched Jen over for a fresh injury, but other than what I had done to her, and scars from old V bites, there was nothing to explain it.

"It could have been worse," Corrina said quietly.

I almost choked. "Worse? It could have been worse than this?"

We stood over Jen's bed, in the makeshift hospital that had once been a church. It was dark, but it was not quiet. Even though the night had cooled, the air felt suffocating. There was this smell of sweat, dirt, unwashed sheets, old wood, the vinegar-like disinfectant Corrina used. Jen whimpered in her bed, lost in a terrible memory, but she wasn't alone. This was where we cared for the Faints and any sick Feebs. Two other beds were being used by Feebs. A dozen other beds held the town's Faints. If it wasn't for the ropes tying the Feebs down, they would have hurt themselves or others. Just like Jen had tried to do. Just like I had done.

"It's not your fault," Corrina said.

The spiked coffee Betty had served me sat on my tongue like a layer of bitter paste. It was too dark to see the expression on Corrina's face, but I knew her well enough that I could guess. She would be feeling sorry for me. She would be worried and thinking about how to make me feel better. But Jen was the one lying there, missing an eye for the rest of her life. Because of me.

I stayed beside Jen until she came back to herself. Maybe only an hour had passed, maybe it had been longer. There was no way for me to tell anymore except that it was still dark outside.

Corrina told Jen what happened. Jen cried and apologized to me. A candle lit up her bandaged eye enough to show where blood was already soaking through. Jen drifted into sleep. I threw up on the floor.

I was there on my hands and knees, smelling the mess I'd made, tasting the acid that stung my throat. I should have never left my Faints. None of this would have happened if I'd just stayed away. That's when I noticed a person standing next to me. The outline of thick jeans, a bucket resting against the knee. I looked up. Dylan held the bucket and a few rags.

"It's okay," Dylan said. "We know what it's like. Go rest. I'll take care of it."

His words moved me into action. I would not make him clean up after me. I held out my hands for the cleaning supplies. He handed them over, but still went down on his knees to help me mop everything up. The wood floor snagged my clothing and forced splinters into my hands. The pain only made me scrub harder.

When we finished, I followed Dylan over to Corrina. He rested a hand on Corrina's shoulder and she leaned into him for a moment. There was a whole row of candles on the table to light up what she worked with—glass containers, rubber tubing, bottles, strips of cloth, thick textbooks open to various pages, bowls filled with dark substances. Dylan handed me a glass of water and I used it to rinse out my mouth.

Corrina worked steadily, even though there was hardly any light to see by. The moans of those in the fevers became like white noise, interrupted only by the clink of glassware as Dylan helped her. I decided to slip away before I could ruin anything else.

A board creaked under my step and Corrina glanced over. "Help me with this."

I wanted to pretend I hadn't heard her request.

I went to her side. A candle heated one of the beakers. Steam evaporated off the top as the liquid bubbled. She checked one of the books, her finger smudging the page. Corrina had requested we bring back any medical and plant books whenever we scavenged.

She brought a container to eye level while measuring out a portion of the dark liquid. Several bowls were filled with dried bits of different plants. She pushed one to me. "Grind this up." She picked up the bowl and ceramic stick and showed me to use this sort of circular movement.

I took the bowl and copied her motions. The stick created this grinding sound against the bowl. It felt good to be useful.

After a few minutes of working in silence, I couldn't hold back anymore. "What is all this?" The table looked like something out of a mad scientist experiment.

"I'm trying out different plants from the garden to see if it has any effect." She didn't have to say on the infection. There was nothing else it could be for, not with three Feebs suffering behind us.

"I thought we still had drugs," I said.

Corrina transferred the heated liquid to a third container. Dylan grabbed up another bowl and began grinding.

"We won't have them forever and they're not working like they use to." Her forehead was pinched and even in the low candlelight, it was easy to see how exhausted she felt. She worried about all of us like how I imagined a sister or even a mom might worry.

Dylan caught her gaze. There was something in his eyes, the way he looked at her, as if prompting her. She opened her mouth. Closed it. Opened it again. She took the bowl from him and dumped its contents into the dark liquid.

"Corrina," Dylan said.

"I know," Corrina said, not looking either one of us in the eye. "But what good will it do?" she whispered. "I wanted at least one of us..." The beaker was frozen in her hand in mid-air. Her other hand moved over the table full of glassware as if to brush hair off Dylan's forehead. A beaker tipped and crashed to the floor, scattering glass shards into the darkness.

Dylan grabbed Corrina's hand and held it away from the candle flames. He didn't say a word. He kept his gaze on her face. His eyes shined in the candlelight until she came back. She shook off the spell like a shiver.

"You're turning Faint." It wasn't a question.

"And me as well," Dylan said.

It was like I could see the shape of this huge jigsaw puzzle, almost all the pieces had been fit into place, and someone had tipped it onto the floor. Until now, the double infection had kept Feebs from losing our minds. But everything we had learned about how to survive in this terrible world wasn't working anymore.

"Why are Gabbi and Ano going V, but the three of us going Faint?" I said. "What makes the difference?"

Corrina knelt to pick up what glass pieces she could find.

"You're going to cut yourself," Dylan said.

"I can't just leave it like this," she said.

He came around the table and guided her back to standing. "It can wait until morning, but this," he motioned to the table, "this can't."

She sighed and bit her lip. She looked so young in that moment, in the dark, in the candlelight, surrounded by beakers and bowls and books. Others like Leon were going all vigilante at the chance of a permanent cure. Gabbi was losing it. I was hiding in my room.

Corrina was making herself sick to find something to help us.

"We think it's about exposure," Corrina said finally.

"What?"

"We think the difference between going Faint or V is how many times a person has gotten reinfected with blood from a V. Reinfected with the Lyssa virus," Corrina said.

I thought about all of Jen's old scars.

"The more Lyssa virus in your system," Dylan said, "The less the bacteria can do to fight it off and the more out of balance things get." He hadn't let go of Corrina yet. It looked like if he did she might fall to the floor.

My mind whirled with this new information. "But then we just need to do a blood transfusion, right?" Maybe it worked the other way too. Maybe someone going Faint, someone like me, needed blood from a V.

The sadness on Corrina's face should have clued me in, but it was so simple, so obvious. My heart pumped in excitement. It could give me back my life, my control, make me no longer a burden to my friends.

"We can use Molly. She's the strongest. Give some of her blood to Ano—"

"We tried all that," Dylan interrupted. "It doesn't work. It doesn't do anything."

I looked back and forth between them. Of course they had tried it.

Just like that my hope vanished. I should have known better. People like me didn't deserve second chances.

Corrina seemed to collapse within herself.

"Help me get her sitting," Dylan said.

We eased her to the ground. The glass crunched as we brushed it away with our shoes. The wood floor smelled damp and dusty at the same time.

Corrina waved us away. "Finish it for me, Dylan. You know it can't wait."

Dylan got up and began working at the table again. I stayed on the floor next to Corrina, using my shoulder to prop her up. She was warm and her eyes looked glassy.

"What can't wait?" I said.

She paused, as if thinking about how to answer my question.

"I'm making something I hope will reduce the effects of the memory-fevers." She wasn't exactly lying to me, but her cheek twitched in a certain way. She wasn't telling me the whole truth. Before I could press her about it, Dylan returned.

"It's done for now." He lifted her up, one arm under her knees and the other around her back. Her head leaned against his chest. It was as if his words had given her permission to sleep. Her eyes closed. "It needs time to cool. I'm going to get her to rest."

When he finished positioning her on a cot, we checked on Jen and the other sick Feebs, and then on those caring for the Faints. I asked him what he thought Corrina had been planning to tell me. He shook his head. "Maybe in the morning. Only she knows what she was going to say." And then he wouldn't offer another word about it.

I finally let him send me away. I took a candle to help guide me back to my Faints. The streets were empty, the air was cold and damp. Leon and the others were long gone.

My breathing sounded too loud, my steps explosive. I raced up the stairs and held my breath while I knocked quietly on the door. I sent out a wish to the universe for Ricker to be asleep. There was no answer and my hopes rose for a moment. I went to turn the doorknob when it magically turned for me.

Ricker leaned against the edge of the door, my candle throwing deep bags under his eyes. He stooped over as if having just awoken, but it looked like a carefully prepared stance.

"Hi." My voice sounded hoarse, but I hoped he wouldn't notice. I stepped around him. Another candle was lit on the kitchen counter and was melted almost to the nub. He'd been waiting and worried.

My Faints were all tucked away in bed and their combined breathing created a soothing white noise that relaxed me. They were familiar and safe and I knew how to take care of them.

Molly's foot dangled free from under the covers. I set my candle down next to Ricker's and tucked her foot back in, smoothing the cool sheet for her.

Ricker still hadn't said a word.

I gathered my courage.

He remained by the door, though he closed it behind him. He had stuffed his hands in his pockets and stared at the candle flame. Lost in—

"Ricker?" I rushed to him and shook his shoulders. He felt hot beneath his shirt, like he was running a fever. My head hurt, aching from Jen's earlier violence. I shook him harder. "Ricker!"

He blinked, slow, long, like he was asleep on his feet. He rubbed his face.

I dropped my hands and stepped back to give us some breathing room because just for a second I had wanted to wrap my arms around him and bury my face in his chest and listen to his heartbeat and breathe him in.

"What the hell happened, Maibe? Are you okay? You were gone for hours and it's been getting crazy out there. People sound like they're going nuts." He picked up my candle and waved it close to me. "You're hurt!"

"I…" I wanted to sound strong, brave. I would just tell him what happened and then we'd figure out what to do next. Tears overwhelmed me and tracked down my cheeks and my crying hurt my throat so that I only wanted to cry some more.

"Okay, okay. Hold on." Ricker held the candle away and pulled me into him. His strength and friendship meant so much to me. "Just tell me what happened."

I explained about Gabbi and the meeting and how badly it went. I explained about Leon and Bernice and Nindal and the others, and then I explained about Jen.

He listened without saying a word. He had me pause for a moment so that he could drag a chair over to the sink. I sat in it and he used both candles to give him enough light to examine my neck and scalp. He squeezed cool water through my hair and into a bucket to wash away the crusty blood. Sensations that mixed pain and pleasure began to course through me. I had never been so well taken care of.

He got on his knees and examined my hands, turning them over in his own, stroking my skin, noticing the crust of juices I didn't want to think about. He used a fresh bowl of water and a towel and gently placed my hands in the bowl to soak.

He picked up one hand and washed it like it was fragile glass. When he was finished he interlocked his fingers with mine for a flash and then let go.

I stared at his dirty blond hair, the white part his hairline made, the sweep his hair made on his forehead.

He reached for my other hand, washing it with the same care, and then picked up a clean towel to pat my skin dry. He looked up then, eyes large and meditative.

My heart pounded and my feet felt funny, like pins and needles. He stayed there on his knees, the darkness lifted only by the guttering candles that showed the messy towel, the water bowl in his lap, the way he stared at me. I cupped his cheeks and moved my fingers to tangle in his hair. He closed his eyes for a moment and then opened them again, the pupils large and drowning his irises.

I leaned in and touched my lips to his and he pressed me into him and turned the kiss into something deep and endless that twisted my stomach and made my body burn and the light grew brighter and fiercer and—

The harsh afternoon light cut between us like a sword. Alden stepped back, his shoes kicking up dust. He wiped his mouth, the mouth I had almost kissed, with the back of his hand as if wiping away a disgusting bit of food. He repositioned the mask to fit snug over his uninfected face. The safety shield's plastic glinted in the sunlight, blinding me.

I didn't remember what I was going to say. Alden and I were on a hill overlooking Camp Pacific and we had been sitting next to each other, close to each other, almost touching. He had pushed his mask up to make it easier to talk about everything. He had looked at me long and deep and steady and I didn't think. I had leaned in.

"I'm sorry," Alden said, and he did look sorry, but also disgusted, like he'd eaten something sour.

"I just…" But I trailed off again because my mind was a blur of emotion. A burning embarrassment threatened to swallow me up like I wished the ground right then would do.

"I don't know what I'm doing," Alden said. "I wish…I wish I was okay with this. I wish…" He looked around in the air, desperate for an answer. He looked away. "I wish you hadn't gotten infected."

"If I hadn't, I'd have gone V long before now!" I said, a prick of anger taking the edge off my embarrassment. Gabbi had warned me, she had told me Alden would be like this but I hadn't believed her. You couldn't catch anything from a touch. If you really cared about somebody, what did it matter what they looked like?

But it mattered to him.

"I know." Alden hung his head, and then raised it and stared at me with a fierceness that scared me. "I know."

The afternoon sun faded. The candlelight guttered and then flamed back to life. Alden's face vanished. The embarrassment from the memory-rush remained.

Shadows danced across Ricker's face and on the wall behind him.

"Maibe?" Ricker ran his finger down my cheek, burning a trail through my tears.

I swallowed and gave him a small smile. "Hi."

"Where did you go?"

I shook my head. "It's nothing."

His eyes narrowed and he dropped his finger from my skin. I wanted to return it to my face, but I didn't. Part of me still wished it was Alden kneeling here in the candlelight.

Ricker pressed his lips into a grim line. "It's Alden, isn't it?"

I closed my eyes and turned my head. Was I really so easy to read?

His footsteps drifted away, paused, returned.

I opened my eyes.

Ricker leaned over and kissed me on top of my head. He sighed. "Goodnight, Maibe." He walked out of the room and quietly latched the door closed behind him.

I sat in the chair for a long time and tried to think of nothing at all.

I failed miserably.

ALDEN

*He turned away. He couldn't look at her, not when her face
showed the pain she felt. The pain he made her feel.*

"Why do I bother you so much?" *Maibe said.*

*He couldn't help how he felt every time he looked at what the
infection had done. It made him break out in a cold sweat, to
think about touching her veined hand or seeing the lines streak
across her skin like spiderwebs. As if the blood pounding underneath, full of virus, full of bacteria, full of these things that had
turned some violent, some into sleepwalkers, and some, like
her, into both and neither, could burst at any moment and take
him over.*

"Wouldn't you rather not be sick?" *he said finally, lamely. When
he didn't look at her, he loved her. At least he thought he did. But
maybe he didn't, because if it were true, would it matter what
she looked like?*

"I don't think so," *Maibe said, shivering.*

"*You don't mean that—not really.*"

"*Everyday you risk getting infected by something worse. At least I'm protected.*"

"*I don't see it that way.*"

"*So you feel free to go anywhere? If you come across a V or a Faint you're not afraid?*"

"*You're saying you're not afraid because you're a Feeb?*"

Maibe shifted closer to him, not enough to touch him, but enough for him to feel the heat from her. Enough for him to know she was alive. Sick, but alive. Not dead, not an animal like his father wanted him to believe.

"*I'm less afraid,*" *she said.* "*And you would be too. I can still die, but I can't be turned into a V. I don't have that fear.*"

"*I thought you said you were already dead.*"

"*We ARE already dead,*" *she said.* "*Some of us are further along than others. That's all.*"

"*What does that even mean?*"

She shrugged. "*All that matters is doing the right thing even though the sky comes crashing down.*"

"*So if you really believe that, then that's why you don't go out anymore? Why you stay in town and take care of your Faints instead of rescuing people who need it? Losing them wasn't your fault. It was months ago, Maibe, and Corrina says you're only leaving that room once every couple of days for food.*"

"*I tried, Alden. I tried for months to go back out. I can't. I...*"

He lost her then, just for a moment. That blank look that came onto a Feeb's face when a memory took over—it was on her face now. She was lost in some memory—that memory. She never talked about it, but it came back to haunt her often enough that Alden knew what had happened with the Garcia family.

Everyone knew what had happened.

He was sorry then for bringing it up. He was one of the few people who could coax her from the cave she'd made out of that room with the Faints. The two of them had been having a nice time, for all that he could barely stand to look at her. He wondered for the millionth time how much longer she had, how much longer any Feeb had. No one knew exactly what the two infections did to the body long term.

She came back. Her eyes had stayed open the entire time, and she mumbled under her breath, but it hadn't been one of the bad ones—one of the times when she dropped to her knees and sobbed and sprinted away somewhere to hide until Ricker tracked her down and brought her back.

The spark in her eyes returned and she refocused on him and breathed in and out, long and deep. She stood up and stretched her arms above her head, then to her side, then down to her feet.

Three Feebs walked by them on the sidewalk. They stopped for a moment and stared. It happened often enough—he was a novelty. An uninfected in Feeb town. Most uninfected would have shot a Feeb on sight these days, his father included, and that didn't take into account the Feeb-haters who'd made it their mission to clean up the world of Vs, Faints, and Feebs. They called themselves zombie hunters and rode around with flags and guns and vehicles when they wanted to draw Vs to them. They went on foot when they stalked Faints and Feebs. He figured they called themselves zombie hunters because it made the killing easier, like something out of a video game rather than real life.

One of the women stared at him with longing. Maybe it was his skin, his eyes—sometimes it got intense, especially if he tripped one of them into a memory of a son or younger brother. The woman shivered and came back. She nodded a hello to Maibe and they continued walking.

"They like you. They like seeing you," Maibe said. "You remind them of before."

Alden shook his head.

"But if you don't become a Feeb, you're going to become something worse than that."

"I've been fine so far," he said. "Two and half years later and all."

"You've gotten lucky."

"Maybe not."

"Maybe you can't see it, but I do! I've had to take a V bite before to keep you from getting infected. How many times has one of us terrible, horrible, disgusting Feebs stepped in between you and a V so that you wouldn't be turned?"

"Stop it, Maibe."

"I will not stop," Maibe said. "You're being stupid. You're being irresponsible. It's the best protection you could have in this new world."

"Now you're sounding like Tabitha."

Maibe froze, her hands above her head in a stretch.

Tabitha and her son Kern had taken over an entire camp and tried to turn everyone into Feebs. Alden's father had almost shot Maibe in that chaos, on purpose. He would never forgive his father for that.

"Sorry," Alden said, but Maibe turned away, and he realized that he didn't much notice the lines in her face, that he'd rather there be a million veins and wrinkles to touch than to have her angry with him.

"I think you should go back," she said.

"Maibe." He'd come to see her and tell her there were rumors

of a cure. Rumors strong enough that his own father believed they might be true this time. The camps were falling apart and his father was bugging out. Alden planned to tell Maibe he was going after the cure for his mother, but also, mainly, for her.

"Your father must be wondering where his precious uninfected son is by now. You have to rebuild the human race and all, right? Make sure it stays pure and untainted, right?"

"Maibe."

She looked over his shoulder and her eyes widened.

"Alden, I mean it," she said, her tone different, no longer angry. "You should leave right now."

He looked over and lost feeling in his hands. They were on the edge of town at their usual spot, and it was pretty safe, because most of the Vs had died off from starvation by now, but not absolutely safe, because nowhere was absolutely safe anymore. There was a V. One that was freshly turned, the fat not yet burned away to skin and bones because a V forgot to eat in the midst of all the rage.

He stood up and the movement caught the V's attention. He cursed. Maybe he could scale the gutter pipe onto the roof in time, but it looked slippery and likely to peel off the wall once he was halfway up. Maybe he could lock himself in a room somewhere, but the closest ones all had large windows.

Maibe ran past him, a stick of some kind in her hands. Alden screamed for her to stop because she might get infected. But then he remembered she was already infected and this was what she meant, this was exactly what she meant. He was useless to her. But if he could cure her. If he could bring her over to his side—

A curtain of darkness fell over his thoughts. Suddenly he felt like he was sitting again, but this felt like a chair, not a sidewalk.

His arms were strapped down, his ankles were strapped down. Something around his forehead held his head down.

He cracked open his eyes and blinked away the crust and shut them against the bright dome of light that seared into his brain. The memory of Maibe had been so real but he was in a room, he was in that room, with the speaker box and the shining glass eye and the gray vent—and the three voices on the other side. How could he be here now when he had been so completely there with Maibe a moment before?

"Where's Maibe?" he shouted. "What have you done with her? Where is she?"

"Did we...Did he just come out of the fevers?" A woman's voice from his left. She was in the room. A soft glow edged her white suit. "We brought him out of the fevers. This worked much faster than before. The blood must act as a sterilizing agent. This could be it, Dr. Stoven. Check the saliva levels. Check—"

"Yes, but the cost..." A man's voice. To his right. Soft, but excited. "We cannot rush the results."

"What results?" Alden said, the words getting stuck in his throat as if he hadn't used it in a long time. Their voices were familiar, but was it because he'd heard them often enough now through the speaker box, or because he knew them from somewhere? His vision cleared a bit. Two white suits with plastic shields over their faces leaned over him.

"Of course. We will repeat the procedure and confirm. Reset the machine."

"Excellent."

Silence. The two shifted away, the whirring sound of their respirators muffled their talk. Alden's heart fluttered.

"This is good work," Dr. Stoven said. "No one looked at the

different load levels of blood and saliva. The Lyssa virus must cause the fevers and the bacteria subdue it."

"No, Dr. Stoven, they battle for balance in the brain," she said. "I believe it's their interactions that cause the fevers."

"But surely the rage episodes—"

"This is promising," the woman doctor interrupted, "but we must refine it. Bring out the next batch of Lyssa virus."

Alden strained against the bonds. They were going to give him V blood? His skin crawled at the thought of someone else's blood mixing with his own and infecting him with the terrible rage. He arched his back, pushing off the bed. "Let me out of here!"

One of the white suits came back. "Alden Bennings, please rest now." The woman doctor.

"How do you know my name?" And then all of a sudden he recognized the woman. "Dr. Ferrad?"

Dr. Stoven returned to his bedside with a needle full of blood—except it wasn't blood. It couldn't be blood because the liquid was almost clear, like cloudy water.

Dr. Stoven plunged the needle into a sort of drip-line and connected it to Alden's arm. Next he uncoiled a thin tube. The liquid inside this tube WAS red. He held up the tube and twisted at something near the end. "Time for connection?"

Dr. Ferrad glanced at her wrist. "We must give the viral load adequate time to complete two cycles of binary fission. Ten minutes should suffice."

"How much is required?" Dr. Stoven said.

"All of it," Dr. Ferrad whispered.

"What are you doing? Tell me what you're doing!" Alden wrenched himself against the straps again. The edges dug into his flesh, cutting off the feeling, turning him black and blue and *red, making his veins stick out like a Feeb.*

Veins like a Feeb.

He froze, back arched in the air, and then slowly lowered him-self flat onto the bed. His insides grew cold. His stomach flipped. He blinked once, and then again. He stared at his hands, and arms, not understanding why they looked, why did they look...

He began to scream.

CHAPTER 7

THE NEXT DAY, I paced the old hotel room for hours. Freanz, Molly, and the twins seemed to sense the tension. They reacted to my every movement with involuntary twitching. There were no new broken windows, just the gaping hole as a reminder, but every time they settled down enough for me to leave and check on Jen, one would start up again.

By the end of the day, the walls felt like they were closing in on me. The wallpaper was faded and dirty, the floor covered in scratches, food was ground into the cracks. Why hadn't I noticed any of that before?

I filled a bucket with water, took a rag, and spent the afternoon scrubbing every surface until all of it shined, but my mind strayed to Jen again and again.

When I finished feeding everyone dinner and settled them down for the evening, I sat by the broken window. A slight breeze gave some relief to the stifling heat. I drummed my fingers on the sill, watched the sunset change colors.

Just as I decided to chance leaving there was a scratch at the door. Molly mumbled and her foot slipped out from under the covers. I repositioned the sheet on my way to answer the knock.

Corrina stood there, smiling, but the smile did not reach her eyes. She was taller than me and her wild hair was long and dark and framed her face almost like a lion's mane.

"Is it Jen?" Fear struck me like lightning.

"She's okay," Corrina said quickly. "Not any worse, at least. I thought you might want to see her."

I closed my eyes and breathed out the knot that had formed in my chest.

"Also—"

"What?" I said.

"I thought you would want to know. Ano and Gabbi are gone."

"Gone where?" But even as I asked, I knew the answer. Ano and Gabbi had gone for the new drugs without me. I was a coward for not going with them.

"These new drugs might be exactly what we need," she said.

"But we still have plenty of the old drugs."

"We have enough for the next few months, if we're careful," Corrina said. "But they're not working the same as before."

"But they're still working."

"For now." Corrina's face was drawn as if she hadn't been sleeping much. The orange light from the sunset cast a weird, sickly glow on the lines and wrinkles of her infected skin. "I'll watch your Faints for you if you want to see Jen."

I tumbled out of that cave of a room, down the stairs, and onto the wooden sidewalk before realizing I hadn't thanked Corrina. But it was too late to go back and I thought maybe even if I tried my body wouldn't let me. The air felt cool and clear outside. The openness shocked me awake and I couldn't return to that dark room. Not yet.

I hurried down the block. The sunset cast the sky and buildings in an orange glow. Ghost-memories crowded the streets. It was like a silent movie, except this movie ran in color. Jen stood in front of me, her face contorted in rage, both eyes staring at me. Leon and his crowd milled around, opening their mouths as if shouting, but no sound came out. I hurried past all of it. I couldn't bear returning to the hotel room, but I feared becoming frozen in the street, my brain betraying me, freezing me in one spot until someone else put me away with the other Faints.

I took deep breaths and broke into a run, hoping the exercise would beat back the symptoms. And it did a little bit. The ghost-memories became just a little more transparent.

I pushed myself into a sprint and hoped that somehow I would find Jen in her bed, awake and feeling better, her eye suddenly healed and all of this a bad dream.

When I got to the church, I skidded to a stop and took in gulping breaths. Even though the air was cooling off, my run made me sweat. Stone blocks propped open the church doors. The sunset changed everything to pink now with hints of gray. With the remaining light, I could see Dylan and a few others inside, moving from bed to bed.

I stopped before my shoe hit the first step. Suddenly I couldn't go in there. My brain dipped into the Garcia family memory-rush. My muscles trembled and I felt that familiar cry on my lips. I was able to step back, and then take another step and another. I was down the walkway and back onto the street before I could force myself to stop. I silently cursed. If I ran away now what would that tell Jen? She'd think I didn't care. She'd think maybe I did this to her on purpose.

Dylan and the other Feebs still hadn't seen me outside yet—too busy with their patients. The outhouse was around back. I decided to give myself a few minutes to make sure the memory-rush was gone.

The dry, yellowed weeds crackled under my footsteps until I reached the path worn to bare dirt behind the church. The outhouse was next to this shed where we stored a lot of the medical supplies. The shed was a dark green. The outhouse was painted white like the church. I hurried to the outhouse door and grabbed the shovel and bucket of sand and wood shavings.

Suddenly Leon and Nindal appeared. It felt like the double infection was laughing at me. I had run just a few blocks, but even so the memories felt overwhelming. My skin crawled as I told myself this wasn't real. They weren't real.

The green shed doors were open, the lock dangling, broken from one handle. Leon passed a box into Nindal's waiting arms. Nindal shifted from foot to foot as if dancing to an imaginary song and passed the box onto someone in the shadows. The beard that had grown in on Leon's face made him look rougher, meaner, like maybe he wouldn't think twice about hurting you if you got in his way.

I told myself to move. I told myself to ignore the tricks my brain was trying to play on me. Another part of me whispered this really didn't feel like a trick. Except that's what the infection fooled you into thinking—that what you saw was real.

Leon passed another box to Nindal and left the shed with a third box in his arms. He shut the doors and the two of them walked away, disappearing into the twilight like they really were ghost-memories. Because that's what they had been. That's what I told myself, even if part of me didn't believe it.

I set the bucket and shovel down. I hurried into the church to check on Jen. I didn't say a word to anyone except to repeat in a whispered voice, "I'm sorry." But Jen didn't hear me. She slept with that bandage around her head and I couldn't bear to wake her.

FOR THE NEXT THREE DAYS, I stayed holed up with my Faints. I went through the motions of the meals. I pointed them in the direction of the bathroom and let their memories do the rest. I chatted about nothing that mattered. I put them to bed and tried to read a book in the last of the light, but kept not understanding what I read. I tried to decide if what I had seen at the shed had been real.

When the sun woke me on the fourth day, I couldn't stand it anymore. Corrina needed to know about what I had seen, even if it turned out to be a ghost-memory.

Once the rope had linked us all together, waist-to-waist in a train, I led my Faints down the three flights of stairs and left them in the care of the church-turned-hospital. I was the only one in town who took care of Faints full time. Everyone else willing to help rotated through the hospital on shifts.

The morning was crisp and cool. There was a wet smell of dew in the air. The pale blue sky was cloudless. Birds chirped in several trees that shook with their movement. I saw the community hall from down the block. It was over two stories tall, though it only had one level.

I entered that cavernous space and yet it somehow still felt claustrophobic. The hall was used mainly for morning exercises. Today it seemed as if less than half the town was there—maybe fifty people. Many had yoga mats and spaced themselves out in rows. Gabbi stood on a little stage that had probably once held piano recitals and school plays. She often led the exercises because of all the classes she'd taken at the fitness centers during her time as a runaway.

My heartbeat increased as I took a position in the back row.

So they were back and no one had bothered to tell me. Not even Ricker.

Gabbi kept everyone moving, even while we focused on breathing and thinking, but thinking in such a way as to put obstacles around memories and to flex mental muscles that could push back anything that crept forward. Every moment flowed into the next without stopping. We worked from our head to our toes. My breathing deepened and moved like a waterfall up and down my spine. She changed the elevation a number of times. Bends, planks, lunges. The muscles in my arms and legs woke up, my head cleared. Our breathing filled the empty space above our heads, all of us silent and working together toward a common goal. To control the zombie in us.

Sometimes we lost someone anyway. The person would go still, but eventually returned, and resumed. No one spoke, and yet we were together. My body opened up and so did my heart. I had not felt such belonging in a long time.

Mayor Helen took the stage after Gabbi finished. She had been middle-aged when she turned and her plumpness made her very grandmotherly. The town had elected her during a group vote last year. Gabbi didn't like her and Mayor Helen didn't have much use for how Gabbi went about things either. Corrina always played interference between the two of them.

Ricker, Gabbi, and Jimmy stood together in a huddle off to the side. Only Ano was missing this morning, but I didn't think much about it. Everyone skipped morning exercises at some point. I hadn't attended them for months.

"I have an announcement," Mayor Helen said. "People have been leaving and I know some of you are considering it."

Conversations erupted.

"There's a cure!" someone shouted.

"There might be." She held up her hands for silence. "There's rumors of it, yes. But that's all it is right now. Rumors. Notwithstanding the few people taking care of the Faints this morning, or those in the fevers right now, who you see around you—that's our town now."

People gasped, including me. Several dozen people had left, just like that, over some rumor, after we'd done everything we could to rescue them and give them a safe place to live.

"The first group left three days ago."

This comment unsettled me. Three days ago was when I had left the hotel to visit Jen. Three days ago was when I had seen Leon and Nindal's ghost-memories at the green shed.

"More left the day after, and a third group just last night. They've taken supplies, stuff we had been holding in trust for the entire town. Food, medicine." Mayor Helen looked like she saw something so broken she couldn't see any way to put the pieces back together.

"But if they find the cure—it'll be worth it," Betty said from the middle of the crowd.

"We should have given them more," said an older man I

didn't recognize.

Others joined in, their talk crowding the air.

"They just took it," Mayor Helen said in a loud voice, chastising everyone into silence. "We would have supplied them. We would have—but fairly. But they didn't ask, they didn't care, they just took it and didn't think about what it would mean for the rest of us still here, still trying to keep all this together."

"What she's saying to you," Gabbi said, separating herself from Jimmy and Ricker, "is they took all the drugs. They left nothing for the Faints or for us if we go into the fevers."

It was like I'd just put together enough of a puzzle to see what picture it was forming, but the picture was horrifying. I had never seen Leon before that night in Betty's store. I had never seen the two of them carry boxes around. Leon and Nindal hadn't been a ghost-memory. I'd watched them take the rest of our medicine and I hadn't done anything to stop them.

The mood in the room shifted. There was still a sense of desire, of fervency, to go after the cure, but the new situation began to dawn on people. We would watch our neighbors slowly turn on us and know our other neighbors had helped it all along.

"But we can get more," Betty said. "Can't we?"

Mayor Helen didn't answer. The silence extended and filled the space like the chatter had just moments before.

"We tried to get more," Ricker said.

The room stilled, as if we all decided to stop breathing at the same time.

"We should go after the cure!" Betty said.

Mayor Helen nodded slowly, sadly. "That's a choice you can make. Maybe it's even the right one, but think about it for awhile yet. If you decide to leave, don't just disappear on us.

We'll share whatever supplies we've got left."

People broke up into groups, some leaving, some shouting at each other, some just looking around, bewildered. I was one of those. Stunned, dizzy from all of it, trying to work out how I felt and going nowhere with it.

I gathered my courage like I was collecting broken cobwebs and went over to Gabbi and the others. I told them what I had seen Leon and Nindal do. I told them what I had done—nothing.

Gabbi looked at me with hooded eyes. Ricker grabbed my hand and squeezed it before dropping it again.

"Where's Ano?" I forced my mind not to think about all the horrible possible answers to that questions.

"He's in the fevers," Jimmy said. "He got bit by a V."

Bewildered, I said, "But how's that even possible? They're starving out, slow, bumbling around like zombies from *Night of the Living Dead*."

"This was a fresh one," Ricker said. He didn't look at me with judgment like Gabbi did. Mostly, he looked tired. "It was probably an uninfected that finally got the V virus."

"Or it was a Feeb turned V," Gabbi said.

"You don't know that," Jimmy said.

"You don't know that it's not true either," Gabbi said.

"But who's with him?" I asked. "If you're all here, who's staying with him during the fevers?" We never left each other alone during the fevers and we never spoke about what we heard or saw when one of us went through it.

"Corrina and Dylan are with him right now," Ricker said. "I'll be going back next, and then Jimmy."

"I'll take a turn," I said. "I'll go next."

Ricker tilted his head, thoughtful. "There's something we

need to tell you."

"What happened on the raid?" I should have been there with them, with Ano and Ricker and the others. I should have helped them. But even as I thought the words, I resisted them. The fear came raging back to gulp me down. It wasn't my place anymore to go out there. It wasn't where I needed to be.

"There was medicine," Jimmy said. "The right kind—the kind the healer wanted. But someone else had gotten there first."

"You went?" I said.

"I'm not a little kid anymore, no matter what you think," Jimmy said. "I was on the street long before you!"

"Not by much," Gabbi said.

"Stop it," Ricker said.

"Jimmy, just tell her," Gabbi said. "Tell her all of it if you're going to tell any of it."

Jimmy opened his mouth, closed it again, then said. "Alden was with them—"

"What?"

"It wasn't Tabitha's people or Sergeant Bennings, it was somebody else. But…"

"Alden's been taken," Gabbi said.

Noise, like the whirring of an engine rose higher and higher. I realized it was the blood rushing past my ears, drowning out other sounds.

"It was a mess, Maibe," Ricker said. "We got there and it was crazy. The whole world is pretty much empty with people and yet there was Alden and he was alone—at first."

"You talked to him?"

"He said he was searching for the cure," Gabbi said.

"But that doesn't make any sense," except that it made perfect

sense, but I didn't know what else to say, only that I had to say
something to fill the void that threatened to consume me.

"Alden was there," Gabbi said. "He knows we're all going
Feeb-crazy. He said he left to look for the cure on his own. For
you. Then this group of uninfected took him."

"Sergeant Bennings," I said. "It must have been his father's
people."

Gabbi shook her head. "It wasn't. I didn't recognize any of
their faces. It wasn't Sergeant Bennings."

"But who else—"

"The only reason we got out was because of those Vs,"
Ricker said. "The uninfected had pinned us into a corner and
demanded to know what we knew about the cure—"

"The goddamn cure," Gabbi interrupted. "People can't stop
talking about it."

"Because it's got to be real," Jimmy said. "We have to help
them find it."

"They had plenty of guns," Ricker said, ignoring Jimmy. "I
figured that was going to be it for us, but all the noise had
attracted fresh Vs—maybe ones from their group that had
recently gotten infected. I don't know. But it was enough for
us to escape."

"Except Ano got bit," Jimmy said.

"We don't have any medicine," Ricker said, an anguished
look in his eyes that I didn't understand. The medicine eased
the symptoms, made people come out of the fevers faster, made
the memories less intense, allowed the Faints to come back
enough to help us help them, but there had been no medicine
in the beginning. We knew we could make it through without
the medicine.

"He'll come out of it," I said. "Maybe it'll take longer than it used to but we always come out of the fevers."

Gabbi didn't respond. That wasn't like her and it scared me.

CHAPTER 8

THE INSIDE OF THE METHODIST CHURCH looked different in the daylight. Less spooky but more depressing. Its wood-planked floors, high windows, arched ceilings, and stonework walls was the only place big enough and secure enough to set up lines of beds dragged in from surrounding houses.

The church-turned-hospital was small, but had plenty of room for us Feebs injured or sick by regular diseases like the flu. It was where we cared for moms and new babies, those born infected—seeing ghosts and dealing with memory-rushes even before they could speak. The hospital was also for the town Faints who could be triggered into eating and drinking and using the old outhouse. The Faints who were so comatose that they refused to eat or drink—there wasn't much we could do except make them comfortable and make their end as painless as possible.

Most of us took shifts in the hospital at some point, as if

we could somehow get rid of the guilt of surviving when our families and friends hadn't.

The church smelled like old wood varnish, decades worth of dust, and a vinegar disinfectant. Lines of baby food jars, some empty, some filled, were set out on two tables near Corrina's experiments. Not more than half the beds were filled. We'd lost five Faints to dehydration in the last heat wave and to a general sense of giving-up-ness that had taken over, as if the bacteria in their bodies had surrendered.

Gabbi marched across the creaking wood boards, passing by all the Faints in beds covered in bright colored sheets—striped, solid, animal print. She stopped at a bed near the back. Ricker and Jimmy trailed after me. Ano lay in the bed, his sheets sweat-soaked and tangled, his hands and feet bound to the bedposts by rope. Corrina sat alongside him in a stiff wooden chair, applying a damp cloth to Ano's forehead. His brown eyes were closed, his lips pressed together, his forehead wrinkled and his thick brows pinched as if in deep concentration, or pain.

"How is he?" Gabbi asked.

Corrina shook her head. "He's been in the fevers all night." There was a hunch to her shoulders and dark circles under her eyes as if she'd been awake most of the night.

The first fevers after infection sometimes stayed for weeks, but after that, the fevers hadn't ever lasted for more than half a day.

"What can I do?" I asked.

"Sit with him," Corrina said. "I can tend to a few others if you sit with him for awhile."

"You need help," I said. "I'll stay, I'll put in more shifts. I'll—"

"It doesn't matter," Dylan said, coming up behind Corrina.

He rested his hands on her shoulders. She leaned back into him. "They won't eat or drink without the medicine," Corrina said. "We're losing people everyday. I thought things could get better. I really did." She stood up and wandered off as if in a daze, shuffling her feet like a zombie. Dylan followed her.

I took Corrina's chair and grabbed Ano's hand. He strained against the ropes, eyes wide and wild and unseeing, looking out past the beds and the church walls. He began talking in Spanish. A fast, guttural Spanish that dropped vowels and cut off words. He gripped my hand, squeezing the bones until my fingers twisted and I yelled out in pain.

Gabbi tried to push down his chest. "Ano, Ano, be calm, be calm...shshshsh."

Dylan and Corrina rushed back. Between us all we managed to get Ano back down, but he wouldn't stop talking. I didn't understand most of what he said, but he sounded like a child again. Someone was hurting him and someone else he loved. My heart constricted. This was a sentence worse than death for someone who had not once in these past three years given up on doing what he thought was right.

"He keeps remembering this...this moment with his stepdad." Dylan drew his hand across his face. I realized he must be able to understand Ano. Every word of it.

"Don't say anything," Gabbi said fiercely. "He wouldn't want anyone to know. He—"

"I know," Dylan said. "I know it. I will never say anything."

"It won't last for much longer though." I hoped by saying it out loud it would come true right then. Guilt cut me deep and I began to babble. "He'll come out of it. It'll stop any second now."

Gabbi stared at Corrina until she looked away.

"I'm sorry," Corrina said. "I just knew things were so hard for you, I didn't want to make it harder. It's not like we can do anything about it so what's the point?"

That look passed between Dylan and Corrina again—the one they'd shared the night I hurt Jen. When we had worked by candlelight and I swore Corrina wanted to tell me something else.

"Tell her," Dylan said, looking at Ricker.

"You knew about this?" I stared at Ricker in disbelief.

"Corrina didn't want you to know," Ricker said. "She knew you were taking things so rough, she didn't think this would help. I promised her—"

"What's going on?" I almost screamed the question.

"We were hoping for the new drugs," Corrina whispered. "Then there would have been nothing to tell."

"The fevers aren't lifting anymore," Gabbi said. "If you get bit by a V you don't come back out anymore."

CHAPTER 9

SOMETIMES MY UNCLE WOULD HOLD BACK a word I needed for a crossword puzzle, the one word that was just out of my reach, because he wanted to see the light that would dawn on my face—that's what he called it, the light—when I discovered what I needed.

"If Alden was going after a cure," I said, "maybe he knew something we didn't—"

"Or maybe he's desperate and stupid," Gabbi interrupted.

"But even besides that," I said. "Whoever took him is looking for the cure. They took the drugs we need with them. If we go after the cure, we'll find Alden AND the medicine that Ano needs—that we all need."

Jimmy looked at me like I was finally making sense, and that scared me. I didn't look at Ricker.

"There's got to be other places that have the drugs the healer wants," Ricker said.

"Where?" I said.

Ricker looked at me, an unreadable expression on his face.

"You know there isn't," Gabbi said quietly. "It was a brain research lab. It was their experimental stuff."

"How did anyone even know it was there?" Jimmy said.

"The healer was one of the uninfected," Gabbi said. "He was part of the camp system working on a cure for them until he turned into a Feeb. The uninfected had all those spots mapped out."

"So whoever took Alden—they must have been part of the camps," I said, thinking it through. "He didn't recognize them, but they knew who he was."

"We have no idea where Alden is," Ricker said.

"We'll go back to the research lab. We'll go back to where he was taken," I said. "Maybe there'll be clues."

"Maybe we'll get ourselves killed for someone who's already dead," Ricker said.

"This is for Ano," I said.

"Is it?"

Fury rose inside me. "Don't even. You know me, Ricker. You know—"

Ricker closed his eyes. "I know. I'm sorry."

"We have to find them for Ano," I said. "And if we find Alden and we're able to save two people we care about and who've helped us survive this far, then what's wrong with that?"

Ricker didn't say anything.

"You keep saying we." Gabbi spoke carefully, as if testing each word in her mind before letting it out. "But you've already told us a million times that you aren't going anywhere. Why do you keep saying we?"

She knew the answer. The look in her eyes told me she knew the answer to that question, but she wanted me to say it out loud—to commit to it in such a way that I couldn't back out. Maybe if I said it out loud, maybe the fear that made my insides quake would settle down enough for me to breathe again.

"I'm going too. I'm going out there to get the drugs for Ano." I glanced at Ricker. "And to look for Alden. With or without you—I'm going."

I put as much force into the words as I could. The roar of my heartbeat settled down enough for me to hear Ano's hallucinations again. This was the right thing to do, I felt that, even if it brought my world crashing down around me. "But I really want you to come with me."

Gabbi smiled, almost vicious. "Since you asked so nicely—I think I'll come along for the ride. Someone has to keep you from getting killed, after all."

"Come on." Ricker avoided looking at me and rested a hand on Jimmy's shoulder. "We need to pack."

"I have something that might help," Corrina said. "I'm so sorry. I didn't want you to go."

"I need to go," I said. "I have to go."

Corrina nodded. "I'll bring you what I have."

Everyone left except for Gabbi. She settled into the chair next to Ano. I knew she wouldn't budge from his side until one of us took her place. It was just me and Gabbi again, like old times. I should have been uncomfortable, what with the waves of judgment coming off her, but that had never stopped me before. I wasn't going to let it start now.

ALDEN

The halls were dark in this section. Emergency lights halfway down the walls glowed red behind their hard plastic casings. The bucket made his arms ache from the weight of the food inside— packet after packet of dehydrated food brought back to life with water. Even though the food wasn't meant for him, his stomach grumbled because he hadn't eaten breakfast yet. The metal handle bit into his hands and turned them numb. He wished his brain would go numb, but it never stopped.

He walked down the hallway until he came to the next door. At head height there was an opening with a metal grate. The noises from the other side of that grate always disturbed him because they sounded so human even though he knew—they were chimps.

He banged on the door with his fist. The noise reverberated down the cement hallway. The chimp chatter increased until it filled the whole world.

He checked to make sure the two young chimps had gone into their feeding cage. He liked the chimps. They were usually caged in pairs or even trios. They would screech and chatter and play together, tumbling around on the ground because they had no idea how terrible the world was now. He envied them for that.

He slowly turned the steering wheel-like handle on the wall. He wanted this part of his morning chores to take as long as possible because he was dreading what came at the end.

Finally metal clanged shut on the other side. Everything smelled like monkey piss in this section even though their cages were open to the sky on the other side. He rested his hand on the door and grabbed up the bucket again, but then stopped and stared at his skin.

His uninfected skin.

Clear, smooth veins and bruising beginning to fade. His head was clear, his memories under control—though he would never forget how the double infection had made his brain betray him again and again.

They had put him under anesthesia and everything went blank for the longest time. He woke up and swore he heard echoes of someone screaming and they said it was side effects from the infection that would dissipate because they had cured him. They had the cure.

But it only worked for Feebs, not for Faints like his mother. It had something to do with blood and saliva and all the fluids that made his stomach feel queasy. He forced himself not to dwell on any of that. Maibe could be cured—if he could figure out how to escape with it. Whatever it was.

That was the problem. He had been cured of the Feeb infection, but he didn't know how.

He opened the door, left the food, released the chimps from the feeding cage, then moved to the next one until he repeated the process over a dozen times. This was a chimp research facility back before the Lyssa virus even existed. The place had lasted all this time under Dr. Stoven's care, all other research projects abandoned except for whatever might lead to a cure—and then Dr. Ferrad had showed up.

Alden closed the door and dragged his feet to the last door, using up a full minute to walk the ten feet. This one was the same size as the others, but there was only one individual inside it. A girl.

He looked forward to caring for the chimps, mucking out their cages, watching them play. He felt sorry for the Faints he helped take care of—a whole wing of them strapped to beds with drip lines and beeping monitors. They reminded him of his mother and the awful things his father had done to try to save her over the years. They reminded him of Maibe and how she slowly disappeared into herself. There were at least a dozen uninfected who ran the facility. He was allowed to interact with them now that he'd been cured. But there were Vs here too and the girl in this cage was one of them. The worst one.

He pressed his hand against the cold surface of the door and told himself to just get it over with.

There was a giggle behind him.

He dropped the bucket, the food spilling onto the floor. He whirled around and saw her. Kailyn—Dr. Stoven's crazy brat.

"What are you doing?" she said, her voice high-pitched. She was maybe ten years old. Today she'd worn a pink dress like out of a Disney movie—with ruffles at the sleeves and a thick petticoat. It matched her blonde pigtails and turned her into a grungy sort of Alice in Wonderland.

"My job," Alden said. "You know this is my job."

She rolled her eyes. "FYI, I'm pretty sure your job isn't about just standing there and looking super dumb at the door."

"I wasn't."

"You were too," she said, her eyes wide, a vicious smile on her lips.

After he'd woken up cured he had been harsh with her when she tried to make friends with him. She dumped all this salt into the food bucket one day, which made some of the chimps throw up. They blamed him. He yelled at her, and then they yelled at him. He learned the hard way that she liked to hold grudges and that Dr. Stoven really didn't care as long as she kept herself out of trouble.

There was a whimper on the other side of the door.

Kailyn giggled again.

He was going to teach her a lesson. She should take things seriously. This was nothing to joke about.

"You want to feed this one?" He gathered the food back into the bucket and held it out.

Her eyes widened behind her glasses until they became like huge, round lenses. They reminded him too much of the camera's eye that had watched while they turned him into a Feeb.

"I'm not supposed to," she said.

He shrugged his shoulders. "You're right. Dr. Stoven always says this stuff isn't for little kids like you." He waited to see if she was smart enough not to take the bait.

She held out her hand. "Give it to me."

The bucket weighed barely anything because it was almost empty now. It swung at her side, hitting her leg once. Her face, her uninfected skin, had gone even paler than usual.

He banged on the door. The V girl was aware enough to know that was the sound of food and she was only going to get the food if she put herself away. That was the problem. That's what weirded him out so badly about her. She was more aware than other Vs. Not by much, but enough.

He looked carefully through the grate to confirm she was in the cage. After all, he didn't want to kill Kailyn, just scare her.

He turned the wheel, then unlocked the door. This room was different, more like a hospital room than a chimp cage. Her bed and blanket had been torn to shreds in a fit of rage at some point. The V girl looked healthy except for the crazy light in her brown eyes. She seemed only a few years older than him. Her hair was in mattes around her face. Her fingernails were dirty. She wore a hospital gown that looked three sizes too big for her.

"Go on," Alden said.

Sweat broke out on his forehead. Both of them were staring at him. But her stare was different than Kailyn's. She looked at him like he was prey.

Kailyn stepped into the room with the bucket. Her legs shivered. He pushed her in further. She screeched and whirled around. "Don't touch me!"

"FYI," he forced out, the tremble in his voice betraying his fear, "I'm pretty sure just standing there and looking dumb isn't going to get her fed."

Kailyn gave him an evil look. "I'm fine. Just don't touch me. You might still have Feeb germs lurking around you. Just because they say you're cured doesn't make it—"

A hand shot between the bars of the cage and grabbed at the bucket. Kailyn was so shocked, she forgot to let go. She was slammed into the bars. The V grabbed both pigtails and held

Kailyn inches away from her face.

Alden shouted and threw himself between the two of them. The V didn't budge. He hit at her arms and wrenched Kailyn away. He tumbled backwards, but didn't fall because the V caught him by the shirt. He prayed for it to rip. Kailyn wailed behind him, but he couldn't see her. The V brought him close, her breath harsh, her brown eyes huge and fixed on his face.

"Ricker?"

This stunned him. It wasn't a common name. There was only one person in the world he'd ever met who had that name. She couldn't—

She pulled his arm through the bars and bit him deep on the flesh of his bicep. The pain seared into him like fire. Panic flooded his hearing with a roar. She still held his arm. She was going for another bite.

Her pupils contracted.

She let go of him and he fell hard onto the cement, bruising his tailbone. She stepped away until her back was against the stone wall of the other side, as far from the bars as she could get. She covered her bloodied face with her hands.

Alden cradled his injured arm in his lap.

Kailyn got down on her knees next to him and tried to peel back his sleeve.

"Don't!" He jerked away.

"I'm sorry. I'm sorry. I didn't mean—"

"Get help, Kailyn. Hurry."

CHAPTER 10

THE HEALER'S HOUSE WAS COLD. The walls were thick with the stink of incense. Freshly brewed tea steamed on the table in front of us, the tendrils floating up in lazy arcs.

He wanted everyone to call him a memory healer. I told myself every good zombie movie had their version of a person with the answers, but that didn't mean I had to like it.

Beaded curtains, tea leaves, cotton paisley throws everywhere, a cat twining around the table legs, a dozen eclectic rings covering his fingers. I half expected a crystal ball to come out next. I decided he must have always wanted to be a witch doctor, full of potions and motions that were faker than the special effects head when Quaid's disguise had malfunctioned in *Total Recall*—the original, please, not the remake. Now that the world had ended, this was his chance.

When Dylan had come to relieve Gabbi from Ano's bedside, I'd said goodbye to Freanz, Molly, and the twins. I collected some food and water in a backpack and now there was nothing left to do—except to leave. But Gabbi wouldn't leave until we visited the healer. Ricker told me she'd been seeing him every time before heading out of town, like he was a sort of good luck charm.

Gabbi had wanted us to come because I think she believed in it a little, probably more than a little. Angels and demons and Mary—Gabbi talked about it all in her fevers. She never admitted it outside the fevers, so I dared not bring it up.

The healer used a metal circle, rusted, almost like a basketball hoop torn off its backboard, and a ruler with bells attached. He turned circles around us while chanting. His assistant, a much older Feeb who walked with a limp, waved smoking sage over our heads and sprinkled water onto our hands and faces. They both wore shades of green, because green was thought to calm the memories. Red was for Vs and a sign of violence. Blue was too calm, too close to how Faints lived. Green was for life, for growth, for energy, for control. Green was for fakes.

I sighed and caught Ricker's eye. He smiled. He had been upset with me about too many things, but he could never stay mad for long. His shirt hung big on him, highlighting the weight he'd lost because of infection, or cold, or too little food, or all the above. He needed to eat more, rest more, laugh more.

The chanting grew louder, to almost a shout, then a silence that was almost stunning. My ears rang.

Gabbi remained still. Eyes closed. Face tense. She wanted peace, I knew that's almost all she searched for—those moments when she could calm the emotions that always seemed to boil up inside. She and Kern were made for each other in that way, if only his mother, Tabitha, weren't so terrible a person.

The healer rang a final bell. He took up the food Gabbi had brought in trade.

"Thank you," Gabbi said.

I realized it didn't matter if I believed in anything he did. Gabbi believed it, and maybe that's what mattered.

We walked outside, onto the creaking wood porch, down the rotting steps lined with rickety railings and flaking paint.

Jimmy waited, hopping from foot to foot with impatience. "Corrina's in her garden. She wants us to meet her there."

Gabbi went ahead while Ricker and I grabbed our backpacks—barely halfway filled with some of the supplies Leon and the rest hadn't stolen.

The path to Corrina's garden was overgrown and green. She carried buckets of water for it everyday from the town's reservoir. A waist-high gate separated the garden from the rest of town. Hedges grew along the edge, creating a semblance of a fence. I knew behind those hedges deer-fencing had been strung up, otherwise many of her plants would have been chewed down to dirt. The wooden bars of the gate were made out of stripped branches. A triangle of branches formed the center of the gate. This was not the food garden for the town but Corrina's personal garden.

The shadows of the surrounding forest seemed both to somehow protect this spot and yet hide monsters in its depths. The faint smell of licorice floated in the air. Gabbi and Corrina stood in the sunlight, examining a wooden frame made out of the same branches as the gate. The bars of the frame towered a good foot above their heads. Bundles of flowers and other herbs hung upside down from the branches like decorations.

Their heads were bent, almost touching. They looked

comfortable with each other, like they often worked in this garden together. Like they were friends doing something important. My heart ached. I had made myself stay away for so long. I wasn't really part of this circle anymore, not how I was, not how I desperately longed to be again.

Gabbi noticed the three of us first. She stood and turned away. As if thinking better of it, she stomped back, little puffs of dirt kicking up from beneath her shoes. "Just because you've decided to come along now doesn't make it okay how long you stayed away."

"Gabbi," Corrina said, a warning note in her voice.

Gabbi whirled on Corrina. "Don't even start. You're the one who made us all keep the secret from her. You said we should leave her alone. You said to give her time."

"Calm down!" Ricker yelled at Gabbi. I didn't understand that—amping her up wasn't going to help. He moved as if to step between Gabbi and Corrina.

Gabbi bared her teeth. I held my breath. Those few moments of peace I thought I'd witnessed between the two of them had vanished into smoke. In its place was the old Gabbi I knew, except this one was more dangerous than ever, ready to go V at any time.

"Gabbi, we were having a moment. Go back to the moment." The look on Corrina's face became just a little too dreamy. She swayed, closing her eyes. The purple flowers in her hand tumbled to the dirt, releasing a lavender scent.

I pushed Corrina and sent her sprawling. I feared it wouldn't be enough to snap her out of the Faint episode. I didn't dare touch Gabbi, didn't dare look at her in case it made her erupt into violence.

Corrina gasped and opened her eyes. Jimmy helped her up.

Ricker was breathing hard like he'd just run a mile. He handed Gabbi her pack like nothing had happened and glanced my way. Dark circles surrounded his eyes. "She's okay."

"Maibe…" Gabbi said, but she couldn't finish.

"I missed you too, Gabbi," I said, even as her earlier accusation settled heavy on me. Maybe she hadn't meant it, but I still deserved it. I'd hidden away with my Faints. I'd watched Leon and Nindal take the medicine. I hadn't stopped any of this from happening.

Corrina held out four pouches for us to take and suddenly I felt so angry I almost shook. She made everyone promise to keep things from me. They listened—even Gabbi, the person you could count on to tell you the truth no matter what.

Corrina opened one of the pouches, revealing a plastic baggy full of leaves that looked like just blowing on them would make them disintegrate. "Steep in hot water for ten minutes. If it works, it might lessen your symptoms for a few hours. There are enough for three doses each."

"If it works?" Ricker said.

"What is this?" Gabbi passed a pouch around to each of us.

"Plants from my garden," Corrina said. "Cinnamon, chile peppers, ginseng, a bunch of other plants that support brain function. I'm hopeful it could help, but there's no way to know for sure."

I stuffed the pouch into my pocket. "Let's go."

"Wait." Corrina glanced at Gabbi and Ricker.

"Come on," Gabbi said. "That's our sign to leave them be."

"Very subtle," Ricker said.

"I've been practicing," Gabbi said.

They wandered a few yards away with Jimmy, leaving me and Corrina alone.

"You haven't been yourself," Corrina said. "Not for months."

"That still doesn't mean—"

"I was scared we were going to lose you. Every time something happened and you found out, you retreated even more."

"That's not fair!"

"I'm making it all up? You weren't hiding out with your Faints? You didn't bother leaving that place to even ask what was really going on out here?"

"I…" But there was nothing to finish that sentence with. She was right. I had done all those things. I had wanted to hide and never come back out. I would still be in that room if it wasn't for Ano and Alden.

My anger vanished. I shouldn't be mad at her for making everyone keep things from me—I should be mad at myself for making it necessary.

"After what happened at the camp, we feared it was too much for you." Corrina looked anguished. "I kept hoping if we gave you enough time, just a little more time, then you'd come back to us, you'd forgive yourself—"

"I can't do that," I said. "But I'm not mad at you. I promise."

Corrina pulled me into a hug. "This is not your fault. Blame the infection. It's not your fault they died."

I relaxed into her hug, feeling the warmth and love she was offering. We'd been through so much together. I couldn't bear to contradict her.

Before I walked through the gate, I turned back. Corrina had returned to the drying rack and was tying another bundle of flowers to it.

Another puzzle piece clicked into place.

This was what Gabbi said Mary had always wanted. Gabbi, Ricker, Ano, even Jimmy, they each ranted about a place like this in their fevers. My own memories conjured them up—tying Gabbi down to a bed, Jimmy to a chair, Ricker once to a bathtub.

The bathtub was the most vivid and it crowded out the other memories. It had happened in the early weeks of all this, right after Leaf had been killed. We'd been trapped inside a warehouse where a claw-footed tub had been dumped at some point. Ano and Gabbi dragged it into the middle of the room and tied Ricker down to it because he'd gotten bit by a V. He'd looked so small and helpless, his feverish skin a sickly contrast to the dingy white of the tub.

"We can't do anything until Ricker is out of the fevers." Ano's remembered voice echoed across the space of the garden but couldn't penetrate the trees that darkened its edge.

We'd piled together a bunch of broken chair legs and set them on fire for warmth. I hadn't know them well yet—except that I knew I could trust them. I'd pressed my back against the cold of the tub and waited out Ricker's fevers. My face was the first one he saw when he came out—but before that, he talked about Mary and the garden. A garden like this, in the country, where they could all live together in peace.

But Ano was trapped inside the fevers. The rest of us were on the verge of going V or Faint.

I didn't feel much peace at the moment.

CHAPTER 11

WE STARTED OUT ON FOOT, not because there were no working vehicles, but because engines made noise.

Gabbi walked in front, Ricker was at the end, Jimmy and I were in the middle. The main exit out of town was basically an obstacle course for zombies, like something out of *The Walking Dead*. Burned-out cars were towed into positions meant to slow down anyone trying to weave through. Furniture was turned into piles of scrap that formed little alleys. Dead ends would drop the unaware into spiked pits.

We'd built all this those first few months before rescuing more Feebs. Layers of ash from the fires that burned unchecked during the summers coated everything. It all smelled dead and dusty and forgotten. Symmetrical cobwebs were everywhere—those weren't the ones to worry about. The webs that crackled at the touch and looked like they had been built by a drunk spider, those were the ones to watch for. Jimmy jumped back after brushing against one, slamming into my stomach. I let out a groan.

"Sorry," Jimmy said. His corkscrew hair was plastered to his neck in swirls. Even I could see the fear in his eyes as his brain pictured a black widow jumping out.

I touched his shoulder. "Memory-rush?"

He passed a hand over his face and pushed the damp hair off his neck. "I was in this garage once when I first tried running away. It was perfect because it was full of stuff to hide in and looked like no one had been there for months. I got too close to one." He lifted up his pant leg. There was a puckered scar on his ankle I had always thought came from a V.

We passed through the obstacle course and onto the highway. My friends fanned around me. It felt easy with them, like I was finally in the right place.

We headed for where Gabbi and Ano had seen Alden captured. The place had been a memory research lab for Alzheimer's patients. It would have the *memantine* that could bring Ano back and help the rest of us better control our symptoms. Or it could all be gone now, taken by the same people who had captured Alden. We planned to find out.

Most of the Vs had died years before, but the uninfected supplied the virus with enough fresh meat that we needed to remain watchful. Maybe Leon's group was out here turning V too. Tabitha and Kern's group was around somewhere. They knew about our town but never bothered us. We weren't looking for a cure—plus the town was full of Feebs who Tabitha had infected against their will. She wasn't welcome.

The afternoon warmed up. We had at least several more hours to go. Trash littered the highway. Leaves, weeds, actual paper. Everything yellowed, brittle, ready to burst into flame from the heat. The trees offered some shade but we didn't want to go too deep for fear of what might come out.

Ricker caught my eye and smiled. I smiled back because I knew it would do no good to hide. It must have been as clear as the sunlight hitting my face—I wanted to be outside and doing something. Not that taking care of my Faints wasn't doing something. Molly, Freanz and the twins would have a snack soon and I would have thrown open the windows by now to let in fresh air and light and gaze out on the hillsides. But they wouldn't know I was gone, and here—these steps my feet took—it woke up a part of me I'd thought dead.

The bushes shook like a bear lumbered through them. We crouched because it might actually be a bear. The animals had come back. Not everything, but enough—birds, squirrels, raccoons, coyotes.

Gabbi set down a knee and brought out a crossbow with unconscious ease.

Three figures emerged from the bush, low to the ground—not bears. They saw us and sprinted toward us.

Ricker stood beside Gabbi, holding a machete, saved from some abandoned garage last year. He said he liked the weight of it in his hand. There were guns, we could have carried guns, but we didn't. Guns drew more Vs to you, and let everyone know where you were. Better to run than fight. Better to put down a V from up close than invite more to join in. Other Feebs thought differently and carried guns wherever they went, but whether it was right or wrong, we didn't.

"Help us!" the one in front shouted.

This did not impress Gabbi. She leveled her bow.

The two men and a woman halted several yards away, but close enough to stun me into action.

"They're uninfected," I shouted.

The three uninfected drew weapons. We scrambled away as if following the moves of a dance. It WAS a sort of dance, the way Gabbi and Ricker had learned how to avoid raids and ambushes and traps when they were runaways.

Jimmy disappeared into the trees. I dove into the bushes. My skin burned as it scraped against gravel. The crushed leaves released a burst of pine scents. I put the pain out of my mind as I catalogued the moving shadows, the shouts, the way the leaves shifted and revealed something that shined like metal pointing right at my forehead.

"Gotcha, you dirty monster."

If all feeling hadn't left my body I would have told the guy that I wasn't the dirty one, not by a long shot, not compared to his sweat-stained, dirt-streaked, awful-smelling self. He wore blue plastic gloves, a painter's mask, goggles that sealed so tight to his sweaty face it left indents. Fear did more than tickle my throat, it strangled it. I crumpled to my knees on the carpet of dried pine needles and yellowed weeds.

JIMMY HAD GOTTEN AWAY. We didn't dare say this aloud to each other. But I knew each one of us hoped that he was safe and would find help somehow.

Their campfire was a mess—like now that the apocalypse had happened they might as well be slobs. Gabbi, Ricker, and I sat against trees within the campfire's light, hands tied behind our backs, ankles hobbled to our wrists, exhausted after the miles they had forced us to walk through the forest. By all rights and legends and history we should have been dead on sight. These weren't uninfected from the camps. They were survivalists, zombie hunters, Feeb-haters.

But we were being walked into the ground, for what reason they wouldn't say. We had stayed in the forest so it was hard to tell if they had moved us away from or closer to our original goal—the brain research lab. Every time Gabbi demanded an answer she got a jab in the stomach until finally she threw up a little blood and zipped her mouth in that way that said everybody better leave town fast. Gabbi was liable to explode the first chance they gave her. Whether or not it was a real chance, or one that would get us all killed—that was a different story.

Ricker was pale, like all the blood had drained from his face, but there was a hard light in his eyes like he was remembering something bad.

There were six uninfected. They laughed quietly among themselves as can openers appeared from pockets. The woman dug a grate into the coals and one of the men balanced the cans over the heat. I suspected none of that food was meant for us but my stomach growled just the same.

"Are you going to feed us or do you plan to kill us by way of starvation?" Gabbi said.

One of the men brandished a stick. "Shut up."

Gabbi spit. Her saliva shot into the air and landed well short of his shoes, but he jumped back like a snake had bitten him.

Another guy came up, hands gloved, mask on, carrying a cloth. "We're done with that now. Zach, get back to stirring the cans. If those beans burn, you owe me a week's worth of food." Zach retreated, tossing his stick aside.

Gabbi received a blow across the cheek and the man pulled the rolled-up cloth around her neck as if to choke her. Ricker shouted. I pushed myself against the tree, squatted, and then jumped. The rope yanked me down and I landed on my chin in the dirt, the breath knocked out of me. I gasped and the air rushed back in, clearing my head. Two of the uninfected pinned Ricker to the dirt, pressing his face into the ground with rifle points. Gabbi now sat upright, nose bloody, mouth stuffed with a rag tied around her head.

The men pulled me up by my ponytail. I let out an involuntary screech. My head burned as if set on fire. Ricker moved and got kicked in the stomach.

"Stop," I gasped out. "Stop. I'm fine, Ricker. I'm fine."

"So she does speak," the man pulling my hair said. He let go.

I slumped onto my knees and wished that Gabbi could just keep her mouth shut sometimes.

"I thought for sure she was mute. Most skins are," the woman said, leaving Zach to stirring the cans. She wasn't wearing any protective gear and stayed well back from us. "I would have taken you for one of the crazies," she said to Gabbi, "but the skin always tells the truth, doesn't it?"

The man who had kicked Ricker said, "I still don't understand why this time is different. Why haven't we killed them yet, Perkins? The bounty can't be worth that much. This is crazy risky. I haven't been this close to a creeper since—"

"Shut up, Hugh," Perkins said. "They can hear you."

"Oh, come on. They might look human, but they're as dumb as dogs now. You know the infection messes with their heads," Hugh said.

"You don't have a clue," Perkins said. "She'll take whatever we round up. Whatever's left. You don't even—"

"Remember Sven last summer?" the woman said quietly. The mention of Sven's name froze the group in some common memory of grief, not unlike a memory-rush, but I decided not to mention this out loud since my scalp still burned.

"June, you need to leave off now," Perkins said. "And stop talking around them."

They returned to a huddle around the fire. Even though it was summer, it cooled off fast at night in the forest. I scooted back over to Ricker and Gabbi.

"Keep separate," Perkins said, looking over his shoulder. "Keep away from each other or we'll stake you down now instead of later."

I stopped moving. He turned back to the fire and dug a spoon into one of the steaming cans.

Something metal glinted out of the corner of my eye. I tilted my gaze in Gabbi's direction. I hadn't looked at her yet, didn't want to look at her. Sometimes her temper got us all in trouble. My burning scalp, Ricker's punched stomach, her bloodied mouth. But there was a flash again, the firelight bouncing against an object in her hands. She stared at the group around the fire, freezing whenever one of them glanced up.

She had stolen a knife and was cutting loose her bonds.

I bit my tongue and scolded myself. I should have known better. Gabbi didn't always go about it the way others might want, but she didn't do things for no reason. She had goaded them into getting close enough for her to grab a knife.

The rope dropped away from her hands. She quickly loosened the rope around her ankles and brought the knife around. Instead of applying it to Ricker's ropes next, she slipped into the forest shadows.

My mouth dropped open and then I closed it again. We'd been through too much for me not to trust her. Whatever she did, it was going to be a bad plan, but it might get us out of here. I needed to be ready when the moment arrived.

Perkins looked back again, but must have decided not to count, or maybe the shadows were playing tricks on him. He returned to his can of food like nothing had changed.

In the flickering light, Ricker scanned the edges of the darkness. I did the same on my side, turning my head slightly, listening for movement over the crackling logs and murmurs of conversation. There, on the edge of the firelight, a shadow emerged, low to the ground. Metal flashed and Perkins fell backward with a shout.

Gabbi appeared in the firelight, pressing the knife against Perkins throat. "Stay back."

The others tumbled away as if someone had thrown burning coals in their faces. The food cans spilled their steaming contents into a puddle, making the fire hiss with the sound of burning beans.

"You're in big trouble, little girl," Perkins said, his Adam's apple bobbing around the knife's edge. He closed his fists.

"Don't." Gabbi pressed the knife deeper into his flesh. "One cut is all it will take, honey baby. Don't you know I spit on this thing just a second ago? You left some smudge marks that needed cleaning."

June gasped. "Perkins!"

"Hello, Perkins. I'm Gabbi. Nice to meet you, by the way."

I struggled with the ropes around my wrists, twisting and wrenching. I ignored the burning ache in my bones from the strain. Ricker scooted over in the dirt and we worked on untying each other's hands. Gabbi against six of them. Not good odds. But if we made it into the dark we could disappear. It would be cold, we'd likely get lost, but as long as we escaped, we could find our bearings at first light.

"You won't leave here alive," Perkins said.

"I thought I was already dead?" She rolled her eyes as she said it. Her short, spiky hair stood out straight in all directions.

Suddenly masked figures darted from the forest. The embers scattered. Gabbi and Perkins were knocked aside. She fell flat on her back. He fell on top of her. I shouted for Gabbi to get up and run.

My hands were still tied together.

I was going to lose it.

I was going back to the refugee camp, to the mandarin orchard and the clear sky and the way the dying girl's eyes had reflected such trust in me until the very last moment.

Hands lifted me by my shoulders, but my feet were unsteady, slippery on the leaves. "Get up, Maibe."

A familiar voice. I knew who belonged to that voice, but the knowledge wisped away like tendrils of steam.

Something sharp slashed at my ropes, once, twice, catching my skin the third time, opening up a line of fire.

My hands were free.

I didn't dwell on it, only somehow distantly noticed that the firelight seemed impossibly full of people trampling each other. I barreled into Perkins and threw him off just as his punch landed on Gabbi's chin.

I helped Gabbi sit up. Blood reddened her lips and teeth. She spit a glob onto the dirt and coughed. I looked around for

Ricker. He had pinned the woman's arms behind her back in a sort of wrestling move. To her credit she wasn't yelling, but she was struggling. I jumped up, thinking I would find the rope from my wrists and we'd tie her and then run off.

Someone else stepped forward and yanked the woman away from Ricker.

"Hey!" Ricker said.

The man pressed his boot in between her shoulder blades. "Be still or it will go bad for you."

My mind whirled. His back was to me, the firelight casting shadows against a red plaid shirt. I knew him and the feeling in my stomach wasn't a good one.

"Kern?" Gabbi said.

"Good to see you again, Gabbi." Kern didn't turn as he said it.

Others, his people most likely, had taken out our captors. One lay on the ground, face down, blood pooling on the dirt. The scattered fire had caught and now burned at half a dozen spots in the little clearing. The shadows moved wildly, jumping from face to face, shirt to shirt, trees to mouth to cold eyes. Kern's people stamped out the fires until just one remained. Two of the uninfected had knives held to their throats by the masked people. One of the masked people uncovered—

Tabitha.

Of course.

Kern's mother, the leader of those who had taken over the prison long ago and forced the Feeb infection on everyone at the camp.

Gabbi stalked over to Kern, her face bloody, her expression hard. She swung out a punch. Kern caught it. He said something and the words came out like a love song, dancing in the firelight from his mouth to her ears. Sparks of gold flew off Gabbi's body and into the air around the two of them. As if the electricity that ran their brains had suddenly manifested outside their bodies and joined together.

All thought disappeared and a feeling of calm replaced it. Peace, joy, numbness. To be still like a stone. To invite the water to hit and wash over me and onto the next rock, unmoving, yet taking a part of me with the water to spread out in the world—true peace. I did not understand how I had not known this before. So simple a thing, this being still, this dwelling inside the memories of good things.

"Is she okay?"

The water whispered this. Water could cast shadows as this water did now over me.

"Maibe?" My name was like a caress of mist on a hot morning. "Maibe!" This last call splashed me, moved my rock, made me tumble.

Shapes transformed out of the water—five, six, ten. One shape was close. Another rock. No. Something else. The thing that was calling me—not water.

Ricker.

"She's gone Faint." That voice. I remembered. Kern.

"What do you know? How could you possibly—"

"We're all Feebs, Gabbi. It's happening to all of us," Kern said.

"It's not supposed to happen to her."

I turned the part of my body that was no longer a rock and my nose ran into a neck and I realized his arms were around my shoulders, holding me up from falling. Words hot in my ear. "I am here, my love."

I forced words out around the rock in my throat. "Take it

back, Ricker."

He pulled away a little so that the firelight bounced off his eyes. "There you are."

"Ricker."

"Not my love, then. Only someone I love, like any of the others." His arms tightened around my shoulders.

"Better," I said.

"For now," he said reasonably, as if noticing it had started to rain, which it had not.

CHAPTER 12

THE SMELL OF BURNING BEANS made me wrinkle my nose. Tabitha stepped into the firelight. She surveyed our pitiful group—Gabbi next to Kern, me and Ricker sitting on the ground. I saw Jimmy in the shadows and my heartbeat increased because I didn't know if he was real or a ghost-memory.

"You're lucky we were tracking them." Tabitha was worn, gray, wrinkled, veined. A Feeb that was old to begin with. She had helped us, when we'd first been captured. She acted on our side, acted for the good of the camp, to search for a cure, to bring together infected and uninfected. But what she'd really wanted was more power and revenge on Sergeant Bennings.

"Why would you be tracking them?" Gabbi said.

"We have made it our job to know where and how many Feeb-haters there are," Tabitha said. "You should have done the same."

"Please spare me," Gabbi said.

"What happened," I said low enough for only Ricker to hear. I shook off the last of the feelings of the rocks and the water and the peace they had brought. "What happened to me?"

Gabbi argued with Kern and Tabitha in the background. Jimmy stayed real for the moment, glancing back and forth between me and Gabbi, his corkscrew hair swinging in time. Ricker's hands felt warm on my shoulders even through my layers of clothes. I did not pull away.

"It's what they said. You went Faint." His smile disappeared into a worried frown. "You froze. Like they do. You went blank in the middle of everyone fighting and wouldn't come out. What did it feel like?"

I tried to describe it to him. The water, the rocks, the immense peace in being still. He became more worried as I talked, so I stopped. "It's nothing. It's better now, right?"

"Right." But his voice contained an odd note that told me he wasn't sure about that.

"What are you going to do with these uninfected?" Gabbi said, drawing my attention back to the drama unfolding before me. I saw now that Tabitha's people had our captors tied up and laid out on the ground like a row of sticks ready for the fire.

Jimmy came over to us and spoke so that only we could hear. "I didn't know what else to do. They found me and I knew you guys were in trouble—"

"It's fine, Jimmy," Ricker said. "You did just right."

So he was real. He had to be if Ricker could talk to him too.

"None of your concern," Tabitha said, answering Gabbi's question.

"We're looking for the cured one," Kern held up a hand. "Mother, you know Gabbi and them are too. The word is out.

Don't try to deny it, Gabbi, you aren't a very good liar."

"I have always been an excellent liar." Gabbi stiffened and tilted her head as if daring him to say otherwise.

"Not with me," he said.

I waited for Gabbi to say something back, but she kept silent. He had hit closer to the truth than she would ever admit—except in the memory-fevers. During those first two years, when we were rescuing Feebs and battling Vs, she'd go down in the fevers and reveal that she met up with Kern sometimes. We had never told her. We valued our lives too much to confess knowing something she clearly didn't want us to know. It made me wonder what they had heard from me.

Better not to ask.

"We think these uninfected have him locked up," Kern said. "Especially since—"

Perkins spit into the fire, making it hiss. "We have no such monster. There's no cure for the likes of you except death."

Tabitha flashed a knife, slicing her arm and Perkins' cheek. He howled, slapping his hand over the wound. The Feeb holding Perkins' stumbled, going down on one knee, his mask coming off. Dark eyebrows slashed his face into thick diagonals.

"Nindal?" I said.

Kern shouted for his mother to stop.

The uninfected woman, June, screamed and struggled against the knife at her neck. It dropped away and the Feeb stood and backed up. "That ain't right, cutting him like that. Infecting him—that's not what you said."

It was Bernice, from the store. Bernice and Nindal were here with Tabitha and—

"It's done," said a voice behind Tabitha—Leon. He strode

over to June and threw her back into a sitting position. "Hold it together or you're next."

Tears streamed down her face even as she did what he commanded.

Ricker and I just looked at each other.

"Do you see them too?" Ricker asked.

I nodded.

Ricker shook his head. "This is bad."

"Has Leon always been working with Tabitha?" I said.

Ricker didn't answer except to hold me closer to him.

Perkins rocked on the ground with his hands wrapped around his knees. Though it was a shallow cut, his cheek bled all over his clothes.

Kern stopped shouting and now he just seemed sick to his stomach like Bernice and Nindal. More people crowded at the edges of the firelight. Murmured conversations. Leon's whole group was here—with Tabitha.

"You didn't have to do that," Leon said quietly.

Tabitha just looked at him. "You have no idea where this cured one is." It wasn't a question.

Leon considered his next words and whether he should say them at all. He eyed Perkins and the sweat that had already broken out on his forehead, a signal that the memory-fevers would tumble over him soon. Uninfected blood reacted so quickly to the infections. He flicked his glance over me and Ricker. He shook his head. "Let's get this over with."

"DO YOU THINK WE WOULD TELL YOU ANYTHING?" Zach sat cross-legged on the ground, his hands bound in front of him.

"You're a bunch of dirty creepers who don't deserve the quick death waiting for you at our hands." This was Hugh who spoke up.

I waited for Tabitha to pull out her knife again but she looked bored, like she couldn't be bothered.

"Are we dead or going to be dead?" Kern said. "You really need to make up your mind."

"This is tiring," Tabitha said. "We do not need all of them. Tie these four to the trees. We'll take these two." She pointed to Hugh and June. "We will allow you gloves if you would like, but one way or the other, you will take us where we want to go."

Zach shouted insults and threatened revenge as the uninfected were tied to the trees.

The adrenaline of the fight had worn off. The deepening night made me shiver. My sweat felt ice cold. My feelings of unease, of how good it had been to be a stone, tempted me.

Gabbi stood unmoving against a tree. Jimmy was next to her, almost leaning into her. Ricker helped me over to them. Shadows surrounded us, talking in whispers. Gabbi had this funny look on her face, like she feared the shadows would turn into monsters, but more than that, like she feared if that happened she'd crawl into a ball and cry like a child. We were surrounded by people who could go V at any moment, but that had never scared Gabbi before. This was different, this was a memory.

Jimmy held out a hand against her arm and she flinched. He kept his hand there for comfort until she finally grabbed and squeezed it.

"Welcome back," Jimmy said.

"That was a bad one." Gabbi glanced at me. "The same one I relived at the fairgrounds when I climbed those stairs."

I wanted to tell her she had always been the bravest person I knew. That I wished I could be as brave as her. That I had survived this long only because she'd tried to protect me all this time. I opened my mouth to do it—to tell her how much I cared, but then Kern shouted for everyone to move out.

Gabbi's face hardened and the moment was gone.

The forest was full of this rhythmic breathing like some musicless soundtrack for a movie. The breathing got louder and more dangerous and that's all you could hear—the zombie on the other side, barely held back, scraping its fingers into raw meat on its way out to you because it had all the time in the world and you didn't. None of us had any time left.

"We should go with them." I lowered my voice to keep this conversation private.

Ricker stared at Tabitha. The hair on the back of my neck raised. He looked so mean, so angry. But it must be a trick of the shadows. This was Ricker. He was kind, careful, gentle.

The darkness swallowed Gabbi up except for her flashing eyes. "We can do this without them."

I wanted her words to be true. I wanted Tabitha's craziness to disappear into the forest.

"Maybe we should go back home," Jimmy said.

I ignored Jimmy's plea and Ricker's dangerous expression, focusing instead on Gabbi because I knew what made her tick. I knew what I needed to say to convince her. "But we're looking for the same thing right now," I whispered. "If we don't go with them—if there really is someone who's been cured—and they find him first, then what?"

I let her imagination answer the question. Tabitha would find the cured one, talk to him, take him, find the cure, control it, keep it for herself. I didn't think the cure even existed, but they did, and Alden did, and it was too much of a coincidence. It felt like we all were headed down the same path. If we followed them, maybe Alden and the drugs we needed would be at the end of it—

"All right," she said.

Kern flicked his eyes in our direction. Ricker waited until he looked away before speaking. "We go with them in order to watch them. Otherwise they'll be watching us."

"I said all right," Gabbi said

"I know," Ricker said.

The fire hissed and sent up plumes of white smoke as Kern smothered it with dirt. I coughed until my insides ached. I was hungry and sore. I wondered how much worse off Alden was and then tried not to think about it.

First went Tabitha. Leon fell in line behind her. Bernice and Nindal and most of the other Feebs came after that. Kern took up the rear with a few others. He'd given up on getting Gabbi to talk to him for the moment, but that didn't mean he'd given up on her.

We fell in line. Me behind Gabbi, then Jimmy, then Ricker. We didn't know where Tabitha was going. It didn't seem to matter to Leon or anyone—or maybe they already knew. They followed her and we followed them. Bernice and Nindal wouldn't look at me, like they were too ashamed. Zach and the others, including the newly infected Perkins, were left behind.

Our group wasn't very quiet. Several torches made even more of a spectacle. We walked, our breathing and steps falling into a rhythm that never blended in with the night. We were intruders in this wild place of trees, of leaves that crackled underfoot, of the cool humidity that gathered as plants breathed out a sigh of relief from the heat.

"Stop here," Tabitha said. We huddled together, surrounding Hugh and June. In the torch light, their faces were pale beneath the masks she'd let them wear. They shivered from it, from the repulsion they felt, from the fear. It was real in them—this fear of us, of what we might do to them, of what we could turn them into.

"This will take a while," Tabitha said. "You may want to sit." She motioned Gabbi to the ground. Of course Gabbi didn't move.

"What are you going to do them?" Gabbi said.

Tabitha wanted these two uninfected to lead us to the cured one, maybe Alden too. How did Tabitha plan to get the information out of them?

"I won't let her torture them," I said to Ricker. "I won't stand by and become part of whatever she's going to do to them. I won't, Ricker. I won't." My voice became louder after each word until people began to look at me.

"Maibe," Ricker said.

"Whatever you plan to do," I said, talking directly to Tabitha. "I'm not going to let you hurt anyone else. Get that straight right now."

"You're Maibe, right?" Tabitha said.

"You know her name, bitch," Gabbi said.

"Gabbi!" Kern said.

"Do you really think you could stop me?" Tabitha said, arching an eyebrow that threw her eye into inky blackness.

I watched Bernice and Nindal instead of responding. They knew what she was capable of doing. We hadn't made it to the prison in time to stop her three years ago. She'd infected everyone there, turning them into Feebs. Bernice and Nindal had been there. She'd infected them.

Nindal's eyebrows formed a V on his face and Bernice flushed red and tapped his fingers against his stomach. They knew what I was remembering. She'd betrayed them, but here they were, following her like it didn't matter what she'd done before.

Ricker placed a hand on my arm. I looked up. His kind eyes suddenly held so much anger. He was remembering the prison too. How Spencer had gotten himself killed, how I'd escaped with Alden, how Sergeant Bennings had almost shot me. His fingers dug deeper into my skin until it became painful. I tried to pull his hand off. He let go, sending me tumbling to the ground. He stepped forward, the machete appearing. Metal scraped against leather and belts. Tabitha's people had unsheathed their weapons. Two more held sticks. Bernice stumbled into the shadows but Nindal froze with his mouth gaped open.

"Stop," Tabitha said.

Her people froze.

"We are not planning to hurt them," Tabitha said. "We will not touch them."

"Now why don't I believe you?" Gabbi moved to stand in front of Ricker's machete. She turned to face him for a long second, looking hard in his eyes. Then she whirled around, showing him her back.

The shock of realization poured over me like a bucket of cold water.

Gabbi was trying to protect him.

Ricker was going V.

I held my breath and counted the seconds. After a long minute, he lowered the weapon.

"You don't have to believe us," Kern said. "It's still the truth." He sat on a log. Tabitha and the others followed suit.

We were missing something.

"Are you going to tell us what's going on?" I said.

"Are we going after the cure or not?" Ricker said.

"It really is so easy to make you angry. You should see to that," Tabitha said.

I placed a hand on his shoulder for comfort, or, I don't know, maybe to hold him back if I needed to. He shook it off.

Gabbi opened her mouth and I waited for the curse word that was about to drop.

"Stop it, mother," Kern said. "Tell them."

Tabitha held up her hand. "My apologies. All right. We are waiting here—possibly all night—at least for the next few hours, while the rest of my people track down wherever the uninfected have holed themselves up this time."

"We'll never tell you anything," Hugh said.

"Shut up, Hugh," June said. "Just don't talk at all. Not to these filthy animals."

"You should listen to her, Hugh. She's right," Tabitha said.

June's face was almost comical. Her face scrunched up like she just bit into a lemon.

The torchlight flickered, changing the shadows on Tabitha's face to make her look normal one moment and infected the next. "It happens that we don't need your help," Tabitha said. "We didn't need it to begin with. Or, it might be more accurate to say that you have already helped us get what we needed."

"What are you talking about?" Hugh said.

June whirled on him. "Hugh. Shut. Up."

"You two were just a diversion." Tabitha paused, then turned her attention to Gabbi. "We've been following them for awhile. It happens I think this little episode with you will send the others from their group scurrying back to camp much faster now."

"There is no cure for animals like you," June said, spitting the words out from between her clenched teeth.

Tabitha let a small smile play on her lips.

"We want the same thing as you," Leon said, almost apologetic. Bernice and Nindal sat on either side of him, their faces long and exhausted. "Nothing more. We don't want to be sick anymore. I'm sure you can understand that."

CHAPTER 13

IN THE MORNING, AS THE DARK SKY turned pale and the clouds went from gray to a soft pink, two of Tabitha's people showed up. They said the uninfected camp was close by—somewhere in the same town we'd been headed to search for the *memantine* and for clues about Alden.

I turned over to find Ricker staring at me. So much pain filled his eyes. I reached out for his hand. He flinched when I touched him. I wanted to destroy whoever had done that to him.

"I'm so scared I'm going to hurt you," he said.

"Ricker." The lump in my throat made the words come out as a croak. Tears filled my eyes but I furiously blinked them away. I would not add to his pain and let him think he had made me cry. "You won't hurt me."

"You don't know that." Gabbi laid on a bed of pine needles, hands tucked behind her head. She looked up at the soft pink clouds that checkered the sky.

"You would never hurt me." I spoke to both of them. I put all the confidence I still had left into those words.

Gabbi snorted.

"Jimmy," I said.

He didn't respond. All three of us looked at the same time. He lay there, on his own bed of pine needles, a smile locked on his face. His dark eyes were staring at the sky, unfocused. His breathing was shallow. He clasped his hands over his heart like it might burst from happiness.

Gabbi scrambled up. Pine needles flew into the air, releasing their astringent scent. She shook his shoulders until his head bobbed up and down on the ground.

"Stop it, you'll hurt him," I said.

He didn't come out of it. Now the others discussing the camp noticed our commotion. Leon walked over like he didn't have a care in the world. I swore I saw a sneer on his face, but then he became grave. He scratched at his beard and shook his head. "It's a terrible thing. Someone'll have to stay behind with him. Don't look like he's coming out of this for awhile."

My anger made adrenaline rush into my veins. I jumped up, fuming. Nobody knew how to take care of a Faint. Nobody cared about them or took the time to try to understand them. They were locked in, sleepwalking maybe, but they weren't unreachable. You could get them to respond if you knew what to do.

I spotted water in an old plastic milk gallon jug and grabbed it up. Bernice exclaimed and held out his hand as if to take it back. I marched over to Jimmy and dumped it on his face, careful not to get any up his nose. He spluttered and woke up and cursed me with words I didn't even understand.

Gabbi helped him sit up and Ricker slapped him on the back a few times. I dropped the jug at Bernice's feet and dared anyone to say something.

Leon bent over, picked up the jug, and set it back onto the log.

"I don't think we've officially met." Leon held out his hand.

I realized he wanted me to shake it. But I couldn't. If I moved they would see me shake.

He lowered his arm and smiled to let me know he wasn't offended. "You're the girl who saved a bunch of us, aren't you?"

My throat locked up. I wanted to run into the forest and never let anyone see me again.

"Yeah, she is," Gabbi said from behind me.

"Lots of people owe you their thanks, and their lives," Leon said.

It felt like the entire camp stopped and stared at me. Their eyes raked over my hair, my skin, my clothes. Some of them probably thought no way a girl had done all that. Others like Bernice and Nindal, they knew, and they maybe remembered how I'd rescued them.

But I remembered the Garcia family and how the girl's braids had wrapped around her head like a crown and I couldn't take it anymore or I might burst. I turned my back on Leon. A puzzle piece clicked into place and I turned all my thoughts onto it to help me ignore the stares. I knelt next to Jimmy, Ricker, and Gabbi.

I nodded toward Hugh and June. "Could these uninfected be the ones who have Alden?"

Gabbi looked up, surprised. Ricker's face drew in on itself.

"Ricker." I feared I had set him off just by saying Alden's name.

"I'm fine," he said. "I'm thinking about it, Maibe. It's a good question. It can't be coincidence that the uninfected camp is so close."

Hope flickered inside me for the first time in an eternity. To see Alden again, to see him smile, to hear his laugh, to know he was alive and safe—

He nodded at Gabbi and Jimmy. "What do you think?"

Jimmy didn't respond other than to look at Hugh and June really hard. Even that took effort. He was still half gone.

She shook her head. "It could be. I can't be sure though."

"If it's them," Ricker said, "it's not any of the ones we've run into so far."

"You're sure?" I said, my hope shrinking at his words.

He shook his head. "I'm not sure, Maibe. It was so fast. How can I trust what I may or may not have seen when anyone of the people here right now could be a ghost just as much as they could be real?"

There was silence for a long moment as the four of us looked over the people in camp. Most of the time you could tell which ones were ghosts by the faint silvery edge to their shapes. Sometimes you couldn't.

"They might have been the ones to take Alden," Gabbi said. "It could be them."

WHEN WE CROSSED INTO THE TOWN, the streets were quiet and empty. The town had once boomed during the Gold Rush and then much later had reinvented itself as a tourist attraction. But that was before the infection spread.

Ivy had grown up along the walls, creeping across the streets and covering windows. There was no wind. The heat felt more intense here, further down the mountain from Dutch Flat. Leaves lay thick and dry and crumbling on the ground. The place felt empty. It could have been empty—Faints and Vs long dead—except Alden had been captured here.

My palms sweat with the intensity of our silence. Stones scattered nearby and every time so far it had been an animal, but the entire group, four of us, several dozen other Feebs between Tabitha and Leon's people, kept waiting for it to not be an animal.

Suddenly a shadow the size of a person slid around the corner of a building and into the street ahead of us.

"Do you see that?" I said.

Ricker shook his head. "Nothing."

I sighed. A ghost-memory, then.

"What about the roof of that building on the left?" he asked, tilting his head that way.

I saw a faded red trim sagging over a stucco wall. "No."

"Maybe we should take the herbs Corrina gave us," he said.

I shook my head. "Not yet. It's not bad enough yet."

We reached the spot where the research center should have been. Leon and Kern went in first—except there wasn't anything to go into. The place had burned down. A pile of black sticks, white ash, and melted glass that marked the former windows.

The blood drained from Gabbi's face. Ricker wore a grim expression. Jimmy blinked really fast, like he was holding back tears. I wanted to throw up. We all knew what this meant. There was no medicine left for us. No medicine for Ano.

Kern, Leon, and a few others sifted through the ruins, but they found nothing. When Kern abandoned his search, he came and stood in front of Gabbi. His shoulders hung low and ash had streaked his cheeks and forehead with ghostly gray marks. Gabbi just stared at him, like this was somehow all of his fault. He lifted his hand to brush hair from her cheek but she turned away.

"There must be something," Tabitha said.

Kern looked at his mother. Her face held an expression I had only seen once before—on the night Spencer had killed himself, when she'd told us she was sorry for our loss. We hadn't known then the terrible things she was capable of then. This look on her face surprised me now. The pieces clicked into place.

"How many people?" I said.

Tabitha closed her eyes. "Ten of us. There are ten of us who are too sick now."

"We needed this too," Kern said. "Just as much as you."

"No," Tabitha said. "There's still a chance."

"It's gone!" Gabbi said, her voice too loud in the stillness of our loss. "All of it's burned. There is no chance left!"

"Gabbi, listen," Kern said, his voice rising. "There's still—"

"Kern!" Tabitha said sharply. "Move everyone out."

Kern hesitated. Gabbi turned her back on him.

He walked off to call Leon and the others away.

I stepped forward, glancing at Ricker. He noticed it too—the way Tabitha had cut Kern off.

I stepped in Kern's path. "What are you keeping from us?"

He opened his mouth, caught his mother watching us, shut his mouth again.

"Don't pull that crap with us," Ricker said from behind me.

I waited for Gabbi to join in. If anyone could get it out of Kern it would be her—but there was nothing. I looked over my shoulder. She had walked far down the block and stood at a street corner looking off into the distance. I almost called out.

Ricker placed a hand on my shoulder. "Something's up."

Me, Ricker, Kern, Tabitha, everyone—we caught up to Gabbi. She pointed to a flat, empty lot set in between two brick buildings. The lot backed up to a hillside that rose pretty much straight up into the sky. The top of the hill was lined with trees. In the middle of the hill, on level with us, was a metal door that stood ajar, as if opened to thin air, but on the other side it was dark except for a small light. I tried to understand what I was looking at.

"Is anyone else seeing this?" Gabbi said.

The door was an opening in the hillside. It led into the hill, into a type of cave.

"I see it," I said.

"The door, right?" Kern said.

"And the lights," Gabbi said, coming up to stand next to me. "There's lights."

"It's real," I said.

Tabitha and Leon locked eyes on each other and a silent message passed between them.

I tried to understand. This must be the uninfected camp. Or at least Tabitha and Leon thought it could be. Maybe the uninfected had taken the medicine to keep us from getting it. Maybe they had even burned down the research center. Maybe they had Alden inside, even now. We needed to figure out what to do and when to do it. We needed to watch and plan. I thought next Tabitha would tell us to hide.

Hugh fell on his knees. He shouted and his voice boomed, destroying the silence. "Lock it down! The infected are here! Lock—"

Leon punched Hugh in the gut, cutting him off mid-sentence. Hugh fell onto his side, gasping for air, but it was too late. Above the cave entrance the bushes shook.

Tabitha shouted and motioned her people forward. They brandished sticks and clubs and knives and guns. They ran silent, swift, their afflicted skin harsh and ashy under the summer light, like young people dressing as old people for Halloween.

"They can't be serious," Gabbi said, her eyes wide, her voice almost a whisper.

Ricker fell to his knees next to June and Hugh and began working away at their bonds. They shouted, struggled, fell over onto their faces in the dirt.

I realized—they thought Ricker was going to kill them. A deep stillness settled over me. This world was full of pain and death and even the good you tried to do didn't count for much now.

The ropes dropped to the dirt. "Get out of here," Ricker said.

June and Hugh scrambled away from us and from the fighting.

Booms sounded. Jimmy shouted for us to take cover. Gunfire. Their side, our side—it didn't matter. The guns would bring along any Vs still left alive. Some of Tabitha's people fell to the ground. Most kept running for the cave's opening. Kern and two others stopped to fire back.

A shooter tumbled from the trees above the cave, slammed onto the ground, and lay still.

The gunfire continued and I wanted to clap my hands over my ears like a three-year-old. Jimmy was right. We had to hide, but I couldn't get my body to move. Part of me knew what was happening. Shame filled me because I was letting all of them down again.

I was pushed onto my side. June and Hugh reappeared, sprinting now for the cave. They waved their hands around and I swore they shouted something about Vs but then June was cut down by her own people. I watched it—the burst of light from the trees two stories above us, the way the bullet threw June back as if punched in the gut, the blood that sprayed, how Hugh kept running.

The first of Tabitha's people were swallowed up by the cave's dark entrance. Then a couple more. And then another blur sprinted away.

Gabbi.

She ran to the battle.

No. She ran to Kern. He sat upright in the dirt, a block away, halfway between us and the cave entrance. He held a bloody hand to his arm. He wore a dazed look on his face—blank, in the grip of some memory that would make it impossible for him to think and move out of harm's way.

"Gabbi!" I shouted this and I shouted at the peace that rose up inside me. I shouted for it to go away because I didn't deserve it because my friends needed me because I would rather die than let them down again.

I pushed myself up from the dirt, but Jimmy grabbed me and held me back.

Ricker crept along a building and then another, moving closer to Kern and Gabbi but staying out of the gunfire.

I fought against Jimmy and slipped away. I followed Ricker and Jimmy followed me. The battle disappeared from view when I ran past the corner of a brick building. Fragments of brick flew off and hit my skin, like a burst of heat, as if someone had taken a cigarette to my cheek.

I sped along the wall to where Ricker crouched. He started up at my noise, fists ready to fight, then saw it was me. It felt like the whole ocean roared in my ears.

He crawled around the corner. I followed. Jimmy's breath was hot on my neck. Kern still sat on the ground, but now instead of holding his arm, he raised his right hand. He fired off a shot into the bushes above the cave entrance. A man and rifle tumbled out, flipping once in midair.

Gabbi yelled and dragged Kern back, hooking him under the shoulders. He let himself be dragged. The three of us scrambled out to help, each taking a leg or shoulder. We ran with him around the building's corner, behind the safety of a brick wall.

Kern took gulping breaths, his face white as a sheet, his Feeb skin shiny in the harsh sunlight. A vein in his neck pulsed.

"What were you thinking?" I said, rounding on Gabbi.

"I wasn't." Gabbi's face was pale and she wouldn't look at me. "Otherwise I would have left him for dead."

That shut me up, but Kern didn't look like it mattered to him. Maybe it was normal for them. I couldn't understand how she could, how they could...I wanted to punch Kern in the face. Instead I yelled at him. "Do you know how many people have just died because of you?"

"You have no idea what's really going on here," Kern closed his eyes and leaned his head back against the brick building. "The *memantine* was a backup plan. Dr. Ferrad's done it. The cure is real and they don't want us to have it. Now is someone going to help me tie off this wound, or are you all going to watch me bleed to death?"

CHAPTER 14

WE WORKED FAST. Kern was propped against a brick wall. Ricker ripped part of his own shirt into strips and I tied up Kern's wounded arm. The bullet had passed through muscle and gone out the other side. As long as the wound didn't get infected, he would survive it. I told myself I could think about what his words meant later—a cure! It was real!—but unless we hurried, we might not survive the Vs surely headed our way.

It was silent except for the birds. The birds were always around now, singing their songs in the cool early mornings or the warm evenings. There were no cars or planes or electricity to interfere. Technically some of it still worked. Sometimes over the past couple of years I could hear an engine's grinding gears if the wind blew just right.

Jimmy and Gabbi stood on lookout at either corner of the huge warehouse that hid us in its shadow. They were barely still in sight of me and Ricker as we worked on Kern. We were on the side of the building opposite the battle that had turned silent. The fighting was over, but we had no idea who won.

Jimmy scraped his foot in the dirt. I focused on Kern's blood seeping through the makeshift bandage. Bright red like flashing rubies. He smelled like forest, like dirt, like fear. Ricker rested a hand on my shoulder and squeezed. I looked.

Jimmy held up both hands. One formed a 'V' shape, the other flashed all five fingers—three times. I looked over to Gabbi. She watched a different street. She flashed the same signs Jimmy did—five times.

Now I heard them. It was a sort of growling that rose up that you didn't notice at first. Background noise that grew and transformed into something vicious. We hadn't seen more than two or three Vs together in at least a year and now there were forty all in one place? The question was on my lips—where did they all come from? But there wasn't any time.

Kern's injury was beginning to clot, but blood still dripped down his arm and into the dirt. He looked pale and unsteady. Ricker and I helped him onto his feet, but he slipped back down to the ground. His eyelids fluttered and his eyes rolled showing us the whites.

Gabbi sprinted back to us. She was slick with sweat and mud streaks and Kern's blood. "We have to get into the cave right now."

"It's too quiet in there," Ricker said, but there was no heat in his voice. We couldn't fight off forty Vs at once, no matter how slow or weak they might be at this point.

"We don't have a choice." Gabbi propped Kern up, using her shoulder to brace him under his arm. Ricker took the other side as I helped. We dragged Kern to the end of the warehouse and paused at the corner to see if our path was clear.

Ricker glanced over his shoulder and froze. "Jimmy!"

I looked behind us. The noises had grown now, unmistakably. Growls and screeches and the snap of teeth. Jimmy stood still at his lookout at the far corner of the building. He leaned against the brick and showed us his side profile. Too still. Too dreamy. A half-smile on his lips.

Acid burned my throat and my hands became slick with sweat. He was going Faint again.

Ricker moved to drop Kern.

"No!" I said. Gabbi and I couldn't move Kern alone. Ricker knew it. "I'll get him."

Before Ricker could protest I ran off after Jimmy. Gabbi shouted at Ricker to move his ass.

My feet pounded the dirt, kicking up puffs of dust that formed haze in the air. My heartbeat pounded so loud in my ears it drowned out the growls. One V came into view and another tripped into the dirt close behind him. Jimmy felt a mile away. I pushed myself harder. Even from this distance, the Vs moved like I did. They looked normal. They looked fresh.

I shouted at myself to go faster. I felt like my heart might explode. Jimmy stood there, with his curly hair like a halo around his head, his lanky body thin and covered in scratches, his face dreamy, his muscles relaxed and lazy because he couldn't see what was closing in on him.

There was shouting behind me. Time slowed down. There were five Vs now, strung out yards apart from each other. One of the Vs was still facedown in the dirt from falling. Sweat poured off me and I swore I saw drops of it fly into the air and scatter into a million tiny rainbows. The drops fell into the dirt and it was the most beautiful sound and I pushed all of it back and thought about the most terrible things instead—Ano trapped in the fevers for an eternity, the girl and her family dying in the summer sun on that hillside, Jimmy about to die in front of me.

I slammed into the first V as he reached out to grab Jimmy by the hair. We went tumbling into the dirt and I tasted a dry, grittiness on my tongue that crunched between my teeth. I punched and kicked and everything was a blur of clothes and teeth and dust that stung my eyes.

There was a sharp pinch on my leg, like it had just been caught in an animal trap, the metal teeth clamping down, tearing, ripping.

I hooked the Vs nose with my fingers and yanked. His eyes flew open—brown, bloodshot, empty except for the anger that haunted them. The trap released its hold. I scrambled away. Rocks scraped my skin raw. Two more Vs ran at us. Their clothes were mostly clean, their sprint was smooth and fast.

The roar in my ears grew so loud I thought my head would burst. The first V came at me again. He shaped his hands into claws. His blond hair was long and beginning to form mats. He had that wild, hungry look in his eyes. Without thinking, I jumped up, grabbed a fist-sized rock and smashed it into the side of his head. He held a hand up as if surprised, then crumpled.

Jimmy still stood, hands at his sides, that half-smile on his lips. I ignored the burning pain in my leg and ran to him. Back by the cave, Ricker sprinted for us, his machete waving in the air, even as Gabbi picked up a rifle and shot at the Vs that came out from the other direction.

The next two Vs locked on me and Jimmy. Ricker was too

far away. He'd never make it in time and my little rock wasn't going to do anything to two of them.

I yanked Jimmy's arm but he didn't move. I screamed at him but he didn't even blink.

My body burned with a heat that made me see things so clearly. I whispered in his ear a list of wonderful, beautiful things. I described chocolate ice cream and parks with green grass and a squirmy puppy with soft, silky fur and how they were all there in the cave, all waiting for him, just for him, and shouldn't we run to it? Wouldn't that be a fun game to see who got there first to play with the puppy?

His leg twitched. The two Vs were within several feet now. Ricker was still too far away.

Jimmy laughed a clear bell sound and before I could blink he ran off. His hair bounced with each step. Ricker stopped in his tracks and his mouth fell open. I sprinted after Jimmy and I couldn't hold back the thrill that bubbled up. It worked! He was going to be okay.

Jimmy ran past Ricker.

My heart dropped into my stomach.

Jimmy was headed straight for the other battle. He wouldn't see them. He wouldn't turn. He wouldn't fight.

Something snatched at my shirt. I screamed, pivoted, saw a V had caught me. Her stinking breath blocked out all other sensations. It smelled like something had died in there. I fell backward. My shirt ripped and suddenly I was free and running as fast as I could in spite of my burning ankle.

Ricker caught up to Jimmy and herded him to the entrance. The darkness of the cave swallowed the two of them. The fighting near Gabbi had stopped because some of the Feeb's had come out to help. When they looked in my direction, they shouted and fled back into the cave too. I dared not look behind me but pushed myself to go faster.

I crossed the threshold. The door slammed closed behind me with a screech that echoed. I tripped over something soft on the ground, flipping and landing on my back so hard it knocked the breath out of me.

My chest heaved as I opened my mouth and gasped for air. The panic in my brain drowned out the pain in my leg.

Suddenly my lungs began to work again. Cold cave air rushed in and I felt such pleasure in just the simple act of breathing.

In and out, in and out.

It felt like an eternity before I realized the thumping I heard wasn't my heartbeat but from Vs slamming into the cave door. My eyes began to adjust to the almost complete darkness.

Shapes appeared—lumps on the ground. Dead people. The one I tripped over was still warm. I jumped up, shaky, needing to get out of that hallway before I threw up.

I walked through the bodies until the passageway opened up to a larger room lit by torches. More lumps on the ground here. More dead.

Gabbi had Jimmy sitting down. She nodded at me while biting her lip. He still had that smile on his lips. He laughed just a little bit and moved his hands in his lap like he was playing with that puppy I'd promised him.

I felt sick to my stomach. Jimmy was like Molly and Freanz and the twins now. I couldn't bear to look at him like that because maybe I'd saved his life but he was still gone from us. Was that what I had looked like to Ricker and Gabbi?

I let low, urgent voices draw me further into the cave. Here was an eating area, rock ceilings braced with huge wooden beams. More uninfected slumped across tables—murdered so fast they'd had no time to get up. The smell of blood and iron was thick in the air. I raised my shirt over my nose and breathed through my mouth.

This room branched off into several passageways. Only one was open. The others were filled with piles of supplies. I followed the voices down the open passageway. My skin felt clammy and cold. Each breath I took left an ache in my chest. My leg still hurt like someone had taken a match and held it against my skin. If the V had actually bitten me, I'd be trapped in the fevers by now like Ano, so I ignored the pain. I could deal with a sprained ankle later.

The passageway led to a room filled with Tabitha's people. She held a torch taken from the wall. They had their backs to me. Their focus was on a man chained by his hands and feet, spreadeagled and lifted up in such a way that his body formed the shape of an X. His head hung down, a shock of dirty brown hair. He looked young, so young—

Alden.

I cried out and ran to him. I pushed through Tabitha and her people, and fell to my knees before him, the cold wetness of the cave seeping deep into my bones. The darkness of this place boxed up my mind.

He did not move.

He was dead. They had tortured him and strung him up like an animal and I was too late.

"I understand their fear of us," Tabitha said behind me. "But I still do not understand how they could have done this to one of their own."

Her words did not reach my brain for many long seconds. My ears heard them but did not understand, not while the rest of me was so shocked by seeing Alden here, his bruised and scratched legs, his dirt-grimed feet, a toenail ripped off—

"Keep searching," Tabitha said to her people and most of them left.

I looked up and saw a face, and for a brief flash, it WAS Alden's face, hazy and fogged and overlaid on this one as if someone had moved the camera too fast while taking a picture. My heart broke into a million pieces. I would never be able to tell him—

And then suddenly, it wasn't Alden's face. It was someone entirely different, someone older, larger than Alden would ever be.

I choked over my breath.

"Maibe." When Ricker's voice broke the silence, only then did I notice that his hand rested gently on my elbow as if I needed to be steadied. Maybe I did.

"Tell me who this is," I whispered to Ricker. "Who do you see?"

He took in the tears on my face and his eyes widened. "It's Perkins, Maibe. Whoever you thought it was—it's not. It's Perkins."

My mind had played an awful trick on me. I had thought it was Alden, but now the fog in my brain cleared.

This wasn't Alden.

"What did he do?" I said, even as my heart began beating again. "Why did they do this?"

Tabitha's face looked worn but determined. "He was going to turn Feeb."

"Because you infected him," I said with a venom that

surprised me.

Tabitha nodded. "Yes, and he'd probably already gone into the fevers."

"But why this torture?" Ricker said.

"Look around," Tabitha said, a hint of exasperation in her voice. She'd always sounded so levelheaded in the prison, so Zen, and some of that was still there, but now with cracks. "Look closer. They were trying to fix him, in their own sick and twisted way."

"They were bloodletting him," Ricker said, his voice in awe.

On the ground underneath Perkins sat two large pans that collected the blood still dripping down one leg.

"They don't believe we're human any longer," Tabitha said. "Why not? Why not try everything that might work to keep one of their own from changing? If you get it out fast enough, maybe you can stop it, or you make the person bleed to death, but either way, you take care of the problem until it's not a problem anymore."

"You say all that like it's nothing," Ricker said.

"It's not nothing," Tabitha said. "But it's of no matter to us."

"You can't mean that," I said.

"We won't be changing their minds. Not you, not me. We've enough to do trying to survive them and the rest of the world."

A shout slapped the walls with its intensity.

Tabitha whirled around and there was a gun in her hand where there had been nothing. Leon, with his full beard and dark shining eyes, appeared in the room with us. "You need to see this."

She followed him out. Ricker and I followed her.

"Kern said you know Dr. Ferrad has found a cure," I said.

"You actually think these people had a cure."

She froze mid-step, then continued. "Clearly not. Their little torture room proves otherwise."

"But you thought they must have it or at least know where. Is that why Leon is here? Because he said he'd seen a cured one? You really—"

"I've seen a cured one," Tabitha said. "A Feeb. Someone who had been a Feeb and now isn't. Leon lied about seeing one himself, but that doesn't make it any less true."

Leon flinched at Tabitha's words even as he led the way down the tunnel. "I knew one existed. I needed help finding him. People needed convincing."

"And where is this cured one everyone claims to have seen," Ricker said. "You'd think he'd be the most well-protected, famous—"

"SHE is out there still. This group of uninfected was hunting her." Tabitha continued down the snaking tunnel that would soon fit us as snug as a cocoon if it continued to narrow. "They don't believe once you've turned you can be brought back."

"Maybe they're right," I said.

"You expect us to believe all this?" Ricker said. "This blood-bath is simple revenge. A cure would be shouted from the rooftops. There'd be no way to hide it or keep it from everyone."

"Believe what you want," Tabitha said. "It doesn't change the truth."

"But it does," Ricker said fiercely. "It does change the truth, and you know it."

IN A SMALL ROOM, ALMOST FULLY ENCLOSED by rock, dimly lit

by smoking torches, several of Tabitha's people hovered over a table spread with papers and other maps hung on the wall.

I approached the table, expecting for someone to bar my way or tell me to stay back. No one did. The papers were thin, almost like tissue, light blue, with dark blue lines drawn with care, and the paper crinkled at my touch.

The designs felt familiar somehow as if I knew the shapes in real life.

I turned to the maps. These shapes seemed even more familiar. Rivers, valleys, streets, highways. Town and city names, landmarks, waterways. I hadn't ever used maps in school, before school ended forever. Gabbi and the others had used them all the time as runaways and I'd gotten really good at map reading—often our rescue missions depended on reading a map and knowing how it matched real life.

This was a map of our area—the River City all the way into the Sierras.

"Do you see it?" Tabitha lifted an arm and lightly brushed a finger over a section of map two-thirds of the way from the River City.

I stepped closer and saw faint pencil markings. They sectioned off Dutch Flat, our town. I turned back to the table drawings and pictured our town and the surrounding hills, the back roads that were still passable, the reservoir that contained our water and the little dam that held it all in.

I rifled through the papers. Different angles, different details.

"This group of uninfected was going to take out your water supply," Tabitha said.

I stood there in shock still trying to make sense of the maps.

"Actually, let me rephrase that," Tabitha said. "The uninfected

ARE going to take it out. The people we fought today, they're just the ones these Feeb-haters left behind. We'd been following a much larger group. Maybe they're already on their way."

Ricker pivoted on the wet stone and ran out. I dashed after him, through the cold, damp tunnel, over the bodies, into the main room. Ricker was talking to Gabbi, throwing his arms around, cutting the air into shapes and punctuation. "And what will they do after they destroy the water supply? Why not burn down the town next? Set fire to our food? Kill anyone they meet along the way?"

"We have to get back!" Gabbi stepped away from Jimmy then back to him.

I knew what she was thinking—we had to leave, we had to go back to Corrina and Ano and Dylan and the others, but how could we keep Jimmy safe too?

"Stop." I put a light hand on Gabbi's arm to convince her to stay in place. I knew better than to use any real force to hold her, but she looked ready to jump away like a scared rabbit and disappear into the trees without thinking about what would happen. "Gabbi, we have to get there fast. But if we're going to have a chance, we have to think about this. Vs are outside, can't you hear them?"

I paused to let the thumping sounds bleed through.

My mind twisted and turned through the different options. Make a run for it, just the three of us and hope Tabitha would magically take Jimmy under her protection. There was no telling how far ahead the other Feeb-haters were or how many guns they might have. Wait and convince Tabitha to help us save the town, but even if they came, we would be slow, too slow, to make it in time.

"The main group of Feeb-haters is far ahead," Kern said, limping over. "The group split off days ago and we didn't have enough people to split ourselves up too."

"You followed the wrong group!" Gabbi yelled. "You followed the wrong group and now everyone we know is going to die!"

Kern looked about to shoot back a response, but I cut him off.

"We need to find some working vehicles," I said, barely thinking over this idea as the words came out of my mouth.

Conversation stopped, but I wondered if I was the one who had stopped, if this were a Faint moment that had stalled me. We huddled around Jimmy like he was our life vest. And maybe he was. All of us fought to protect each other. That's what made everything worth surviving. He was lost now and we would lose each other, one by one, until there was nothing left.

Unless Tabitha was right.

Unless there really was a cure and we could get everyone back.

For the first time in a long time, I allowed myself to hope there might be a chance to fix all of this.

"The Vs will follow us like bees to honey," Kern said. "All the way back to your town."

"We should risk it," Gabbi said. "There are a ton of cars around, we just need a few to work."

Ricker stood up. "There's got to be another way out. This can't be the only entrance, can it?"

"We don't have a choice." I forced my voice to fill with a confidence I didn't actually feel. "We have to try."

"Even if it kills us?" Kern demanded.

I didn't need to look at Gabbi and Ricker to know they agreed with me. It was the right thing to do. It was the only thing to do.

"Even if it kills us all."

ALDEN

"This is the only way to save you." Dr. Stoven held up a needle of dark yellowish green fluid.

Alden wanted to wretch. "But what about the cure? You have the cure. Use it!"

"I thought you understood this part," Dr. Ferrad said. "I'm disappointed."

Dr. Stoven stepped over to his bedside. "The virus and the bacteria no longer stay intact at sufficient enough quantities inside blood cells to catalyze transformation unless you are completely uninfected."

"You're not making any sense," he said. "What is that?"

Dr. Stoven sighed behind his face shield. "If you must know, it's a sanitized mixture of saliva and sputum that contains active virus and live bacteria in sufficient quantities to stimulate the body's immune system, which will then mount a defense that predictably generates the onset of a group of symptoms characterized *as—"*

"It's the Feeb infection, jerk. They're making you a Feeb because you were stupid and almost got me killed," Kailyn said.

Alden looked wildly around the room. It had been her voice, but he couldn't see her. He couldn't believe they would let her in the room with him like this, about to go V, about to be infected with that vial of fluid.

"The cure only works if both the virus and bacteria are fully present," Dr. Ferrad said, bringing him back to the present.

"I don't understand," Alden said in a wail that embarrassed him even though he couldn't stop it. Where was Kailyn? What was going to happen to him?

Dr. Ferrad and Dr. Stoven exchanged a look through their plastic face masks.

He hated how alone he felt. They were the ones who looked like they had come from outer space but he was the one who felt like an alien.

"You're not supposed to understand," Dr. Ferrad said.

Dr. Stoven plunged the needle of fluid into Alden's arm.

They waited and watched and recorded him as he went into the memory-fevers. The needle was not the cure. The needle reinfected him with both the Lyssa virus and the bacteria that together would turn him into a Feeb again.

The worst memory was reliving when he found his mother and no amount of shaking would wake her from her stupor. His father had rested a hand on his shoulder and told him there was nothing to be done. That she wasn't coming back. That she was sick somehow from this bacteria that was supposed to have saved people from the Lyssa virus.

When he came out of the fevers, the room was dimly lit. He'd been sucking on a sour candy from the fair when he was six. That sourness still sat on his tongue, puckering his lips. The walls were a sterile, dark gray. That stupid lens and speaker box and heating vent that never worked stood in judgment over his head. He wanted to smash it all to bits.

They forbid Kailyn to speak to him.

They didn't cure him right away.

They said it was because the cure was hard to make and it cost a lot. But that didn't make sense—money was useless now. How could the cure cost anything? They didn't say they kept him Feeb as punishment for putting Kailyn's life at risk—they didn't have to say it.

He couldn't get used to it. The skin. The memories. The way his brain kept betraying him.

And then there was the V girl who somehow knew Ricker's name. Every time he thought of it, he lost feeling in his fingers and his heart sped up. She was a V but she had spoken. Not only that, she had said the name of someone he knew.

He had to find out more.

Dr. Stoven wouldn't speak to him but Dr. Ferrad let him work with the chimps and Faints again after a few days.

The Faints needed daily care from the lab scientists—food, IVs, monitors, samples—but no one bothered to turn them to prevent bed sores, so he took it upon himself to do just that during every meal time. It was like touching death, twice everyday, but he made himself do it. Maibe would have done so much more for them.

Plus, he needed the doctors to trust him again. He needed to *see the V girl.*

They finally let him take care of her again. Alden figured it was because there were so few people left. Sometimes uninfected showed up at the facility and he would catch glimpses of them in the halls or at the common dining area, but then it would be like they vanished into thin air. He would never see them again.

He couldn't see the V girl now. Her door had a food slot at the bottom which he pushed the tray through. Everyday he crouched on his hands and knees and tried to talk to her. One time there was a glint of an eye on the other side. A hand snaked through and scratched his cheek, ripping it into ribbons. He patched himself up and kept trying.

He attended to the Faints and chimps as best he could. A part of him feared that maybe they weren't going to cure him this time, so he threw himself into whatever they asked for. He became their errand boy, their chimp-feeder, their stall-cleaner. He scrubbed and cleaned and prepared and dropped into his bed each night exhausted. But the fear grew with each passing day. Why did they hold back the cure?

He fed her, whoever she was, this girl who knew people she shouldn't have. He pushed the tray through and tried to talk to her and then moved on. When it was time for the next tray of food he removed the used one—that sometimes came back bent or dented or scratched—and replaced it with a fresh one.

After a week of this, five uninfected arrived. Their voices filled the cement dining hall with overwhelming sound. They were toasted, given all the best food because they'd brought other uninfected with them. It was like someone's birthday party in there. They were welcomed without suspicion or caution. Alden didn't understand this. People were dangerous now. It didn't matter whether you were infected or not. But Dr. Ferrad and Dr. Stoven didn't seem to care. They sent Alden to prepare rooms with fresh sheets but told him to stay out of sight so the new uninfected wouldn't have to look at a Feeb's skin.

He burned with embarrassment and anger but did as he was told. He was glad Maibe wasn't there to see him just roll over like that. Even the little he knew of Gabbi, he knew she would have thought him less than nothing for not standing up for himself.

He listened in the darkened hallway during their dinner. Goosebumps rose on his arms from the cold and his feet fell asleep as they laughed and shared stories by candlelight and wine. Dr. Ferrad made a speech about how her scouts looked for people in order to bring them back here where it was safe. That they were close to a cure and wanted as many people as possible to be a part of making history.

He realized this must be how he'd gotten captured. Dr. Ferrad sent her people out to collect other people and he'd been caught in that net.

The next morning, Dr. Ferrad stopped him on his way to his chores. She placed a gloved hand on his shoulder because he was still a Feeb and she didn't dare touch him barehanded. He had the food bucket in one hand and the V girl's food tray in another. He must have been standing there, frozen in a memory. Dr. Ferrad said his name and shook his shoulder like it was the tenth time she'd done it.

"Alden Bennings, you need to come with me now."

He set down the bucket and tray, but then paused. "They'll be hungry."

"Never mind that," Dr. Ferrad said. "It's time for you to receive the cure."

She led him to the gray room and strapped him down to the hospital bed. For their own protection, she said. Not his.

"Why now?" He said this in a fit of anger even as he wanted to hug her, thank her for finally, finally taking this burden from him.

She didn't answer him except to continue hooking up an IV line and two thin tubes that disappeared into the dark shadows of the room.

The light glinted off Dr. Ferrad's plastic mask. He'd worn one very much like it when protecting himself from the infected. Had he looked as funny as Dr. Ferrad looked right now?

Probably worse, he decided. She looked tired but confident. He suspected he'd looked like a coward.

CHAPTER 15

THE DEAD AROUND US WENT COLD and the Vs outside kept smashing themselves against the door. Leon, Bernice, and Nindal, and many others from the town were still alive. They clustered around each other, somehow keeping themselves separate from Tabitha's people even though there wasn't that much space.

Ricker, Gabbi, and I hovered over Jimmy and planned how to run with him when the time came. Kern stayed by our side, his bandage an inky black in the cave light. He didn't talk much and he sat down a lot, but he helped with Jimmy.

It took hours to find another way out of the cave. The other entrance was at the end of one of the passageways blocked with supplies.

We waited now in the darkness lightened only a little by the sunlight that filtered through the opening. We didn't know what was on the other side, only that at least there was no thumping.

Everyone worked to clear the way and then we were outside. The sunlight, the heat, the brightness were all shocking, almost painful.

Bernice and Nindal carried Jimmy between the two of them almost like an apology. Ricker helped me walk. There still hadn't been a chance to look at my leg. Gabbi was in front of us, Ricker's machete in her hand.

We were above the cave now, in the middle of the forest. Wind fluttered through the leaves. Sunlight dappled the brush at ground level. The sudden heat brought goosebumps out on my skin. There was a moan and a figure darted from one of the trees but at first no one reacted. A ghost-memory. I was seeing a V that wasn't there. He raced toward us, his features distorted in rage, his hair dirty and tangled, his muscles straining with his sprint as if he thought that if he could just make us go away, so too would he banish that rage.

The noises around me softened and then stopped, people and trees became just shapes and colors.

Ricker shouted. He ran for the V and a part of me understood this did not make sense, not if the V were a ghost-memory. The V barreled into Ricker and they both fell onto Kern. Bernice and Nindal ran, jostling Jimmy around. Gabbi yelled and slashed at the V with the machete.

Kern twisted around on the ground, pulled out a gun, angled it, pulled the trigger. Blood misted into the air. The V toppled over.

People streamed out of the cave. They spread out and began firing. Shadows moved from around the trees. The forest was full of shadows and moaning. It was beautiful how desperate we all were to stay alive. Ricker loomed, blocking out everything except for the sweat that plastered his hair to his head and streamed rivulets down his cheek. Dirt smeared his nose and chin. Blood droplets spattered his face like freckles. He said something as if from down a long tunnel. "Maibe, you've gone Faint again. You've got to snap yourself out of it. We have to run!"

I understood his words but there wasn't time to explain.

"Come on, Maibe." He slapped me, a sharp blow to my right cheek that flared lights in my eyes. I waited for my aunt to appear, but she didn't and I was so happy about that. The world tilted and I was flying in the air, flipping over. More shouts and more gunfire. I stared at something yellow with red spots, scuffed from fighting—a bullet casing that sparkled like gold in the sunlight.

I reached my hand out to grab it but couldn't reach. I was folded over someone's shoulder. This thought tickled the edge of my brain. Ricker's belt was eye level. The rise and fall of his steps jarred me. His jeans were dusty and threadbare. He was stronger than I remembered. He carried me like I weighed nothing.

He began to run. I wanted to tell him I was fine. I wasn't going Faint, or at least I wasn't going all of the way Faint. This felt different somehow—my head was clear even as my leg burned, even as his run bounced me like I was on a roller coaster ride. His shoulder dug into my stomach like the safety bars had when I'd ridden with my uncle. I pictured my legs dangling across his chest and his arm latched over my knees to keep me from falling. I wiggled my toes like a child on a carnival ride.

Suddenly there was a shout and I turned weightless. The ground rushed to my face as if I were flying into it.

I KNEW I WAS AWAKE EVEN THOUGH everything was still black—I no longer felt numb. I was no longer weightless. My nose pressed into something firm and musty smelling. A low humming sent vibrations into my body.

I pulled my head back a few inches. Light flooded in, revealing ribbed upholstery fraying at the seams. There was a dusty, cracked window. The ceiling cloth was torn and hanging down. Shapes and colors passed by the window, slow but steady.

I sat up and the movement made my head throb. I put my hand to my scalp and it felt crusty. My hand came away with flakes of dried blood. I was in some sort of van, in the back seat. The van crawled along faster than I could walk, but slow enough to avoid all the obstacles on the road. One person sat in the middle row. Then there was the driver and another passenger in front. A sharp edge jabbed my thigh. I looked down—the metal shape of a seatbelt latch. As if on autopilot, I grabbed the seatbelt and clicked the metal together.

The person in the middle row turned, showing me a profile. His face was familiar, yet strangely out of reach. Maybe that meant I still wasn't in control yet. Fear snaked up my spine at the thought that maybe I would be gone for good, but then that very fear calmed me. In those worst, stone-like moments, I was at my most numb. All fear and guilt and anger had washed away. These terrible feelings told me I was back—fear was my friend.

"What's happening?" I said.

"You weren't out for long this time," Ricker said. "I just couldn't wait for you to come out of it. I tried, Maibe."

I remembered the slap and then him running and me flying.

"I made you drop me, didn't I?"

"We had to get out of there."

"You're dodging my question."

He rubbed the back of his neck. "There was a V running straight for me. I was so angry. I wanted to rip the V to pieces. I...I think I threw you to the ground." He looked sick to his stomach. "I was filled with so much hate. I knew if I could just get my hands around his throat that everything would feel better." His neck muscles clenched and he jutted out his chin as if trying to fight off some inner demon. It all rushed up in me at once that maybe he was about to lose it again, this time inside a car full of people.

"I didn't drop you," he said. "I threw you off."

There was a thump on the side of the van, hard enough to make it rock.

Fear squeezed my stomach. "What was that?"

"Vs," Ricker said. "There are so many obstacles in the road. We're driving slow enough—sometimes they catch up."

I examined the rest of the passengers and the driver. "Where are Gabbi and Jimmy?"

"In a different car. With Kern and some of Tabitha's people." The lines on his face deepened as if he were an old man filled with burdens too great to bear. "Maibe...Kern was bit. Four others of Tabitha's people were bit as well...It's bad."

"They're trapped in the fevers," I said, not asking a question. "They're trapped like Ano and they're not coming out until we find some medicine."

Ricker closed his eyes and he wiped furiously at his cheek.

I grabbed his hand. Things were going terribly wrong, but I felt like I was regaining some control. I felt better, more myself than I had in weeks. He'd slapped me and I hadn't lost myself. Not completely. "I'm still here, Ricker. We'll find what they need. We will."

Another V slammed into the van. The driver swore.

"Do you think these Vs were Feebs like us?" Ricker said, but it wasn't the question he wanted to ask. I could read it in his eyes. What he really wanted to ask was if I thought whether he would be next.

I sat up and held his face with both of my hands. "You could never go V." I kissed him deeply until his mouth relaxed. He wrapped his hands over mine and pulled me into his warmth. I drowned in the kiss. He took a hand away, the cool absence breaking my focus. I felt a hand in my hair, running fingers through it, holding me gently, and then more strongly.

"Ouch." My head throbbed where I'd hit it.

He sat back as if slapped. "I'm sorry. I'm so sorry, Maibe."

"Stop it. It's okay."

Another V threw herself at the windshield. A window from the car in front of us rolled down. An arm snaked out and the muzzle of a gun flashed twice. The V flew off the windshield, leaving behind streaks of blood.

"Well, that kind of ruins the mood, now doesn't it?"

He tried to smile at my joke but it didn't reach his eyes.

"Ricker." I grabbed his hand again.

He squeezed back and then pulled away. "It doesn't matter. We'll all turn V or Faint. We're all dead either way. Isn't that what you always said?"

CHAPTER 16

"WE'LL TAKE CORRINA'S MEDICINE," I said. "We'll take it and it'll work."

He didn't respond.

"I know I said that." I pulled out the pouch of herbs Corrina had given me and searched the van for any sort of container we could use as a cup. "I'm not taking it back. We're dead or might as well be but we still have to do what's right. We still have to help people."

"Why?" Ricker said. "No one's helping us."

"Tabitha—"

"She's doing this for her own reasons," Ricker interrupted.

He was right. She might have decided to help us at the moment, but it wouldn't last. "Because," I finally said.

"Because why?"

"Just because, Ricker." I held out my hand for his own pouch of herbs. "Because we have to."

He hesitated, as if ready to argue with me some more, but then pulled out the pouch and handed it over.

The driver passed back a water bottle. We created a makeshift stove out of a hand lighter and a small metal container from the trunk and did our best to make the tea. It was bitter at first and then turned sweet by the end. We passed around the water bottle now filled with tea to everyone in the car, using up all of Corrina's gift. We didn't feel any different, but then again, we had no idea how long it took to start working. If it worked at all.

Another hour passed and we covered all the ground that it had taken two days for us to hike. The Vs stayed with us. Three of them had busted our windshield at this point. The V mob formed a growing entourage that fell behind as we gained distance on clear stretches of highway and caught back up as we slowed to maneuver around obstacles.

The cars discussed plans across walkie-talkies. Tabitha wanted to use the Vs like something similar to what Spencer had done to get inside the Cal Expo fairgrounds years ago—draw in a big mob of them to do the fighting for us. I did not think it was a good idea. The only way to the reservoir was through the town itself, drawing Vs into where we didn't want them to be. We'd have to wind into the hills and be a slow-moving target for anyone waiting for us down at the reservoir. The hills were steep and would leave us few places to hide. The direct exit to our town was blocked by the layers and layers of obstacles we'd placed there.

The vehicles made their way through our carefully constructed path. I wondered how Tabitha planned to get in contact with the town and warn them about the Vs. There was still a gate to get through.

But the gate that should have been closed—it was wide open. We lost the Vs around a corner, but it was only a matter of time before they would catch up. The lead vehicle stepped on the gas and we followed in a rather stately line, weaving in and out of the town's cottage-style ranch houses. There wasn't a single Feeb walking around.

I held my breath as I examined the windows for signs of life. Was there anyone left in town to care for the Faints and for Ano? My hands became clammy at the vision of him lying in that hospital bed, shouting out, no one there to help. Where were Corrina and Dylan?

Movement shifted the curtains of a second-story window. A hand pushed the curtains aside and for a brief second Corrina stood outlined by the white window frame, raising her hand as if in hello to us. Or was it as a warning to ward us off?

A boom sounded. Something kicked up asphalt in front of the lead car.

Uninfected streamed out of the houses and stood on the rooftops, the late afternoon sun glaring behind their backs. The first car swerved and slammed into a telephone pole that had long ago turned into a posting board for photos and messages to dead loved ones. The vehicle in front of us veered to the right and wrecked a fence before skidding to a stop in a front yard, the passengers dashing out, Gabbi included.

A bullet smashed through the driver's side window of our van. Glass flew, our driver's head lolled to the side. I ducked down, the noises more terrifying now that I couldn't see what was going on. I scrambled over to the van door and inched it open. Ricker was on the floor, watching me. The van had stopped near the large oak tree on the corner of the block.

Bullets whizzed past the opening, throwing shrapnel from the tree, the dirt, a wooden fence, the street. I rolled out of the van and against the tree, the shade cooler than the van had been.

The gunfire petered out and stopped. People began shouting.

Someone pointed a rifle barrel at my face.

I moved slowly to see who held the rifle. He hadn't shot me yet, so maybe if I didn't him give him a reason, maybe he wouldn't.

But then I realized he was a she. A woman held a rifle at my head. She was dressed in fatigues faded from dust, heat, the wear of years. Her combat boots had seen better days as well. The heat left large sweat marks on the army green T-shirt she wore under her bullet-proof vest. She even wore a military helmet. There were several dents in it along with a chip off the front. A wisp of blonde hair fell across her forehead and there was something very strange about her skin. Veins and mottled skin—like a Feeb's—yet faded, as if getting washed away.

"Hello, Maibe."

I started at my name. Now I looked her full in the face. I'd been looking at all the details, missing the big picture.

I knew this woman.

"It's Jane. Don't you remember?" She smiled, as if that would make everything better and I wouldn't notice the rifle still pointed in my face. "Don't move!" She shifted the rifle to point above my head, at whoever appeared behind me.

This had been Corrina's best friend. When Corrina and Dylan had let me into the RV, she'd already been there. She'd slept with Dylan before the world fell apart and told Corrina at the worst possible time. She had left us while we were being turned into Feebs. She had sided with Sergeant Bennings and hadn't been seen for years. Alden would have told me if she had come back. He would have.

"Do you know where Alden is?"

"The girl does have a voice. Still talk about zombie movies too?"

I cringed at the disdain in her voice. She was the worst kind of person. Someone who liked to laugh while she stabbed you in the back.

"What do you want?" Ricker said behind me.

"Get up," she said. "Don't worry, I'm not going to kill you. Yet." She smiled. "That's gotta be a line from a movie, right?"

"What's wrong with your skin?" I said.

She stepped back and motioned for the two of us to stand.

"Nothing another week or so won't fix up."

CHAPTER 17

THEY GATHERED US INTO THE CHURCH with the Faints. Tabitha's people, those now trapped in the fevers like Ano, were brought into a back room and laid out on the extra beds. Kern was put in a bed next to Ano and tied down to the frame. Bernice and Nindal carried Jimmy to a different bed in the Faint section. Ricker and Gabbi followed. Three of Tabitha's people had died, others had been injured in the brief fight with the uninfected. Corrina and Dylan treated them as best they could.

Tabitha was on her knees, her hands behind her back. Leon was with Mayor Helen. They both stood next to Sergeant Bennings as if they were no longer enemies. The world was pretty much empty and yet all these people had come to the same spot—for what, the cure? But the cure wasn't here. It had never been here.

The shifting politics made my eyes swim. I didn't understand why Sergeant Bennings was here, why Tabitha was on the ground, why we weren't prisoners or already dead, why Jane of all people was alive and cured. The cure!

Even thinking those words made my heart skip a beat. There was a cure. I had denied it and yet there Jane stood. Everything that had marked her skin as sick was fading away like it had never existed.

My thoughts strayed to Alden and what he would think of me, of us, if the Feeb skin he hated so much were to disappear. Then I saw Ricker at Jimmy's bedside and my feelings became all mixed up. I focused on the cure. Things would somehow get better now. Somehow.

I decided to figure out this puzzle in front of me. I had always been good with puzzles. It helped take my mind off how I'd killed my mother during childbirth, how my aunt had died from a throat cancer that took her ability to speak but not to slap, how my uncle had cared for me until the Vs killed him. I was the bringer of death. That's why my father had named me Maibe because it meant grave.

But even so, my uncle had cared for me as if I were a wounded animal. He'd brought me puzzles, sometimes jigsaws with beautiful landscapes and vivid colors, sometimes puzzles I held in my hand and needed to separate in a special way. He set me onto these tasks and I would work for hours until I figured them out.

The cure must be so close. I would figure this out, find the cure, and bring it back to my friends.

I stepped carefully over to Sergeant Bennings and Mayor Helen. The only people under the guns were Tabitha's. I would try my best not to change that.

"You need to know," I said. "We did not kill your people at the cave. Me and my friends—we were there, but we didn't kill anyone."

"You and your runaways, you mean." Mayor Helen's tone wasn't kind.

Sergeant Bennings looked me over. He had his son's eyes, but there was a hardness to him that Alden never carried. He was taller than both Mayor Helen and me. His beard was thick and salted with gray.

"We've helped everyone in this town ten times over. If it wasn't for Gabbi and Ricker and Ano—Mayor Helen, you should know—"

"Please stop speaking, Maibe."

Her words burned my mouth shut. I forced myself to become a polite young woman, like my aunt had sometimes beaten me into being. I had learned to fear her, but I had also learned the power in silence. I could not risk saying the wrong thing, not when Sergeant Bennings was the one with the power of life and death over us.

"You have always been a good girl," Mayor Helen said. "You took the best care of your Faints. But a cure is within reach and Sergeant Bennings and I have come to a necessary agreement."

"Did he tell you he had planned to blow up our water supply?" Tabitha said.

"That was as a last resort," Leon said.

"In case an agreement was not possible," Sergeant Bennings said.

"But it is possible, is it not?" Mayor Helen said.

Sergeant Bennings inclined his head.

I couldn't hold back this time. "You've been working for Sergeant Bennings?"

Leon scratched his beard and stared at me until I looked away.

"Don't be dumb, girl. We know each other from the camps. I was uninfected once and Sergeant Bennings is a good man. As soon as we got to town today and I saw he had the cured one, I told him I'd help any way I could."

"You've always been trustworthy," Sergeant Bennings said. "There's a real chance now. We find the cure, we can start putting things right again."

"She knows where it is?" Leon said, looking off toward Jane.

Sergeant Bennings shook his head. "She doesn't remember."

"But she will remember," Mayor Helen said. "She must."

"She's trying," Sergeant Bennings said. "I'll give her that."

A BOOM LIKE FROM A BOMB sent vibrations through the church. Mayor Helen flinched. Leon looked at me like he'd forgotten I was there. Sergeant Bennings hadn't forgotten though—he flicked a glance my way, an unreadable expression in his eyes. I went cold at that look. He was hiding something.

"Another attack. They're going to kill us."

"We have to get outside."

"They blew the reservoir!"

"We are drawing away the Vs." Sergeant Bennings voice boomed like the bomb, stopping all other voices. "We have set interval charges to go off throughout today to draw the mob away from the town."

"The camps are destroyed," Mayor Helen said, speaking to what was left of our town now crammed into the church between Faints and uninfected with guns. "Sergeant Bennings' people are in need of fresh food and a new home. Our home."

"They want to live with Feebs?" Tabitha said from her position on the floor. "They tried that before. It didn't work out so well for us."

Mayor Helen paused then, a pained expression on her face. "In exchange for our lives and a chance at the cure, we will be going to work for Sergeant Bennings and his people."

"What does that even mean?" someone shouted.

"What about our Faints? Our sick?"

A growl erupted in the back. There was a scream. A shot was fired. The noise seemed to suck the air out of the room. People moved away, opened up space.

Betty lay on the ground.

The blood darkened her navy blue shirt to match her black shorts.

The soldier raised a hand and said, "She went V, Sergeant Bennings, there was nothing I could do."

Sergeant Bennings nodded. "Some of you will be forced to leave, for our own protection. Some of you will be allowed to stay and continue to do the good farming work you've started here. Those of you too sick to work…will also be allowed to stay." But he didn't say for how long and everyone heard the unspoken threat anyway.

"But what about the cure?" Corrina demanded, stepping away from a bed. "You didn't have to kill her. Why did you kill her? You have the cure, so give us the cure and we won't be a danger to you anymore. We'll be able to care for our sick."

A shout of agreement rose up.

"Calm down, people!" Mayor Helen yelled.

Leon left and talked quietly with Bernice and Nindal. They slipped out the back. I looked around, wanting to tell someone, anyone because it seemed like their leaving meant something even though I didn't understand what it could be. Then I noticed that Sergeant Bennings had watched them go. Tabitha was old news—made powerless again. They were working for whoever had the best shot at the cure.

"We want the cure! We want the cure!" This became a chant. People punched their fists in the air. Voices filled the space. The Faints protested with us by becoming restless in their beds.

Sergeant Bennings held up his hands for silence, but the chanting continued for several more rounds before dying away.

"I don't have the cure to give you."

"That's a lie!" someone yelled.

"No. It's the truth," he said. "Tell them, Jane. Tell them what you remember."

She'd showed such a brave face when she was pointing the gun at me, but my snap judgment of her wasn't totally fair. She looked worn out. The Feeb markings on her skin had faded, but her eyes looked haunted. She'd survived in this insane world for three years just like the rest of us.

"I was kidnapped and infected and cured." She looked at everyone, except somehow not at Corrina and Dylan, as if she couldn't bear to acknowledge their existence. "I was infected on purpose and then cured on purpose and then I found a way to escape. I don't know what they did. I don't know where it was, but it's out there. We just have to find it. We can find it."

A thick silence filled the room.

"So there's no cure?" Ricker said into the emptiness.

"There is a cure," Sergeant Bennings said. His eyes flicked to me. "But we don't know how to find it." His lip twitched at the end, almost unnoticeable, almost nonexistent.

He was lying.

CHAPTER 18

SERGEANT BENNINGS ESCORTED ME to my old hotel room. Ricker and Gabbi had protested leaving me alone with him, but they had guns and we did not. I still had not puzzled out why he was here. They had Jane. If she didn't remember where to find the cure there was nothing we could do to fix that. His remark about farming made me think this was about food but there were still plenty of places to scavenge.

I was allowed to gather a few things, some clothes, some personal items. They were moving all the Feebs out to make room for the uninfected.

He watched me like I was a criminal. Maybe I was. Maybe I had always been one in some form or another. I pulled a bag from the closet and began packing.

"Do you know where he is?"

I stopped. I knew who he was talking about. I pretended not to know. "Who?"

"Alden's been missing for months now. I came here because I thought he'd be here. Because of you."

"He knew I was here. He's come here before. It—"

"He's been here before? He knew where this place was all this time?"

I saw it was too late to take back my words so I didn't. "Yes."

"I cannot believe… Do you know where he is?"

"I do not." I resumed my packing. Lesa would want her favorite shirt with a picture of Dolly the Fish on it. The colors always seemed to register in her eyes.

I was going to wait him out. I was going to keep what little power was left to me and make him ask whatever it was he was trying to ask.

"How often did he come here?"

That wasn't what he really wanted to know, but I answered it anyway, letting him stall. "Once every couple of months. But sometimes I went to meet him."

He opened his mouth. Closed it. Opened it again.

"What did you talk about? What did he say?"

The longing in his voice spoke more than his actual words. He didn't care about what we had talked about. He cared that his son had done all this behind his back, that he'd lost his son a long time ago.

"We traded information, sometimes supplies, sometimes—"

"—I see." His mouth snapped shut.

I zipped up one bag and grabbed a second one, then began filling it with supplies from the kitchen. Cans of food, the fruit we had just picked. The leftover oatmeal. My ankle bumped against a table leg. Pain shot through my body, making me stiffen. I had forgotten about my injury once it had dulled to a low throb, but now it screamed at me.

"I need your help." He turned his back to me and began to rifle through a shelf of books as if embarrassed by this confession. "I need you to help me find my son."

I stopped packing and curled up the leg of my pants. Spots of blood covered it. Part of the cloth was torn.

My fingers froze as I revealed the skin. I began to shake. This didn't make any sense.

Sergeant Bennings picked up a book, flipped its pages, returned it to the shelf. "But how can I even trust that you will find him?"

I stared at my skin, at the puckered flesh, at the indents that formed an irregular oval.

The bite had broken the skin.

The bite had made me bleed.

The bite had been from a V.

Sergeant Bennings sighed, rifled through his pockets, and pulled out a small journal.

Why wasn't I trapped in the fevers like Ano and Kern? I dropped my pant leg down to hide the wound. Maybe it was Corrina's tea. I didn't think I'd felt anything from it, but maybe that was the point. Maybe that's how it worked.

But a little voice inside me whispered that this wasn't a very good lie. Ano had gone into the fevers minutes after getting bit. So had Kern.

Ricker and I hadn't made the tea until hours after I'd been bit.

Sergeant Bennings set the journal on the dining table and stepped back.

I tried to hide the shaking in my hands as I opened the journal.

I stared. My name was scrawled all over it. Again and again, in cursive, in block letters, in big capitals and tiny swirls. There were drawings too, notes, little maps with markers.

Alden's handwriting.

I rifled through the pages, they were as if from a mind gone crazy. Most of it didn't make sense. In the center of one page there was a crude map. This map had been circled by a pencil so many times the marks formed a dark ring, making the paper fragile and smooth.

I recognized the drawing.

It was of a camp. We'd been sitting on a ledge above it. It was where I had tried to kiss Alden once. It was where the Garcia family had been murdered.

Someone had drawn an arrow through the circle, pointing to the camp. In dark, blocky letters, the arrow's label said:

Cure?

ALDEN

He couldn't stop staring at his skin. Wrinkled and veined and ashy—but fading. It would take a couple of days, maybe weeks, for all of it to be gone.

He was back in the hospital bed, legs and arms strapped down. The speaker box and camera lens were his only company, but he didn't even care.

Dr. Ferrad entered through a hatch-type door—this thick, bulky metal that looked more like something out of a submarine than a research facility. She left it open and entered the room, her white suit and plastic face guard so bright it almost hurt his eyes.

When Dr. Ferrad moved to his bedside, he saw Kailyn waited in the doorway almost like she was afraid to come in.

"I won't bite," Alden croaked.

"You might," Dr. Ferrad said. "You haven't received the full dose yet."

Kailyn didn't say a word.

Dr. Ferrad lifted thin tubing—there were two of them, red, full of blood. The tubes were inserted into each of his arms. The blood ran through a machine. The motor that powered the machine hiccuped sometimes. In his dreams, Alden had thought it was someone beating a drum, but now he knew it was the machine's pump.

The lines snaked onto the ground and across the room, disappearing behind a door.

"Does the machine clean my blood?" Alden asked.

"Yes, it prepares it," Dr. Ferrad said.

"What does that mean? It's the cure right? The machine cures the blood?"

Dr. Ferrad stopped checking his monitors. "Something like that." But her words were too careful, there was too long of a pause between his question and her answer.

"The V girl—is the cure from her?"

There was a moan. Alden thought it was Kailyn, but she stared at him with those wide eyes behind those glasses, looking exactly like before. Light glinted off her glasses and sort of outlined her body. She didn't say a word. It was weird she was there at all if Dr. Ferrad really meant he wasn't fully cured yet. She didn't have any protective gear like what Dr. Ferrad wore.

The moan sounded again, but Dr. Ferrad didn't act like she noticed anything. Was it all in his head?

"That would have been ideal. But no, we have not found a way to cure her or use her to cure others." Dr. Ferrad cocked her head. "No, we still have not found the way."

"But—"

"There now." She patted the sheet, but her kindness felt forced, what with the full bodysuit and all. She left, walking right through *where Kailyn stood like she hadn't even seen her.*

Alden realized she hadn't seen her—Kailyn had never been there. What had Maibe called them?

She'd been a ghost-memory.

Kailyn disappeared but his panic remained. He stared at the machine, listened to its hum, and watched his blood flow through it, along the ground, disappear behind a door, and return back to him through the other tube. He willed it to go faster.

CHAPTER 19

I STOOD IN BETWEEN ANO AND JIMMY'S BEDS. My chest felt constricted, as if there wasn't enough air left in the whole world for me to breathe.

They were trapped. They wouldn't get any better unless we found the cure.

I tried to ignore the wound in my leg—the burning that didn't make sense, the fevers that weren't happening.

Sweat poured off Ano, but Jimmy was different. A half-smile stayed on his face. His forehead was cool to the touch. He lay so still, except sometimes his eyelids twitched.

We'd set off to get medicine and now things were worse than before. All that was left was the cure. All we could do was follow the clues Alden had left in the journal and hope they would lead to a permanent cure.

"I know where Alden went."

Sergeant Bennings stood too close. "You know where he is?"

He had followed me into the hospital and waved the guards away when they tried to stop me from entering. He was masked and gloved and he loomed over me. I was the one who could hurt him, infect him, but it didn't feel that way.

"I know one place he's been, which is more than you've got."

"Tell me," Sergeant Bennings said.

"Take me with you," I said.

"I will not travel with sick—"

"You have to take me too." Tabitha was still tied up though they'd moved her onto a chair and next to Kern's bed.

Sergeant Bennings and Tabitha began arguing. Their voices rose in pitch. Sweat formed on their foreheads from the warm air inside the church. The guards at the door stepped forward.

Corrina left a Faint's bedside. She grabbed a bottle and threw it onto the floor. The glass shattered and sent shards in every direction. Tabitha froze. Sergeant Bennings whirled around. His guards pointed guns at Corrina's head. I stepped forward, not thinking. One of the guards shifted to point his gun at me.

"You are both looking for the same thing." Corrina's voice was quiet yet somehow that made her words more powerful. "You are looking for Alden, for the cure, for Dr. Ferrad. Are you not?"

Sergeant Bennings inclined his head. He waved his hand and the guards lowered their guns. "We suspect they are all in the same place."

"We've been following the trail for the cured ones," Tabitha said, her voice also quiet. "Dr. Ferrad is the most likely candidate. She betrayed us when she—"

"When YOU helped her escape," Sergeant Bennings interrupted. "She was close to finding a cure in the camps. We always knew the double infection wasn't a permanent solution. You destroyed our chances—"

"Because you created the infections."

He barked a laugh. "That old conspiracy again? I would deny it, but you won't believe it."

"You can't deny the bacteria are your fault," Tabitha said. "Look at your wife and try to deny it!"

Sergeant Bennings went cold. The look on his face was dangerous. "We created the bacteria to fight the virus. It's the only thing that holds back the Lyssa virus."

Tabitha snorted. "The camps had already been up and running for months before the epidemic devastated the state, the country—the world—for all we know. Kern and I are proof of that!"

"The camps had been around for years," he said, his voice still cold but under better control. "This happened to be the disaster that finally justified the money the government spent on them."

"And your experiments? Your prisons?" Tabitha strained against the ropes so that they formed indents on her arms.

"Strict quarantine procedures with dwindling resources. Life isn't very pretty when the world falls apart."

"There were plenty of resources, you—"

"Enough!" Corrina said.

They stopped. The church door creaked. There was the sharp slap of shoes on the wood floor. Jane appeared, her blonde hair tied back from her face, her Feeb lines almost nonexistent.

"None of you should go," Corrina said.

I saw it, standing close to Corrina like I was, how she stiffened and her cheeks lost their color. Maybe it had been years ago, but the infection must make her relive all those terrible moments between her and Jane.

Corrina glanced over to me. "None of you should go. There-
fore, all of you will go. Maibe knows Alden better than anyone
here and he may be our best chance at finding the cure. If there
is a cure."

"I'm clear proof of that," Jane said, her voice cutting through
the hot air.

"Yeah, you're proof of something," Corrina said. "Whether
that's a permanent cure for us, well that remains to be seen."

Jane stepped forward, her eyes blazing. She lifted her chin
and forced her hands to relax at her sides. I don't think the two
of them saw us anymore.

"Are you calling me a liar?"

Corrina's voice was steady and careful. "I'm saying I'm going
to wait and decide what to think based on what Maibe finds."

They all looked at me. I wanted to drop through the floor.
I wanted to hide in a room with my Faints. I wanted to prove
to Corrina that I deserved her trust, but we'd already failed
three times. We hadn't made it more than a few dozen miles
away from town—caught by the Feeb-haters, then by Tabitha's
people, now by Sergeant Bennings.

"The kid?" Jane said. "The zombie-watching, movie-obsessed
kid? Oh that's classic."

"Think what you want," Corrina said. "It matters nothing
to me."

"Take me and my people with you," Tabitha said, interrupting
the crackling energy between the two of them. "We will help
you find Dr. Ferrad. If you leave me behind, you will regret it."
She glanced over to one of the beds.

A woman lay there, caught deep inside the Faint symptoms.
The IV line dripped liquid into her veins, but she still breathed

on her own. Her pale hair streaked the pillow around her face. The sheet was pulled up to her chin. She must have been brought in by Sergeant Bennings because I had never seen her before. There was something familiar about the shape of her face and the color of her hair.

"You dare threaten my wife?" Sergeant Bennings said. "I should kill you."

It was Alden's mother.

Tabitha bowed her head in submission.

"I live and act as if being uninfected is something worth protecting," Sergeant Bennings said. "That does not make me a monster, but you…"

He raised his hand as if to strike her.

She did not flinch.

He finally lowered it.

"She's right and you know it," Tabitha said. "We all need to find the cure. We all just might know enough about where to find it—together."

CHAPTER 20

IT FELT DIFFERENT THIS TIME. Feeb and uninfected, friend and enemy.

But it was more than that.

We were going to find a permanent cure for all of this.

We walked silently into the forest, us Feebs in the middle so we couldn't run off. Ricker, Gabbi, and I stayed together. Tabitha took two of her Feebs and somehow got Leon, Nindal, and Bernice included. Jane was there, protected from all sides by other uninfected. Her being cured and all, they hoped she'd recognize something eventually.

Sergeant Bennings took along Hugh from the Feeb-haters. He didn't explain why his people had been working with the Feeb-haters. Deep down, I felt sick about it because I suspected they would have taken out a whole town of people because Sergeant Bennings wanted me to find his son.

Ricker wore a small pack, a water bottle latched to the side of it, a light, short-sleeve shirt, thick pants, and hiking boots. A bandanna around his neck, a hiking hat and sunglasses. In the before time, he could have been going for a hike in the hills to check out a waterfall. Now, it was a matter of preventing sunburn, dehydration, and dressing in such a way that you could walk forever. I adjusted the bandanna tied around my neck. Eyes skittered away from mine whenever I looked at the uninfected too quickly. It felt like they were waiting for me to do something to justify putting a bullet in me.

Sergeant Bennings had wasted no time. We'd left town within an hour of when he showed me Alden's notes. Even walking underneath the trees was hot. The sounds made everyone nervous. There were birds, hundreds of birds around us by the sound of it. Dry leaves crunched under us and yellow dust coated our shoes and pants. Water sloshed in the bottle slung around my shoulders. I hid my limp as best I could. The bite on my leg was even hotter than the sunlight. I'd been given no chance to clean it yet. I didn't understand what it could mean so I didn't want to think about it.

We entered a clearing full of vehicles. The pine trees formed a green background against the dead grasses trampled by the cars. Sergeant Bennings planned for us to drive as far as the roads would allow. The hazardous waste camp in Alden's drawings was about 150 miles away, down in the valley. Less than a three hour drive once. No way to know how long it would take now.

We packed into the cars and the engines roared to life. The noise was deafening. The bird noises disappeared, the wind seemed to stop, the trees almost leaned back from us, as if wanting no part of the chaos that would come next.

Our caravan ate up fifty miles of highway and main roads,

maneuvering around obstacles, bypassing wash-outs, snaking through foothill towns when too many accidents clogged the freeways.

Before long the Vs came out—sometimes from the side, sometimes from ahead. They were decrepit, gaunt things you could almost feel pity for. Whatever memories had allowed them enough consciousness to survive for this long wouldn't last much longer.

Our cars easily outdistanced most of them. Others were shot dead and run over. I sat in between Ricker and Gabbi and couldn't help but feel as if the world was ending all over again. How long did either of them have before going fully V? How long did I have before I was trapped like Jimmy? We would get no mercy from Sergeant Bennings and his people.

Ricker pressed his forehead against the glass, closing his eyes for a moment.

"Are you okay?" I said, even as I watched the Vs outside. They had been alive once, they had been loved by someone once.

"Upset stomach," he said. "Carsick, I guess. It always happens—just not in awhile."

"You felt it on the way back from the cave?"

"Yeah, but not as bad. That was a short trip."

"Maybe we should stop," I said.

"I'll be fine."

"But—"

"Stop, Maibe. It's carsickness. It'll be fine." An angry note crept into his voice.

I stopped. Ricker didn't get angry. Ricker smiled almost as much as Jimmy. Ricker was gentle and kind and thoughtful. But the grimace on his face spoke of more than nausea. The tightness of his lips and the lines in his forehead showed tension, ferocious emotions held back—

"I'll be fine. Just leave me be."

Sergeant Bennings turned around and stared at him through his face shield.

"What are you looking at?"

"You," Sergeant Bennings said. "Going V right here in this backseat. Aren't you?"

"And if I was?" Ricker snarled out.

"I will put a bullet in your brain." He pulled the gun out so fast it was a blur.

I gasped, choking on my breath. Should I touch Ricker? Should I say something? Would that finally push him over the edge or talk him back down?

There was a long measured look between the two of them. The driver watched through the rearview mirror, his eyes bugging out behind the mask. I realized with a shock that it was Hugh. From the group who hated Feebs so much they drained the blood out of one of their own. He looked ready to jump out of the driver's seat any second.

The silence stretched. They did not break their stares.

Sergeant Bennings tightened his grip on the gun. Ricker trembled as if his willpower to hold back was breaking. Gabbi looked ready to lunge. My mind went blank. I shouted silently at myself to do something or my friends would die right here and now.

"Good." The word came out like Ricker had opened a release valve. He relaxed back into the seat. "You better be ready."

CHAPTER 21

WE LEFT THE FOOTHILLS and stopped in a town. The brown sign called it Plymouth, population 861.

We stopped because there was no more road. A sinkhole had taken out houses all the way to the base of this sloped hill of yellow grassland dotted with oak trees and crumbling tombs from an old cemetery. On the other side of the road, the pit had sheared a former elementary school in half. One of the classrooms spilled out its insides of desks, books, and papers like a waterfall frozen in time. The sinkhole stopped at the entrance to a large sign that read "Amador County Fair Grounds."

We needed to turn back and find a way around it. Instead, Sergeant Bennings ordered everyone out of the cars. Sweat poured down my face and arms. My clothes stunk. I didn't want to think about the cemetery or the school or the fairgrounds or the sinkhole consuming all of it. Instead I focused on how the skin on their uninfected necks was so smooth, so different from ours.

Hugh dug his rifle point into my back. He motioned me, Gabbi, and Ricker forward. Two other uninfected escorted Kern, Tabitha, and the rest of us Feebs.

I struggled at each step. School had never been a good place for Ricker or Gabbi—for any of the runaways. But I missed going to school. I missed books and learning new things. I missed how the yard duty lady always smiled at me. Alden and I had gone to the same school for sixth grade. We had no classes together, but I had noticed him. He never noticed me. Not back then.

Hugh pushed us on until the road turned into crumbling dirt, splintered wood, broken glass, and twisted metal pipes.

I looked down and it felt like I looked inside the half-digested contents of the belly of a monster. This monster growled as if hungry for more. Debris shifted and groaned. A classroom desk slipped over the edge and tumbled into the darkness.

Soon the sinkhole would eat the entire school. Next it would consume the fairgrounds, the rest of the houses, and then the cemetery at the top of the hill.

The memories shouted at me—the Cal Expo fairgrounds that Sergeant Bennings had turned into a prison camp with human experiments. The high school where we'd lost Corrina and Gabbi and I thought I would die of dehydration while trapped on a rooftop by a mob of Vs.

But those were the easier ones to remember. The memory underneath, the one like the belly of this monster that rumbled with hunger pains as beams shifted, and glass tinkled, and dirt resettled—THAT one had the shape of a stone like those dotting the hill. This stone was pockmarked, pale, and engraved in Arabic script with the name of my mother.

I turned from those thoughts with all the force I possessed. My breath hiccuped. I slowed it down—five seconds to breathe out, five seconds to breathe in.

A voice behind me said, "Company."

The Vs came out of the fairground entrance like a group of cats that had found an interesting scent trail. One fell into the chasm while shrieking her outrage. Dark dots shifted on the hillside. People stood up and began to wander among the tombstones.

Sergeant Bennings signaled. Instead of heading back to the cars, his people shifted on their heels, pulled out knives, machetes, swords, bats. No guns. He wanted to fight it out, but with as little noise as possible. I thought he was crazy. They were all crazy for not running from this.

The Vs from the fairgrounds skirted the edge of the sinkhole. Different ages, different clothes, different genders and ethnicities, but all had something in common. They had a decent amount of weight on them, not the gaunt, practically starving look of Vs who couldn't remember to eat or bathe or how to use the bathroom anymore. They had few injuries among them. Their clothing was threadbare, but mostly intact.

Something about their skin caught my attention.

Was that—

"That's Feeb skin!" I said far too loud.

"Quiet." Hugh smashed the butt of his rifle into my side, knocking the breath out of me.

Ricker pushed Hugh back so hard it dropped him to the dirt. Hugh swung a leg out and sent Ricker face first into the dirt. The sinkhole rumbled deep below.

Gabbi stood at the edge of the sinkhole, staring, nothing but air under the front half of her shoes.

One of the uninfected went down in a series of grunts and wrestling holds with the first V. Another cut a V down by slicing her between the shoulder and neck. Blood sprayed the air and splattered their face shields.

People grunted, cried out, lashed out.

Ricker was still on the ground, his chest heaving. He'd gotten the breath knocked out of him. One of the Vs dove for him. I threw myself at the V even as Hugh delivered a vicious kick into Ricker's side.

I barreled into the V's warmth, into his musky stink, and landed hard on my injured leg. The ground seemed to slip away from me. My feet lost their hold and felt like they dangled in the air. I dug my fingers into the dirt but it crumbled. My stomach flipped and I tasted acid in my throat. I was eye level with the fighting now. A dozen legs twisting, stumbling, falling, smacking, grunting. The sucking noises of knife wounds. Gabbi still stood on the edge of the abyss as if the fighting around her didn't exist. Her face had glazed over, her hands reached out for something that wasn't there.

I shouted the name she only revealed while deep in the fevers. The name none of us were supposed to know. "Cecelia Gabriela Vergara Ortiz!"

She flinched.

I shouted her full name again.

My hands slipped more.

The belly of the monster waited below. I couldn't make out the bottom, only the remains of the house—jagged, sharp, dangerous.

Hands grabbed mine. Ricker's face filled my vision, his expression twisted, his eyes holding a terrible light.

I flew into the air, my body weightless, my stomach turning over on itself. I landed on my side in the dust that painted everything with a blurry golden glow. The V that had jumped for Ricker tackled Jane. He clawed at her as if he were a dog digging for a bone.

Jane's knife flashed out but then dropped from her hand. I scrambled up, ignoring the screaming pain in my ankle, ignoring the terrible light I'd seen in Ricker's eyes. I picked up the knife and drove it into the V's skull. There was a crunch, and a slick, squishy, slurp. The sounds made me gag. The V went limp.

I spit out the acid in my mouth but more returned.

If we had the cure already, I might have saved him.

Gabbi backed away from the edge of the sinkhole. The Vs were dead. Blood spattered every face, every shield, every piece of clothing. A guy cradled his left arm while sitting in the dirt. An almost perfect circle of bites leaked blood onto the dirt.

One of Sergeant Bennings team had been injured—bitten. Infected.

The fight was over, but not for long. The dark figures among the tombstones were coming down the hillside.

"Cut it off, Eddy," the injured man said to the man holding a machete. "Do it now, before it spreads."

"But what if we find the cure?" Eddy said. "We could heal you."

"What if we never find it? Cut it off."

Eddy looked at Sergeant Bennings. Instead of answering, Sergeant Bennings examined the hillside of moving dots. He rested a hand on his gun holster.

"Put a stick in my mouth. Knock me unconscious first.

Whatever it takes, just, just do it now…please."

"It's not that bad," Kern said. "It's not fun, but you'll live—"

"Shut up." The injured man had gone a weird gray under his brown skin. He extended his arm on the ground. In a muffled voice, he said, "Do it now."

Eddy held out the machete as if it were a snake about to bite him. He lowered it. "I can't. I just—"

Ricker snatched the machete out of his hand. Before anyone could stop him, he swung the blade over his head and sliced through the arm at the elbow. Blood squirted. The arm dropped onto the dirt. The man screamed and then fell unconscious.

Hugh raised his gun and locked it on Ricker's face. Kern whipped off his belt and knelt to strap it to the wound. The blood slowed into beads of red that bubbled and dripped on the ground.

Sergeant Bennings stepped forward and pointed a second gun at Ricker's head. Ricker dropped the bloody machete. I held my breath and silently pleaded with Ricker to not move another muscle.

"What the hell did you just do?" Hugh said.

"What you couldn't," Ricker said, his voice sounding normal. "I helped him stay uninfected."

"You made him trade one kind of infection for another," Sergeant Bennings said.

"Someone should take him back to our town," Ricker said. "They'll help him in the hospital. They've got supplies."

"Not antibiotics," I said, unable to keep my mouth closed, my stomach sick at what I'd just seen.

"Not antibiotics," Ricker agreed, "but other things might help."

Sergeant Bennings nodded to Eddy. "You take him back." He

flicked his eyes over Ricker. "You may have just saved his life."

That was as close to a thank you as I'd ever imagined hearing come out of Sergeant Benning's mouth. All because a man would rather lose an arm than become a Feeb like us.

"We should go back too," Kern said.

Sergeant Bennings holstered his gun. A muscle on his neck twitched. He looked over the hillside and the sinkhole. "We're not going back until I find my son."

Sergeant Bennings led the way. His people followed even though his decisions might get all of us killed. I fell in behind Gabbi. She didn't acknowledge me. I had revealed something I'd learned about her in the fevers. I had broken our code, even though it had saved her life.

Ricker came up behind me and I thought about jumping away if he attacked me.

If Ricker attacked me.

I couldn't wrap my mind around this.

Ricker looked at me sideways. "Don't be scared, Maibe. Not yet, at least. I'm still okay."

There was such a note of longing in his voice, my confusion almost stopped me in my tracks.

I felt the tease of Fainthood whispering at the edges of my brain. If I let it take over I wouldn't have to think about any of this. It would all go away and I would feel so much better remembering only the good things.

My throbbing ankle brought me back. I walked faster, trying to banish it all away. Ricker increased his pace to match mine.

We explored the fairgrounds until we found a two-story warehouse with a fire escape. Sergeant Bennings sent in us Feebs to search the building for Vs. He decided we would stay on the roof for the night and let any Vs in the area move on. We'd find a way around the sinkhole in the morning.

Once on the rooftop, they built a small fire. Pink, orange, and gray streaked the sky during the sunset. No trees interrupted the view this high up. It was as if we had entered a painting. Yet there was this imaginary line that separated Ricker, me, Gabbi, and the other Feebs from the uninfected.

They gave us some blankets and made us set up on the far side of the roof from them, as if breathing the same few inches of air was too much. For a long time, Sergeant Bennings stood at the edge looking out at the brilliant light and the destruction below.

Tabitha sat away from all of us. She was cross-legged, her hands resting on her knees, her back straight. She looked like a picture of calm meditation. As if she were thinking about all the ways she could help the world instead of hurt it.

Most of the other Feebs worked on our own little fire and passed around whatever food they'd escaped with from the cars.

Gabbi was at the other corner of the roof as far away as possible.

Ricker sat next to me and I wondered how close I should get to him and what nightmares the darkness might bring him and how I would protect him from the others if he did lose control.

I bit my lip and moved my blanket closer to his. "Hi."

Ricker looked at me, evaluating my hello as if it held a deeper question.

Of course it did.

He talked softly, as if I were the wild animal that needed soothing instead of the other way around. "Sergeant Bennings was going for his gun. His whole body was going tense. He had this mean stare he was giving the guy like he was a rabid dog that needed to be put down for his own good."

"He's right," Kern said. He stood several feet away. I realized he stood halfway between Tabitha and Gabbi. Unsure or unwilling to go to one over the other. "I saw it too."

I tilted my head, trying to think over the scene. I'd only had eyes for the machete and Ricker. I hadn't seen Sergeant Bennings or paid attention to what he had been doing.

"Didn't you see Sergeant's gun?" Ricker said. "He was ready to kill the guy for getting bit. For getting infected."

"But we're going after the cure," I said, remembering the disturbing light in Ricker's eyes. I also remembered how Sergeant Bennings had placed his hand on his holster. I thought he'd been focused on the hillside of Vs. "He believes the cure exists. He's going after it. It doesn't make sense."

"He was about to kill him for having gotten infected," Ricker said. "I had to do something. You believe me, right?"

"I believe you." Although I wasn't sure I did. But I didn't NOT believe him either.

Ricker squinted at me.

"I believe you. I do." This time I said it with more conviction.

Hugh crossed the imaginary line on the roof while slapping on a pair of blue surgical gloves. Two other uninfected walked on either side of him, guns ready. Hugh went over to Gabbi.

I stood up.

She turned her head. Her short hair was plastered to her skin. There was a wild look in her eyes.

I took a step. Kern grabbed my wrist. "Let her be."

I shook him off. He didn't know Gabbi very well if he thought letting her deal with someone like Hugh alone would work.

"Put your hands together," Hugh said. "In front of you.

Ankles too."

"What are you going to do?" I called out.

One of the guns swiveled in my direction. The other stayed trained on Gabbi.

"You're to be tied up for the night so you can't escape—or worse."

"Or worse?" I said.

"Infect us," Hugh said, not taking his eyes off Gabbi as he answered me. "Pull another stunt like you all did today while we're sleeping and can't defend ourselves."

"We're not criminals," I said.

"Depends on whose point of view you take," he said.

Gabbi didn't move. I thought if she did move, it would be an explosion and we'd all die from the blast.

"Right." I held out my hands. "Go for it. Tie away. Whatever."

Hugh left Gabbi and used simple rope around my hands and ankles, then he did the same to Ricker. Next came Kern and the other Feebs.

Gabbi was the only one left untied. They had all the weapons. We had nothing. Gabbi held out her hands while staring steadily at Hugh. He kept breaking the stare and fumbling with the rope. When he finally finished the three uninfected hurried back to their side.

"That's it?" I said.

"He can't believe this will hold us for long," Ricker said.

Hugh returned with a gun and a steaming packet of food. He sat cross-legged on the ground.

"What are you doing?" Ricker said.

"First watch," Hugh said.

CHAPTER 22

THE NIGHT WAS LOUD. Crickets and frogs called out a chaotic drum session. A type of painted gravel covered the roof and dug into my skin through the blanket. Even though I was warm enough at first, it soon chilled. I slept in fits. The ropes dug into my body in weird ways. I dreamed of Dutch Flat and wondered how my Faints were. I hoped Corrina and Dylan were still okay.

I woke the next morning to the sun and uncurled from between Ricker and Gabbi. She wouldn't talk to me, but even still had thrown a protective arm over my waist in the night. I didn't know if she was angry, sad, scared. Probably all of those things at once.

Ricker moaned at the loss of heat and opened his eyes. "What's on the menu?"

"Hot coffee and French Toast dipped in eggs and cinnamon," I said, "and real maple syrup."

"And fresh squeezed orange juice?" He smiled.

"Of course."

We ate the stale crackers, cheese, and sour water passed around. Hugh untied all of us and we climbed down the fire escape after checking for Vs.

The sinkhole had grown over night, taking out more houses, the entrance to the fairgrounds, and our vehicles.

The drum session hadn't been the crickets.

Leon cursed. Tabitha whispered something to him. He went silent.

Sergeant Bennings went to the lip of the monster and looked down.

"I hope he falls in," Gabbi said. They were the first words she had spoken to me since I had called out her full name.

"That's Alden's father," I said.

"That's the man who imprisoned us, who kept Mary from us, who tried to kill us." Gabbi's voice rose in volume with each word until she was practically shouting.

I snatched at her arm. "Lower your voice."

She jerked away and pushed me up against a fence. The metal chain links scratched my skin.

"Gabbi," Ricker hissed.

Nobody paid attention to our little drama except for Leon. His gaze stayed steady on Gabbi, flicking only once to me. Gabbi's fingers pinched my arms. Ricker looked ready to punch her, and Leon, I didn't know what he would do.

"We need Sergeant Bennings," I said.

Gabbi snarled. "I don't NEED anyone. I've survived fine without help from anyone like him. Anyone like you."

Ricker placed a gentle hand on Gabbi's shoulder. She flinched. Her head turned as if she were about to snap at him. I wanted to throw up. Gabbi couldn't go V, not now, not with all of them here. She would die. We would watch her die.

"Gabbi, I'm sorry about your name," I said. "You were standing at the edge. I didn't know what else to say. I didn't want you to die."

Her voice softened. "Maibe?" She blinked. "It's just a name. It's nothing. It's not anything. You're one of the only people who has ever cared enough—sometimes you remind me of her."

Leon stepped closer, blocking us from the sight of Sergeant Bennings and the other uninfected. Something bright glinted in the sun. He unsheathed a knife from his belt. Somehow, he'd kept a weapon from the uninfected. Now he held it out as if ready to use it on Gabbi. Fear shot through me. My heartbeat slammed into my ears, drowning out all sound.

"Mary always cared, even if she was hard on us sometimes. I knew it was because—"

"Gabbi," I said, my voice low, urgent. I tried to keep the fear out of it because I thought if she could hear that, it would only trip her further into a frenzy. "Remember the cure? Remember Ano and Jimmy? We're here for them. We're here and we're alive and we're going to find the cure that will bring everyone back and fix all of this."

Something about Gabbi changed. Her eyes narrowed, her grip became more painful. "You always said we were dead. You said we died as soon as we got infected. What does any of this matter? We're zombies—that's what you said. And zombies are supposed to hurt and kill and—"

"Mary's still out there," Ricker said, putting a sureness into his words that he couldn't possibly feel. But then I looked at the blaze in his eyes and thought that maybe he did believe it. I didn't know Mary, but she was a powerful person to them. She was who this had all started with. She was everything.

"We're not dead." My voice caught in my throat. All the movies I'd watched with my uncle tumbled around and overlapped in my brain. Infection. Change. Death. It was my life. It was thick around us. "I was wrong."

I wasn't just saying these words to talk her down. I really believed them now. We were alive and I wanted to stay that way.

"We need Sergeant Bennings in order to find Mary. You want to find Mary, right?"

Leon crept closer.

"If he dies," I said, "How long do you think it will be until Hugh and the others hurt us?"

Her grip on my arm loosened just a little, but it was enough to get her back. She knew I was right.

Leon's knife flashed in the sky, blinding me.

"No!" I screamed.

Gabbi whirled.

Two figures crashed into Leon. They tumbled to the ground. Dust kicked up and stung my eyes, my mouth, my lungs. Ricker coughed next to me.

Sergeant Bennings and the others ran up.

The dust cleared. Leon was knocked out, knife still in hand, eyes rolled to the whites. Nindal and Bernice held him down.

Gabbi sat on the ground, arms crossed over her chest. She was covered in dust, but she looked unhurt.

"He attacked them," Bernice said without blinking an eye.

I thought the three of them had teamed up, but now I wasn't so sure.

Sergeant Bennings took in the scene. He bent over and

plucked the knife from Leon's hand. "Tie them all up again. No more chances."

WE HIKED AROUND THE SINKHOLE. The rope rubbed just the right way against my pants that it opened up a fire where the V had bitten me. I gritted my teeth and bore the pain as best I could.

On the other side of the pit we lost several hours until we found enough working vehicles for our group. Once we were bustled into the new cars, the landscape moved by in a blur. We ate up the miles in this flat part of the state. You could almost pretend nothing had happened here because it had always looked abandoned.

We didn't take I-5, but instead took Jack Tone Road around Stockton, Manteca, Modesto. We avoided the dense population centers. We passed by fields of dead almond trees, grape vines, rows of industrial warehouses, miles of barbed fencing.

Out here, there hadn't been many people in the first place, and there didn't seem to be anyone now. When we hit Shiloh Road I began to recognize the scenery. The citrus orchards had died off between now and when I had been here last. Eventually we came to a small rise of a hill that felt a certain way, the paper-thin rattle of dried grass sounded a certain way, the stretch of highway and the now dead trees on the other side looked a certain way.

Sergeant stopped and let all of us stretch our legs. He didn't want to enter the camp making a bunch of noise. I wandered to the hilltop, my hobble making it awkward.

The rise allowed me to see some of the camp buildings. My

breath caught in my throat. Ricker grabbed my hand. I flicked my eyes to him for a moment and then looked away. I'd never told him. I'd never told any of them but they knew. We all fell into the fevers but we never told each other what we learned. Never.

"Those trees," I said.

"Breathe," Ricker said.

The orchard, now spindly and transparent and dead, stood between us and the strip of highway. On the other side of the highway was the camp. A slight breeze rustled the dead leaves. Through there I had run and not looked back and had looked back ever since.

"Move, Maibe. You need to move around." He raised my arm for me and knocked his foot unknowingly against my injured ankle. Shooting pain woke me up.

"Move through it. Move through your practice."

I breathed deep, brought my hands together above my head, and then leaned over to allow blood to rush to my cheeks. I stood back up and all of it hit me like a train crash.

"TAKE THE MEDICINE." Ricker held out a steaming cup of liquid. "There were a few bits left. I made it as strong as a could."

The last of Corrina's medicine.

How long had I been in the exercises? How long had I been lost if he'd found the time to make tea? My mind rebelled but my mouth opened. Ricker's face overlaid my visions of the girl and the fence, the father on his knees, the sounds of bullets. I swallowed the tea to keep from choking.

It seemed like only seconds later that my vision cleared. But the sun was at a different angle than I remembered. When I looked down the hillside I saw Sergeant Bennings and his people lounging in the shade of a large metal storage bin. Two played with a deck of cards, others stared listlessly into the heat. Tabitha sat in the shade with her eyes closed, her hands tied together in her lap. Gabbi was in the shade too, away from everyone, staring out into the distance but not really seeing anything.

Then I noticed I sat on the ground, leaning against someone. My legs were outstretched in the dirt, my arms were slick with sweat because I was in the sun. The ropes around my wrists and ankles were dark with my sweat. A breeze increased and helped cool my skin a little. My pant leg had crept up, revealing the angry red of the V bite. I flicked my cuff back over it. But then I thought—why was I hiding it?

I turned around to tell Ricker. I saw bright red skin, like a lobster.

"Ricker!"

"Yes, my love?" he said, not turning around.

"Get in the shade."

"You first."

I snatched the bandanna from around my neck and doused it in my remaining bit of water. Hopefully the camp would have more.

"Bend over." I wrapped the wet cloth gingerly over his burned skin. "Oh, Ricker."

"It'll be fine. I want to know how you are."

"How long was it?"

He paused. "Two hours."

It had felt like only seconds.

"And Sergeant Bennings waited like it was no big deal? Just waited for me to…come out of it?"

"You're why we're all here, Maibe. He believes he doesn't have a chance of finding Alden without you."

"And what do you believe?"

But as soon as I asked it, I knew I wasn't playing fair.

"Ricker, I—"

He shook his head. "It's okay. Forget it."

I held my hand out. He took it and I helped him up, his warmth comforting me more than I thought it should. The wind turned the dust that coated my clothing into a cloud around us. I looked over the landscape. Flat, yellow, the air so hot it distorted shapes, making everything swim.

I grabbed Ricker's arm.

"Maibe!" he said, alarm in his voice.

I dug my fingers deeper into his skin.

"You can't go V. It doesn't make—"

"Smoke!" I shouted.

The orchard was dead. We were surrounded by a field of sticks and leaf litter that had been drying out for three years.

The wind shifted, grew in power. Out in the middle of the orchard, the smoke darkened and thickened like a tornado. Orange flames sprang to life and licked at the sky. Ash began to rain down like snowflakes.

Sergeant Bennings yelled for everyone to get on their feet.

The camp was just on the other side of the freeway, but the fire blocked us from the cars.

The orchard went up in flames like something out of a movie. My brain felt fogged, thick with fear and a headache. I couldn't remember the name of the movie.

Tabitha shouted something about our ropes, but the uninfected had run off.

Ricker and I hobbled down the hill.

Suddenly Tabitha was next to me. She pushed me forward. "Run!"

I stumbled and landed chin first on the ground. I gulped air and got smoke instead. My wrists strained against the rope. Sweat coated my hands, making them slippery, but the ropes were still too tight. I scrambled back onto my feet. Gabbi was tearing at the ropes with her teeth.

I couldn't find Ricker.

"Rick—" My throat felt like it broke apart on the smoke. Ash stung my eyes, making them tear. Nindal was on his knees next to a tree. His hair was like a smudge of charcoal against the trunk. I stumbled over to him, coughing and tripping on the ropes around my ankles.

"Get up!" I screamed this in Nindal's ear. He turned to me. His eyes were bloodshot. They looked empty, so empty.

I blinked. His brown eyes were bloodshot from the smoke. Tears tracked dirt down his cheeks. Ash had gotten caught in his dark eyebrows, turning them white. I used my shoulder and elbow to lift him off the ground.

"Come on." The orange light grew brighter around us. I didn't know how we would make it out hobbled together, only that we had to try.

Hugh ran past. I shouted for help, but he didn't pause. Then Sergeant Bennings appeared and slashed through our ropes. He pushed me forward and linked his shoulder under Nindal's. This knocked his face shield sideways, revealing sharp blue eyes and a mouth locked in a grimace that showed his teeth.

"Run, you stupid girl."

To my left, the flames danced along the tops of branches, like water pinging down a riverbed, but this was fire and wood. I ran through the trees. A figure came up behind me and for a moment it was Alden but then I blinked him away. Suddenly Ricker shouted at Tabitha. Gabbi was at his side.

"Where's Maibe?"

Tabitha ignored him and limped along, as if having twisted an ankle. The uninfected were far ahead now, almost to the stretch of freeway that would serve as a fire break, if we were lucky. Except for Sergeant Bennings, the other uninfected had abandoned us to our ropes and the fire.

"I saw her," Gabbi said. "I saw her ahead."

"It was a ghost, Gabbi," Ricker said. "She wasn't there. I didn't see her."

I stumbled up to them. Tabitha's hair was full of twigs. Ash coated everyone's skin making them look more zombie-like than ever.

"I'm here."

"I see her." Ricker shook Gabbi by the shoulders. "Do you see her? Do you see her?"

Gabbi pushed him back. He fell onto the ground.

"I see her, idiot. Let's go."

Tabitha had kept walking. We caught up and passed her by. The freeway was a football field away. The fire was so hot and was no longer at our backs. It had swept ahead of us. It was curling through the trees as if it planned to cup us into its hands.

We could make it if we ran.

There was a shout behind me.

I looked over my shoulder. Tabitha had fallen.

Gabbi snatched at my arm. "Leave her!"

I shook her off and ran back. Ricker was close at my heels. We lifted Tabitha up between the two of us.

Gabbi appeared, chest heaving, hair wild and ashy, eyes dangerous. We took a step with Tabitha between us, but she moaned and went limp.

Gabbi cursed loud and long. She grabbed up Tabitha's legs. The three of us carried her through the orchard. Sparks floated in the air—California's version of the glow bug. One landed on my bare arm. It burned the hair, creating a stink that made me gag and a painful burning that left a dark mark on my skin. More orange sparks floated by, following different currents. They landed on our hair, our faces, our clothes, our skin.

Our feet touched the asphalt road. Seconds later, Sergeant Bennings and Nindal tumbled out next to us.

The sparks floated like a cloud of locusts in the sky. They drifted across the four-lane freeway, some tumbling to their death on the asphalt, but most—most caught air that brought them into the waist-high, yellowed grass on the other side.

The grass began to smoke.

CHAPTER 23

GHOST-MEMORIES WHISPERED. The fire was at our backs and burning holes in our clothes. We passed the part of the fence I had dug underneath so long ago. Papers, plastic bags, empty bottles were caught in the fence links, forming an opaque wall along the bottom. Glass littered the guard box and crunched under our shoes as we hurried by. There was a body in a brown uniform. He slumped over a desk, desiccated in some parts, bloated in others, depending on what had fallen in the path of the sun and what had been protected by shade.

The camp was broken into two parts, surrounded by gravel and made out of cement. On this side of the freeway, there was no orchard, but the weeds would still give the fire plenty of fuel.

We needed to get inside.

Sergeant Bennings led us away from the refugee barracks that were little more than wooden shacks. They wouldn't stand for much longer. Gravel paths led off in several directions, twisting through the dead grass like gray snakes before disappearing over a slight rise. We hurried along the gravel path that bent around the base of a small hill. The main building stood two stories tall with thick concrete walls. Rust stained the outside in a series of waterfall splashes. Lines of broken windows rimmed the top floor. The door to the main cement building was open, its black rectangle swallowing all light.

Glass, gravel, and broken concrete crunched under our feet, making everything unstable. Tabitha almost slipped out of my arms. My muscles trembled and would fail soon.

Sergeant Bennings dragged Nindal through the doorway. The darkness swallowed them up. The door gave out a long groan as the metal edge of it scratched the stone. I wondered for a moment if we would find Vs waiting inside for us, but then pushed that thought away.

There was nowhere else to go.

We crossed through and the cold, humid air hit me like a slap. I was tumbling down into the carpet, my aunt raising her hand for another strike. I held up my hands to block her and cried out.

"Maibe!"

My aunt disappeared. There was silence except for the crackling fire outside and the way the wind sent flurries of ash and sparks into the air. My eyes began to focus in the dark. I'd dropped Tabitha while in the memory-rush, but she was okay— awake now and rubbing her ankle. Crumbs of metal, glass, and concrete covered the ground. Sunlight streamed in through a series of arched floor-to-ceiling windows. The light revealed pools of water. Pipes ran across the two-story tall ceiling, and drips from them splashed into the pools in front of us. Green moss made zig-zagging paths along the edge of the pools.

A skittering noise brought a bunch of rifles to attention.

Sergeant Bennings' people and the other Feebs were already here.

A small creature, larger than a rat, smaller than a cat, fled across the shadows and lights, disappearing through a far archway where more vines climbed the walls. A few of the uninfected turned back to the dripping water to clean themselves and filter it through their clothing for a drink. Others turned their guns on us Feebs once the animal noises stopped.

I shouted at them.

They had no decency. They had run and left us for dead, not even bothering to cut our ropes. Every step we took was watched, evaluated, scorned. I realized how it must have felt for Ricker and Gabbi to be runaways on the streets. They talked about it sometimes, when the mood hit them just right. The way people hated them, the way peoples' faces changed when they figured out they were talking to a bunch of runaways. The way they'd gotten kicked out of restaurants, run out of parks, rounded up for police questioning just because of who they were.

This was what it must have been like. The eyes watching you. The way they assumed you were always up to no good.

It sat like a weight on my back.

I understood why Gabbi lashed out so much. If you didn't fight back, then you let them think it was okay to treat you like you were less than human.

I understood Ricker's desire to pretend it didn't touch him. They couldn't hurt you if you pretended you didn't care.

I wanted to meet Mary and tell her I knew why she had dreamed of a garden in the country for all her friends to just live away from all of this fear and hate.

I finished my shouting. I couldn't remember ever feeling so exhausted.

Leon and Bernice took Nindal from Sergeant Bennings and leaned him against one of the walls.

Sergeant Bennings said something sharp.

The uninfected lowered their guns. Everyone except for Hugh.

Another word from Sergeant Bennings. Hugh lowered his rifle, but not before spitting into one of the pools.

Gabbi and Ricker just stared at me.

"Where should we go?" Sergeant Bennings said, breaking the silence with his hoarse voice. He was asking me for directions as if I had some secret power that would find Alden.

"I have no idea," I said, my voice barely above a whisper.

Sergeant Bennings looked as if about to call me a liar.

"I need to keep walking. It'll help me think." And avoid the stares of everyone who thought my shouting meant I'd gone crazy. Who knows—maybe I had gone crazy.

At the other end of the large room was a winding concrete staircase. It looked strange, the smooth sweep of its curve against the massive bulkiness of the concrete. Up above were the experiment rooms. I had never seen them, only heard about them from others who had escaped.

Sergeant Bennings stepped through the puddles, his boots sending rippled waves into the moss that lined it. "Turning into a Faint now, are you?" He said this too quietly for anyone to hear except for me.

I followed after him, going around the pools, trying not to disturb any life that had managed to take over where humans had failed. I almost wanted to take his comment as him wanting to start a fight, but there was an edge of worry to his voice. For all he knew, I was the only link to finding his son.

"Exercise helps," I said finally.

"But not like it used to."

"How do you know?"

He didn't answer right away. "It didn't help my wife." There was sorrow in his voice.

Jane walked over. "We should try to find whatever's left of the research. Maybe I'll recognize something."

Sergeant Bennings cocked his head and nodded. "There won't be much left, but whatever there is, it'll be upstairs."

We took the stairs one person at a time in case the concrete decided to give out. On the second floor, everything tightened into a long hallway. One side was lined with broken windows that let the smoke drift in. Glass was scattered everywhere. On the other side was a series of doors. An old fire sprinkler pipe cut the ceiling down the middle like a seam. Piles of dust and leaves gathered in the cracks where the walls met the ground, rounding the edges and narrowing it into a tunnel.

We opened each door in order. Chairs, beds, sinks. A caved roof inside one room. In other rooms the green mold took over in the shade, sucking moisture from the concrete. There were filthy tables with straps, rusting grates over the windows, trays of hypodermic needles, cabinets of tools I dared not open. A decayed body in one of the rooms was splayed out and so old it was impossible to tell the kind of infection the victim had suffered from.

Ricker touched a set of straps with dents that seemed too much like human teeth marks for comfort. We both stared at reddish stains on the walls and floors and wondered what was rust and what was blood.

A growing sense of dread settled into my stomach. This hallway of horrors was where all rules had been set aside for any experiment they could imagine. Everything was given the green light in order to find a cure.

"Sergeant!"

The voice, like a shot, brought Ricker and me into the hallway.

A door led into a large room filled from floor to ceiling with monitors, computer banks, and other laboratory-looking equipment. Sergeant Bennings stood at the far end of the room, rifling through papers yellowed with water damage and spread across a metal table. A broken fluorescent light fixture dangled over him. I imagined it shattering on his head, then banished the thought. If he hadn't cut our ropes and helped Nindal we'd be dead now.

Jane pulled out papers and notebooks from several cabinets.

Sergeant Bennings stood a few feet away. "Do you recognize any of this?"

Jane shook her head. She tore through the pages and let them flutter to the ground. "I...I don't know."

Sergeant Bennings bent down and carefully picked up the papers. Other uninfected picked through the cabinets, drawers, and desks.

When they weren't paying attention I slipped out of the room and back down the stairs. Soft steps gave away that both Ricker and Gabbi followed. I sidestepped puddles and received an adrenaline shock when I startled an animal into sprinting away.

"Where are you going?" Ricker said.

I continued outside.

"Any clues Alden might have left, they wouldn't be inside

here." The sun shocked my eyes into blindness. The dark coolness inside had made me forget. For as far as the eye could see, the sky was a sick brown now. The smoke had blotted out the sun. Orange flames burned the weed-covered hillsides around the camp. We were in the eye of the firestorm.

Sergeant Bennings ran outside, a rifle crooked in his arm. He stopped when he saw me.

I wanted to tell him I wasn't going to run away. I kept myself from wasting the breath and said instead, "You won't find anything in there."

I knew this with a surety I hadn't felt in a long time. I walked up a slope and over a rise that brought me to the top of the ridge. The rolling hills spread out before me. Behind me, the hills ended abruptly at the freeway and gave way to flat, endless miles of valley, now no longer irrigated, now mostly dead, now all burning—and haunted by the memories of that poor family unlucky enough to have gotten me as their rescuer.

I hiked out, crossing another depression and the top of a hill. The fire licked close here. I hurried through a gap in the chain-link fence made by a truck crashing through it. The driver's face was still mashed into the steering wheel, his body positioned like he was praying.

An invisible compass drove me forward.

Behind me I heard the cough and start of an engine. Sergeant Bennings was at the truck's steering wheel. The dead driver was laid out on the ground.

"Everything out here is burning. There's nothing. It's weeds," Sergeant Bennings said.

"We're going to get cut off," Ricker said.

"Let her be," Gabbi said. "She knows what she's doing."

There was only one place Alden would have left me clues. The next hill dumped me onto a ledge that overlooked the camp.

I sat on the ledge, dangling my feet over it, trying this time to trigger a memory-rush and figure out where or what the clue would be.

"This is where Alden and I would meet to map out escape plans." It's also where I had tried to kiss him and he had rejected me so completely.

Sergeant Bennings looked at me strangely. "It wasn't just information? He was…"

"He was helping people you had imprisoned." I forced myself not to think about the Garcia family. "He was helping get them out."

"I knew someone was helping," Sergeant Bennings said, "but I always figured it was someone with infected relatives. I never thought…"

Alden's ghost fuzzed in and out next to me. His feet dangled over the ledge like mine now did. He had commented on how blue the sky looked now that there were no more fires to muck it up. I had talked about logistics, the layout of the camp, where the family was being kept. He had talked about his worry for his mother, how his father shouldn't be blamed for the virus, how he was searching for Dr. Ferrad and the cure and he was getting closer.

His brown hair had dropped into his eyes. I had reached out to brush it away—

"Stop," I told myself.

"What?" Ricker said.

The wind whispered through my hair. Ash fluttered into my lap. There was no sunlight but everything was hot and sweat poured off of me. I turned and saw Ricker had his bandanna high over his nose and he looked so worried and the orange fire on the hillside glowed so bright.

"Go back, Ricker."

He laughed and sat next to me. His movement nudged aside a rock. A paper fluttered from underneath and caught in a prickly stalk of dead grass. Gabbi snatched at it. Sergeant Bennings held out his hand for it. She handed me the paper instead.

I flattened the paper against my knee. It was crisp, yellowed, like it had been enduring the summer heat for awhile. It was a form. A receipt for a shipment of primates. The letterhead said it was from a university research facility just outside of Sacramento.

Sergeant Bennings loomed over my shoulder. "Show Jane the paper."

He made us drive the truck back. It was faster and we needed the vehicle. The dead guy wouldn't mind.

The concrete building gave welcome relief from the heat and smoke though it took a long minute for my eyes to adjust to the darkness.

Jane sat next to one of the pools. She used her finger to stroke waves in the water.

"Do you know anything about this place?" I pushed it into her hands.

We all held our breath as she brought the paper into the rectangle of light.

She scanned the letterhead. Her cheek twitched.

She crumpled the paper between her hands.

ALDEN

The moan was low, painful, and it went on until his entire head was full with it, until there was nothing but the moaning.

He woke to a darkness lifted by three lights. One, the beeping monitor hooked up by patches to his chest. Another, a strip of light setup behind him that only made the room feel colder and more alone. Its light barely illuminated the sheet that covered him from chest to feet. The third, a rectangle that seeped around the door where the twin tubes disappeared, turning it into something like a magic portal.

It didn't seem that far off to him—whatever was behind that door, it was going to make him whole again.

The moaning sound stopped. His ears rang from the silence.

He didn't know what that meant. Was he fully cured now? He tried to examine his skin, but the bluish light only made him look even more dead than when he'd been a Feeb. The room was empty except for the equipment and that speaker, lens, and vent.

Sometimes, in quiet moments like this he felt sorry he had left his father. Deep down, his father cared deeply. His father was frantic over his mother sleeping an eternal sleep.

The moan came back, but this time it had a direction—behind the door where the tubing disappeared. He bit his lip so hard he tasted that metallic sourness again. He struggled to sit up and found he could.

They no longer had him strapped down.

The tubing pumped the medicine into him but suddenly he didn't care. The cure was behind that door. This was his chance to escape with it and take it to Maibe.

He touched his bare feet to the stone floor. Cold shot up his legs. The moans stopped. The sound was not in his head.

He stepped toward the door. The monitor crashed to the floor. He ripped off the remaining patches and tore out the tubes. His arms burned. The tubing squirted dark, black liquid onto the ground. How could this be the medicine?

His lungs ached, like the air in the room was thin, as if he were breathing after a long hike up a mountain. He wavered, dizzy from standing up too fast. Part of him thought he should return to the bed—the moans were a side effect. They were a sign of his brain still betraying him.

He pushed on until he came to the door. The tubing snaked beneath the bottom crack. It looked more like a supply closet than something that would store medical devices. He pressed his forehead against it, hoping the shock of cold would clear his thoughts. Instead a headache began to pound behind his ears.

The liquid grew into a pond on the floor and became a mucky, dark swamp. They said it cost so much. It was going to waste now. Should he collect it? What if it all got used up and there *was nothing left for Maibe?*

He felt so weak, as if from blood loss. Fear struck him like lightning. Were they taking his blood? Were they trying to kill him?

He yanked open the door.

The light blinded him, it was so white, so complete. This dark snake curved along the floor and up a metal bed leg and into the arm of one of the uninfected that had arrived just yesterday.

The moans came from him.

The tubing snaked into his arm.

Alden didn't want to see this. His stomach flipped. He wanted to puke. He wanted to scream.

He understood now what they meant about cost.

CHAPTER 24

IT SMELLED LIKE A BARBECUE.

Gabbi returned from looking out through the doorway. "I think most of them are Feebs who have turned."

We sat next to one of the pools and used Ricker's bandanna to filter the water into something we hoped was safe to drink. The fire had driven the Vs out in front of it—toward our cement island.

"There's more." Gabbi described how the Vs were pressing against one section of the fence because there was nowhere else for them to go. Soon the fence would topple under their weight.

The water dripped through the bandanna into Ricker's cupped hands.

"We'll find the cure," I said fiercely.

"You can't be sure of that," Gabbi said. "No one can be sure of that."

"What else is there to believe in?" I said.

"Ourselves," she said, but it lacked her normal bravado. She looked at Ricker. "Just remember your promise."

"What promise?"

Ricker sipped from his hands. He held my gaze. It wasn't mean, but it wasn't kind either. "We promised not to let each other hurt anyone."

I didn't understand at first. It seemed like a stupid promise, one that we had made a million times, one that we didn't even need to say out loud. Then it dawned on me.

"You would kill each other."

"We would die to keep each other safe. To keep you safe." Gabbi rubbed the list of scarred names on her arm. All of those people already dead.

Ricker had his own list. He took the bandanna from me. "Your turn."

I rubbed my scars before cupping my hands underneath the bandanna. My names overlapped with theirs. Leaf. Spencer.

The cold water dripped into my hands. My mouth tasted so dry in spite of the water. The roar of the fire sounded muffled inside, like maybe it wasn't so bad out there. I understood Gabbi's stony silence now. She wasn't angry with me. She was more scared than she had ever been in her life.

"I won't let either of you die," I said.

Gabbi shook her head. A half-smile formed. "Where's the zombie-girl when you need her? We're already dead, remember? Or did you forget?"

I swallowed around a knot in my throat. "Maybe we are dead, maybe we aren't, but that doesn't get us out of doing what's right."

"Keeping ourselves from hurting somebody else seems pretty

right to me," Gabbi said.

I didn't say anything until both Ricker and Gabbi looked at me. "We're going to figure this out."

Ricker shook his head, flipping his hair over his eyes. Something outside crashed. It sounded metallic and final. The fence.

Ricker dropped his bandanna in the puddle. The uninfected rushed outside. We followed close behind.

The Vs were inside the camp.

A wall of orange flames leapt into the sky behind them. Smoke plumes enveloped some of the Vs, making it impossible to count their numbers. But even the ones we could see—there were too many.

Sergeant Bennings shouted orders. We ran outside and tried piling into the truck. There wasn't enough room. More than two dozen of us. Seven Feebs and the rest were uninfected.

Hugh shouted. "Leave the infected!"

Sergeant Bennings told Hugh to drive. He pushed Jane and two other uninfected into the cab with Hugh. He jumped into the truck bed next. The Vs at the front of the pack saw us and sprinted in our direction.

It was too much. Feeb skin, V hate in their eyes. Bernice and Nindal forced space for Tabitha on the floor of the truck bed while uninfected climbed over her.

Sergeant Bennings just looked at Gabbi and Ricker. "Maibe inside."

I shook my head. "No way." I backed away from the truck. "You find room for everyone or none of us."

"Just go, Maibe," Ricker said.

"Don't be a fool," Gabbi said. "Close the damn truck gate and we'll use the bumper."

The fire's roar grew in volume. Human voices carried on the wind. Angry, vicious shouts.

I jumped into the bed next to Bernice and Nindal. Behind them was Leon, a tire iron ready in his hands. The rest of the truck was jammed with the uninfected, their masks and gloves and long sleeves making it impossible to tell anyone apart.

Bernice slammed the gate closed. We were packed like sardines inside. An uninfected's plastic face mask jabbed me in the neck. Even through the smoke I could smell the stink of their bodies, the way their safety gear had trapped the sweat and made it molder.

Ricker and Gabbi held onto the back. I pushed Nindal and Bernice aside until I was up against the gate. I pressed my hands down on theirs to keep them attached to the truck.

If they bounced off, I was going with them.

The engine roared to life even as the Vs closed in. Uninfected shouted and screamed. I yelled out for the truck to get moving. If Ricker or Gabbi were bit, it wouldn't matter how hard I held on, they'd be lost in the fevers.

Hugh gunned it, fishtailing down the gravel path. Ricker's hands were slick with sweat, water, fear. Suddenly one hand got loose. He was flung halfway off the bumper, closer to the snapping mouths of the Vs that raced for us.

I leaned out, grabbing him back to the truck. Gabbi's hands turned white as they gripped the truck like a vise.

There was a scream. Something pushed into me so hard it pressed the breath out of me. A dark figure dropped over the side and onto the ground. He rolled and scrambled to his knees. His face mask was knocked off. Sweat and dirt streaked his cheeks. His hair was greasy and hung into his eyes. He began to run for the truck. Sergeant Bennings yelled and banged on the roof.

Hugh didn't slow down.

The man tripped and fell in the dirt and the Vs and the smoke consumed him.

A group of Vs caught up to us at the next turn. Their skin was marked like Feebs—ashy, wrinkled, veins pulsing underneath—but their eyes were vacant, bloodshot, angry.

Shots blasted. My ears rang and all other noises disappeared. Two of the Vs lay still on the ground. Three Vs jumped at the truck. One V latched onto the back, between Gabbi and Ricker. His clothes were in tatters. A festering wound on his arm dripped blood and pus that were flung backward into the dust cloud.

The truck slowed and swerved around the guard box. The V was scrawny, but his muscles were like ropes that attached him to the truck. Pebbles kicked up and pinged him in the face. He twisted, growling, and leaned over. His mouth gaped open like it had a laser targeted on Gabbi's arm.

I screamed, let go of Ricker, and shot out my hand. The V crunched down on my wrist, pressing me against Gabbi's skin. His teeth grated on my bones and sparked a matching flame of pain from my ankle bite.

Gabbi roared and kicked out a foot that slammed the V in the gut. Ricker swung a fist that landed on the V's jaw.

I was pulled forward, halfway out of the truck bed.

The V's mouth was still attached to my wrist as he began to fall. The edge of the gate dug into my chest, knocking the breath out of me. Everything went blazing white with spots.

The pressure released as if a trap had been unsprung.

Arms wrapped around my waist and pulled me back into the truck.

I cradled my wrist against my chest.

My blood had sprayed drops across Gabbi's face, Ricker's hands, all down my chest and on the truck. If I looked at my wrist I feared I might see it flop around.

The road evened out.

The wall of fire and Vs dropped back.

Ricker looked at me with such sadness. My heart broke seeing it. Gabbi stared at me with eyes as large as the moon. Her lips moved like she was trying to say something but no sound came out.

They watched me and they knew. Any second now I'd become trapped in the fevers like Ano, like Kern. Tormented eternally with memories of my aunt and everything else terrible that had ever happened to me.

They looked at me like I had just died in front of them.

The truck bottomed out.

My wrist slammed into the metal edge.

Searing pain turned everything red.

CHAPTER 25

EVEN IN THE REDNESS, I heard the voices that spoke over me.

"Wrap her hand tighter than that. The blood hasn't stopped leaking."

"I know how to tie a tourniquet."

A pause. Lowered voices. "Why isn't she in the fevers?"

I tried to open my eyes but my eyes felt like someone had tied weights to the lids.

"Are you kidding me? What does it look like she's in? Are you an idiot?"

"She's just unconscious from the pain."

"I'm awake," I croaked out. My head pounded. My throat felt so dry and scratchy. Water sounded like the most beautiful thing in the world right then. Something hard pressed against my lips. I closed my mouth.

"Drink," Jane said, her voice anxious.

I opened my eyes and my mouth.

We were in a field, bone-dry, weeds yellowed and thorny.

Jane hovered over me. The pupils of her hazel eyes were pinpricks. My heartbeat sped up. What was she doing here? Where were Gabbi and Ricker? I'd been unconscious, maybe I'd even been trapped in the fevers. We never left each other alone. Never. Not when it came to the fevers. I tried to sit up. My head spun and the ash twirled like a tornado around my head.

"Hold still." Short spiky hair wavered out of the corner of my eye.

Gabbi was there, sitting on her heels in the dust.

The world finally stopped spinning.

I breathed out and forced my heartbeat back to a normal rate. We never left each other alone in the fevers. I shouldn't have doubted her.

I gulped down the water. It felt as good on my tongue as I had imagined. It was cool and somehow sweet. It tasted like heaven.

Jane took back the bottle. "That's plenty for now. Take it easy zombie-girl."

"Say it like that again and you'll regret it," Gabbi said.

Jane shaded her eyes in the sun and I swore she smirked just because she knew it would drive Gabbi crazy.

Gabbi stood up in the dirt.

We were in the shade of the truck. Tabitha leaned against one wheel, her leg straight out, her eyes closed like she was sleeping. Dark figures came toward us in two directions but they were still far away. The smoke was this terrible wall of brown and the ash fell from the sky like snow.

Whose bright idea had it been to leave Gabbi with Jane?

"Please," I said. "Just tell me what happened."

"We stopped for water," Jane said finally. "And a map."

"And food," Gabbi said. "Who knows when we'll get the next chance."

Jane looked back at the wall of smoke and nodded at the dark specks moving in our direction. "They keep coming. Like they can smell us."

"They can't smell us," Gabbi said, a sneer on her face. "They're running from the fire."

"So you say." Jane moved into a cross-legged position. Her blonde hair was tied in a ponytail that dropped halfway down her back. Her knees had worn holes through the material of her jeans.

"Do you really not remember?" I said, needing to know. Maybe if I just asked, maybe she would actually tell the truth now that Sergeant Bennings wasn't around.

"I didn't know where the place was until I saw that paper," Jane said. "I don't know how I got so far away, or why, I was just…I don't know."

Gabbi snorted.

"I remember some stuff," Jane said, as if offended. "I got infected after the fairgrounds…There's a gap after that when I was in the fevers, but eventually Dr. Ferrad found me. I know I can get reinfected. I know Dr. Ferrad was the one who cured me—"

"Did you see Mary?" Gabbi interrupted.

"I don't know who that is," Jane said.

"A friend," I said quietly. "She protected them until the infection."

"You don't know what it's been like out there," Jane said. "I was alone after the fairgrounds. It's been so easy for you—"

"Are you insane?" Gabbi said.

"It hasn't been easy," I said.

"You've had each other. I went out on my own." Jane's eyes shined almost like she had tears in them. "I left the fairgrounds alone and I survived."

In the direction of the smoke and the Vs, it was all open field, but on the other side of the truck was a lone gas station. Its sign must have been at least five stories tall. An orange and red rectangle against the sky as a beacon to truckers and families on long road trips.

Suddenly I remembered a different gas station. It had been along the train tracks and the RV had been full of people, including kids. The guy who had owned the RV had a name for it. Lana, Lena.

Luna.

Jane and the driver hadn't wanted me on Luna, but Corrina and Dylan had. We'd stopped at the gas station and I'd run inside with Corrina because even then I felt as if she had a strength that the others didn't. I had felt so alone and I'd known something terrible was going to happen.

I hadn't known how awful it would all get. None of the movies I'd watched with my uncle had prepared me. We thought we would survive it together. He'd been the one to bring me out of my shell after I'd been given up for dead by my father and then my aunt.

It hadn't been enough.

I'd tried to tell the truth, but they hadn't listened at the gas station. Jane laughed me off as a little girl with a big imagination.

"You left me and Corrina," I said, feeling an anger so quick and deep it surprised me. "You didn't care what happened to us."

Jane stood up. Her movement caused Tabitha to start as if

waking from a doze.

"I did what I had to," Jane said. "Do you know why there's a cure at all? Because of me. Because when Dr. Ferrad needed to test it out on a human, I said she could do it to me. They didn't know exactly what it would do. I could have died. I almost sacrificed my life—"

"Because you hated being a Feeb so much." My voice raised even as my headache increased. "Don't pretend you did it because it was the right thing to do. You did it because you would rather die than stay a Feeb."

Jane's mouth opened and closed like a fish.

"Didn't you?" I wanted her to say it.

"I got myself infected and I got myself cured," she said. "I don't have to apologize to anyone for that."

Tabitha pushed herself upright and flexed her injured ankle out in front of her. When she seemed satisfied that it would work after all, she stood up. "Everyone around you is lying. They've always been lying. Why would you ever believe they would start telling the truth?"

I didn't know who the words were meant for. It was something I would have thought Gabbi would say. I wished I had never tried to talk to Jane. I didn't know what to believe.

"What does that even mean?" I said.

"It means she's a bitter old woman who couldn't care less about what happens to other people. Especially her son," Gabbi said.

But even I knew that wasn't fair. Tabitha was here because her son was trapped in the fevers like Ano.

"You can try to bait me all you want," Tabitha said. "I won't bite."

"Dr. Ferrad wasn't lying," Jane said. "She has a cure. She cured me."

"Dr. Ferrad has always been lying." Tabitha shook her head as if disappointed in a student that required her to repeat a lesson. "I tried to work with all of them. Sergeant Bennings, Dr. Ferrad, the council. They repaid me by imprisoning us, by experimenting on us, by creating this hell in the first place."

Tabitha nodded in the direction of the fire and the Vs walking out in front of it. They weren't dark blobs anymore but individual shapes. "Who's to say how long we have until we're all like that."

Another group of dots on the gas station side formed into people—our people. Ricker and Sergeant Bennings and the others were returning.

"That will never happen to me," Jane said.

"Time to go," Gabbi said, helping me up. "I don't want to listen to this crap anymore."

She was careful of my injured wrist. I could look at it now all wrapped with a torn-up shirt from somewhere. I wiggled my fingers. It hurt, but they all moved.

Gabbi had believed me. Gabbi had always listened even when she pretended not to.

"Why am I not in the fevers?" I asked it desperately. I wanted her to explain everything and tell me it was all going to be okay.

"You should tell Dr. Ferrad when we find her," Jane said. "She'll figure it out."

Gabbi squinted her eyes and set her lips in a grim line. "There's probably something REALLY wrong with you."

I couldn't help it—I barked out a laugh. It was a long one that brought tears to my eyes. The salt and the ash stung me, but

I didn't care. I had wanted Gabbi to say something soothing. I had wanted her to lie to me. Instead she said exactly what I needed to hear.

"NOW you tell me," I said between gasping breaths.

Gabbi smiled, and even though it didn't reach her eyes, it was enough. "Ask a dumb-ass question, get a dumb-ass answer."

THE VS FOLLOWED THE TRUCK or moved out in front of the fire. It didn't really matter the reason because the result was the same. We piled back in and drove off—and the Vs followed.

The world burned around us. Flowering bushes towered along the edges of the road, catching fire sometimes just after we passed. Scraggly oaks flared up as the fire jumped the grass and greedily consumed the trees like a favorite snack. Vs who were once Feebs who had once been uninfected streamed ahead of the fires.

Not all of them.

Many let themselves burn like Matilda and her family had done back in that cafe along the train tracks. Back when it had been just me and Corrina, newly infected. Back when the fairgrounds had been a place that was going to save us. Back before I'd known Gabbi or Ricker or Ano or Jimmy even existed.

We finally reached a stretch of road that allowed our pitiful group to gain some speed. The uninfected crowded against the truck cab, away from us Feebs. Tabitha could sit up now, which made room for Gabbi and Ricker. She rubbed her swollen ankle a lot and mumbled under her breath.

Part of me worried she was plotting something. Another part of me thought she must be worrying over her son.

Hours later the truck sputtered to a halt. Hugh jumped out. He lifted the front hood and a huge, white column of steam billowed out. Sergeant Bennings left the truck bed and the two of them banged around under the hood, cursing, until finally the hissing stopped.

Sergeant Bennings unfolded the gas station map on the ground. Moisture beaded on his face. He'd lost his mask back at the compound. The other uninfected hovered around him. Leon, Bernice, and Nindal helped Tabitha off the truck. She took a few careful steps and nodded like she was proud of her body doing what she told it.

"We're close." Sergeant Bennings folded the map and stuffed it into a pocket. "We can walk the rest of the way."

"The Vs will catch up." Leon's voice was low and full of gravel, like it had been years instead of hours since he'd last spoken anything out loud.

"Not if we get moving," Sergeant Bennings responded.

A spark lit up in Leon's eyes like he wanted to start a fight. His beard was peppered black and white. His hands were too big even as he tried to stuff them in his jeans pocket. He was at least as old as Sergeant Bennings, probably older.

Sergeant Bennings told him to go for a walk.

Hugh got twitchy on his rifle. It was several long seconds before Leon listened.

My little miracle bite didn't change anything about what was around us—people on the verge of going V for no reason, a hidden research facility, Dr. Ferrad and the cure.

We left the truck. The hours and miles of being crammed together meant sore muscles—we moved like a bunch of Vs. At a four-way intersection in the middle of nowhere, just a bunch of dead fields in every direction, Sergeant Bennings led us to the right. We passed over a small levee road and down the other side. Off into the distance, something like black metal glinted for just a moment and then the smoke covered it. All of us Feebs had used shirts or whatever cloth we had to put over our mouths as a poor man's filter. All of us still coughed. Even the uninfected behind their plastic masks.

This gravel driveway appeared out of the smoke. Next came the black metal fencing and then—

Green.

A watered lawn—so bright a color while the world burned around us I thought it must be my imagination.

"Do you see this?" I said. "Ricker, do you see this, this...lawn?"

"I see it," he said, almost in awe.

The grass was almost a foot tall. In the middle of it a brown sign had 'California Primate Research Facility' carved into it.

Sergeant Bennings motioned for us to crouch under the shade of a bush. Broken glass and multicolored headlight plastic littered the asphalt from some long ago car accident.

"This is the place." Sergeant Bennings' gaze rested on Jane for a long moment, drawing everyone's attention to her pale face, the ghostly tint to her skin that hinted at what she had been, at least for a short time—infected.

"You recognize this place, don't you?" Sergeant said carefully. She shook her head.

He tilted his head. "Hear that?"

We all held our breath. A high moan echoed across the landscape, like machinery going bad but still managing to do its job. A hundred yards behind us, pulling out from the gravel driveway, a white van appeared. It drove back the way we'd come.

"Uninfected," Hugh said. "I saw them."

Sergeant Bennings motioned to Hugh and two of his people. "Go introduce yourselves. Don't tell them who I am."

"Why not?" Hugh demanded.

"A certain doctor might not think so fondly of me."

Hugh looked about to ask more.

Sergeant Bennings held up a hand. "Enough." He looked over us Feebs. "Tie them up."

"Hey!" Ricker said. "We've done nothing but follow your orders. Every instruction."

"You're still infected."

"Like your wife and probably your son," Ricker said.

Sergeant Bennings held himself so still it was as if he'd turned into a statue.

We waited for what seemed an eternity.

He blinked and motioned for the rope. "Tie them up and out of the way."

They took us seven Feebs further down the road, onto the cool, green grass and under a tree. We were now lower than the road by several feet. I sat next to Ricker and kept myself calm as they tied us up. I hoped Gabbi, I hoped all of us Feebs could keep it together for just a little longer. The cure must be so close now.

"Why did you say that," I whispered to Ricker. "You knew it wouldn't do any good. You knew it would make him want to hurt you."

Sergeant Bennings waited at the top of the road. Watching. The rest of the group came over to wait near the tree. From our position there was no way to see through the smoke or what was happening to Hugh and the other two uninfected.

Minutes passed.

There was only silence except for the groan of machinery.

There was time to wonder how far back the V mob was.

Shouts.

A scream. Shots.

More screams.

Silence.

CHAPTER 26

I WOKE UP IN A WHITE ROOM. White light blazed so brightly it hurt my eyes. White walls blended into the floor so that I couldn't tell where one began and the other ended.

I tried to roll over. I was in a hospital bed. My wrist hurt, my head hurt. The last thing I could remember was being outside. We had been surrounded. These uninfected had worn no safety gear and they'd shot us one by one, but the shots hadn't sounded right. We fell, but there was no blood. When it was my turn the bullet stung, but it wasn't really a bullet. The metal capsule had stuck out where it entered my thigh and the end was this pinkish sort of fluff ball. It made me miss my pink sweatshirt. The sweatshirt had been the very last gift my uncle had given me, but the cloth had fallen to pieces a year after the infection started. I'd fallen into a heap on the ground, thinking about that pink sweatshirt, and then I'd woken up here.

There was a bed next to me. Everything smelled like bleach.

I swore I could even taste it on my tongue. I pushed myself up. This room was full of beds. Gabbi's spiky shock of hair was dark against one pillow, Ricker's dirty blond hair peeked out of a set of sheets. Tabitha, Leon, Bernice, Nindal. We were all together.

A door clicked open.

Someone came in with a clipboard. I didn't know if I was seeing things right. Could it really be Dr. Ferrad? She wore large, orange-rimmed glasses. Her bright blue eyes were wide as she looked us over. Her skin was clear. Uninfected.

Gabbi hissed and jumped off the bed. Her face twisted in this terrible grimace. She ran for Dr. Ferrad with her hands shaped into claws.

The clipboard flew into the air and tumbled out of sight under one of the beds. Dr. Ferrad threw up her hands to cover her face. "Stop! I can cure you!"

Leon scrambled from his bed. The sheets he left behind were coated in dust and ash from his clothes. I thought he was going to join the fight against Dr. Ferrad. He threaded his arms through Gabbi's and pinned them behind her back. This only enraged her. She spit, kicked out, and bucked against him until I feared she might break an arm.

"Gabbi!" I shouted. Ricker and I ran to them.

I didn't know if I should help Leon or Gabbi. She was wild, uncontrollable, gone V. Just gone.

Another uninfected rushed in, slamming the door open. This white coat held a large needle and plunged it into Gabbi's arm. She bucked against Leon again. Her eyes rolled into the back of her head, and then all of her muscles relaxed as she fell unconscious.

"Put her away." Dr. Ferrad readjusted her glasses.

"No!" I shouted it the same time Ricker did.

Both of us stood over her unconscious form, back-to-back. I crossed my arms. My chest shook from trying to breath. This was all happening too fast.

"There's no time for this," Dr. Ferrad said. "The infected you brought with you have finally arrived."

"What are you talking about?" Bernice said. Sweat stood out on his forehead and his face was flushed even though he hadn't left the bed.

"The Vs have come," Nindal said. "That's what she means."

"Yes," Dr. Ferrad said.

"I don't see why we should help you." But there was something in Leon's voice that said he didn't really mean it. "What's in it for us?"

Her blue eyes raked him over with disdain. "I came here in good faith, with no weapons, no guard, to prove to you we are here to help. Anyone who helps us fight off the Vs will get the cure."

Ricker stiffened behind me.

Leon looked stunned.

She had said it as if it were no big deal, as if the cure was a cookie she could just give out when someone acted good.

"You need to move." Dr. Ferrad's gaze shifted back to me. I almost flinched but forced myself to stay still. "Gabbi must go to a different room now that the Lyssa virus has taken a stronger hold in her."

"She'll come out of it," Ricker said.

"She always comes out of it," I said, even though deep in the pit of my stomach I feared maybe she wouldn't, maybe not this time. But I couldn't believe that, not after all that she had done for me or all that we had been through together. We were so close to a cure. My brain was frantically lining up the final pieces of the puzzle, laying them out in a line in front of me, analyzing how to rotate them to lock perfectly into place.

"We do not have time—"

Another white coat rushed into the room. "Dr. Ferrad, they're massing at the East Gate!"

"Just give her the cure now," I said. "Then we'll help."

"Very well," Dr. Ferrad said.

"I must disagree," the newest white coat said.

"Dr. Stoven, do not waste time deliberating this decision."

"I must insist—"

"We're going with her," I said. Neither doctor had brought weapons or guards. We could rush them if we needed to. We could force them. "Stop wasting time."

Dr. Ferrad bent over and retrieved her clipboard. She brushed off imaginary dust from it with one hand. "Dr. Stoven, please escort them to the secondary treatment center." She did not look at Dr. Stoven but it seemed like a message had passed between them.

Dr. Stoven closed his mouth and looked hard at Gabbi's unconscious body. "Help me with her, and hurry it up."

Dr. Stoven and Ricker picked Gabbi up from the floor and left. I went to follow them and the room plunged into darkness. Sirens blared. Red lights came on and cast a terrible glow everywhere.

"Anyone who wants the cure, get yourself to the East Gate." Dr. Ferrad yelled this while running out.

Leon, Bernice, Nindal—everyone followed her.

The sirens cut off, leaving my ears ringing. The red lights

stayed on, playing tricks with my eyes. There was a creaking sound behind me. I whirled around, my heartbeat speeding up.

I thought I was the last one in the room, but there was Tabitha, bathed in a red glow. Fire sparked in her eyes, but in spite of that, she held herself so still, like a statue. I realized she wasn't going V like the rest of them. She was going Faint like me and she had just come out of its spell.

Tabitha sat up and placed her bare feet on the cold floor. "You can't possibly be stupid enough to think she's telling the truth."

THE COMPOUND WAS HUGE. Acres and acres of buildings, outdoor areas, one tall fence that surrounded the entire facility, open fields for miles in either direction. I catalogued all of this as I ran after Ricker, Gabbi, and the white coats. No one tried to stop me. Everyone else was headed in one direction. I assumed it must be the East Gate.

I passed by an outdoor enclosure and the chatter from it made me stumble. There were groups of chimps behind the fences. Their dark faces and human-like hands and bodies freaked me out even as my brain said this made sense. This was a primate research facility after all.

Ricker, Gabbi, and Dr. Stoven disappeared into the next building. I followed on their heels. A hallway veered right and dumped us into an empty cafeteria.

Ricker shouted. Something large barreled into me. I flew through the air for an eternity. The impact knocked the breath out of me. My injured wrist hit the floor and exploded in pain. My ankle throbbed. I swore the ceiling panels swayed as I fought to get back my breath. A large shadow loomed over me, hot stinking breath, wild eyes, saliva dripping in long yellow strands from his mouth. It was a V, inside the building with us, inside where one bite would drown us in an eternity of fevers.

Except V bites didn't trap me in the fevers.

I slammed the heel of my good hand into the underside of the V's chin. Ricker picked up a chair and threw it, sending the V tumbling into another group of chairs.

As the V began to rise a shot rang out. Dr. Stoven had fired the shot. He walked up to the V and fired a second shot. No blood. Only tranquilizers again.

Two more Vs burst in from outside. He took them down methodically. Gabbi was a crumpled pile on the ground, unaware of the chaos around her.

Ricker shook my shoulder. "Help me with Gabbi!"

She moaned as we dragged her away. Red lights obscured signs and made the hallways all look the same. We burst out a Fire Exit door into the bright afternoon sun. The disconnect from inside stunned my mind. I couldn't recognize what I was seeing. People in white coats and tattered clothing all running, some toward buildings, others away, still others toward each other, and then falling to the ground. Blood everywhere.

Gabbi moaned again and tried to hold her head up. We left the white coats to fight the Vs. It was the only thing we could do until Gabbi was safe. She was coming out of unconsciousness now, but would she be herself or like one of the Vs?

"Where are you going, Maibe?" Ricker said.

"I don't know," I said, breathless, but it was almost as if a magnet pulled me forward, away from the noise and the violence behind us, ahead to the screams and chatter of another set of chimp cages. We rushed into the next building, plunging into the red darkness. This hallway had a number of doors lining it. A steel door at the end was slightly open.

Inside it was dark, but at least not the ghastly red of the previous buildings. The air smelled of hay, urine, animal. A play structure's primary-colored plastic sat off to one side behind glass walls. The chimps, maybe half a dozen, all stood or hung from the play equipment, hooting and making noises while staring at us.

Gabbi jerked suddenly. I lost my grip and she fell to the ground, but she caught herself at the last minute with her hands. Her eyes were wide as she took in the hallway, the glass walls, the chimps, the playground. "What's happening?"

"The V mob is here," Ricker said.

"They're out trying to protect the cure," I said. "We have to help, but we have to get you safe first."

I hooked my arm under Gabbi's and pulled her up. I helped her limp toward the open steel door.

"What if there's a V?" Ricker said.

"Then we'll kill it," Gabbi said.

Ricker hurried to get ahead of us. He pulled up the door, then froze. He turned around—all the blood drained from his face.

"I…" He brushed a hand across his eyes. "Is this real?"

I pushed him aside because I knew whatever it was it couldn't be a V. He would have been attacked already. A blue food barrel stood just inside the door. Two people huddled next to it.

"Maibe?" Alden's voice.

My head began to spin.

One of the people stood up. It was Alden's voice, I knew it was his voice. I thought it must be Alden who stood up even though it was hard to tell in the shadows. He walked to me with outstretched hands, but something was wrong with his arms. There was something terrible about his face. It looked like a muzzle was strapped over his mouth and someone had duct taped oven mitts over his hands.

"Mary?" Gabbi said, stepping forward. "Ricker, are you seeing this? Is it really her?"

"I see her."

My eyes caught on Ricker's arm and the puckered skin that formed the name Mary in scrawling childish letters. I looked again. This wasn't Alden. The hair and eyes were too dark.

The person moaned under the muzzle.

"Don't touch her," a male voice said—Alden said.

"What have you done to her?" Gabbi took an unsteady step into the room. "I will end you for hurting her. I will—"

"Gabbi, she's V," Ricker said. "She's V and he probably helped save her life. Didn't you?"

I couldn't stop myself any longer. "Alden, is that you or is it a ghost? Someone please tell me." I trembled, waiting, trying to tell my brain to work, please work, please be right.

"It's Alden," Ricker said quietly.

I knelt on the ground and reached out a hand. "Alden." I touched his cheek, but then remembered. He hated it when Feebs touched him. He hated it when I had touched him before.

He did not flinch away.

I looked closer. Scabbed over scratches marred one cheek. Even in the dim light, he had the same fading marks as Jane.

"You've been infected and cured?"

He barked a laugh. "I guess you can call it that."

CHAPTER 27

"WHY IS MARY LIKE THIS?" Gabbi said, horror thick in her voice.

"It was the only way to be sure everyone could be kept safe," Alden said.

Mary had hugged Gabbi and then pushed her away. She now slumped against the wall and held her head between her legs. No amount of coaxing from Gabbi brought her up.

"Why isn't she able to—"

"She goes in and out of being V," Alden said.

"That's not supposed to be possible," I said. All the years we'd dealt with the virus and it had been black and white. V, Faint, Feeb. All of one or the other, or a mix of both.

Except I realized that hadn't stayed true.

"I don't know what they did to her," Alden said. "Or if they tried to cure her or not. She's the only V here who can partially come out of it."

Ricker kept staring at Mary as if he thought she might vanish into a ghost at any second. "I knew you had seen her, Gabbi. I didn't think you were lying. I knew, but I just never really believed. I never thought. But, Gabbi—"

"I know," Gabbi whispered, her eyes not leaving Mary either. "I know."

"We have to escape," Alden said. "I tried once but they caught me. We have to get out of here while we can."

Gabbi's attention shifted to Alden. "We can't just leave the cure behind." Her eyes narrowed. She still didn't trust him. She never really had. He would always be Sergeant Bennings' son.

"Your father is here," I said.

He didn't respond.

"Alden," I said. "Where's the cure?"

"There is no cure. There never was." He turned his head away from us and stared hard at the blue bucket.

"Don't lie to us." A flush crept up Gabbi's cheeks.

"We're not stupid," Ricker said. "We can see the Feeb marks fading on you. Why would you try to keep it from us?"

Alden's face paled. His hands shook as he used the barrel to stand up. "There is a cure, but it's not worth the cost. It's not worth it."

"You would say that," Ricker said. "You already got it so what does it matter if the rest of us don't, right?"

"Ricker!" I said.

Ricker turned to me. "You can't believe this. You can't just take him at his word. This is too important."

I waited for Gabbi to say something. She always did, but this time she didn't. She looked at me, waiting for me to decide. Could we trust Alden? Deep down, I knew we could. I knew he was telling the truth as he knew it, but what if he was wrong?

I thought about the Vs attacking the compound and how long it would take Dr. Stoven and Dr. Ferrad to notice we were missing. Ano and Jimmy and everyone back home were sick, dying. The cure was here. The cure was within our reach. It was worth the risk—

"Show it to us."

WE CREPT ALONG THE OUTSIDE OF THE BUILDING. The sounds of fighting came from the far end of the compound. It was only a matter of time before someone tracked us down. Dr. Ferrad had kept Mary captured for who knows how long and Alden was Sergeant Bennings' son—too valuable a tool in their war. Even now I felt eyes on us, though I couldn't tell whose eyes— uninfected, V, Feeb.

We needed to hurry.

"What is the cure?" Ricker whispered. "How does it work?"

Alden squinted at the gap between two buildings. He sized up the space, then glanced back at Ricker. His eyes burned with a sort of anger I swore I'd only seen in V eyes until now. "You won't believe me until you see it yourself. Just promise me we'll escape after."

"I'm not going to promise that," Ricker said, disgust in his voice.

Behind us something moved. I blinked, looked hard. Multiple somethings, like a crowd of people. There was no way to tell if they were uninfected, Feebs, or Vs. The only thing I did know was they were headed in our direction.

"We have to go. We have to go," I said, panic making my voice too loud.

Light flared in Alden's eyes. The scratches on his cheek flushed. He blinked, then dashed across the gap. Mary and the rest of us followed.

Mary's movements were jerky, like she moved and then her brain panicked and tried to take it back, afraid she was about to hurt someone. The cycle repeated itself as we passed by a troupe of chimps. There was a pile of hay, more blue food buckets, two metal wheelbarrows tilted onto their sides. They reminded me too much of the one Corrina had used to carry Dylan when he had been in the fevers.

The group of chimps followed us along their fencing and shook the metal when we didn't stop to notice them. Alden took us to this squat building set back at an angle from the grid-like row of sheds. As we approached the door, the chimps went silent.

The fighting noises softened behind us. Smoke filled the sky like thunderclouds. My ankle and wrist ached with each step. The chimps huddled together and watched as if they knew whatever lived in there wasn't right.

The door opened without a squeak. In here, the electricity was still on. No red glow, no flashing lights, no siren to disturb the medical atmosphere of the air. Stacks of paper covered an unmanned reception desk. Ricker pushed on the only obvious door, but it would not move. A key card next to it glowed red.

"Security is rather tight, don't you think?" Gabbi said.

"Never can be too careful." Ricker rummaged through the drawers of the desk. He came back with a letter opener, pried off the card slider, and examined the wiring before jamming the point six inches deep into the device and twisting.

A whirring noise died away, then the red light turned green. With a click and rush of air the door opened.

"How did you..." Alden said.

"I'm smarter than you've ever given me credit for," Ricker said.

"That's not true," Alden said.

I was about to explain it was because he and Gabbi had learned to pick all kinds of locks as runaways, but something held my tongue. The two of them looked at each other in such a way that I knew this was about much more than the lock.

Noises, almost a hint of a melody, drifted through the opened door. "Do you hear that music?"

I sighed with relief when they agreed. My symptoms had not betrayed me for awhile. I could only hope my luck would hold.

We entered a sort of laboratory mudroom, tiled with porcelain that glared in the golden light. White suits and full head gear hung on hooks. Hoses were attached to cylinders of oxygen.

The noises had turned into unmistakable, foreign songs, with a woman singing in a language that was almost familiar. Her melody was both haunting and romantic, the melodies of a string section, hand drums, even an accordion. It sounded like an old recording, like the music on tapes my uncle had made me listen to when he wanted to remember the old country. The music played on a loop through speakers set high in each corner. Over these last three years I had forgotten about music and how it could make you feel. This tore at my heart in a way I almost couldn't stand.

"Oh, god," Gabbi said somewhere off in the background, as if speaking through a wall. "This is the place. They showed up at the railroad station. They had this white tent and they dragged Mary into it. They just surrounded us and took us. They must have brought us here. I remember the chimps when we escaped. I thought it had been the fevers somehow, but I had never seen a real-life chimp before."

"I remember the chimps, too," Ricker said quietly. "Which means it wasn't the fevers."

"We didn't know what it all meant," Gabbi said. "Only that we needed to get away."

"Mary was here," Ricker said.

Gabbi looked at us with wide, haunted eyes. "Mary's been here and we left her. Why didn't we come back?" There was a keening note in her voice.

Mary reached out a hand and rested it on Gabbi's shoulder.

"Mary, Mary. I'm sorry. I'm so sorry." Gabbi hugged Mary and buried her face in her shoulder.

The look in Mary's eyes changed. I waited for everyone to see it, but it all was too powerful a spell—the music, the room, the glowing tiles.

"We thought she was dead." Ricker's eyes searched the walls as if they contained the answers to all the questions he should have asked a long time ago. "We got lost in the fields—in those fields that went nowhere for miles until suddenly we were back at the red boxcar and then things got really bad." He turned to Mary a yearning look on his face. "We thought you were dead."

Mary scrabbled at Gabbi's back with the duct-taped oven mitts. She banged her muzzle-covered jaw over and over again on top of Gabbi's head.

Gabbi cried out and backed away, holding her hands over her head.

Mary moved forward as if tied to her with a rope, swatting her arms around.

I rushed over and helped Ricker pull Mary off. We pushed her onto her back. I sat on her arm and part of her chest while he did the same to her other side. Her legs kicked wildly and slammed into the side of my head. My injured wrist flared with pain. It felt like my ankle wept blood again.

Gabbi sat across Mary's legs so that she was pinned down by all fours.

"Alden, please do something," I said. "Where's the cure? Where's a sedative? Find something."

The veins on his face seemed to pulse. He sprinted through another door. It opened into a type of shower that flipped on hot pink lights. He kept going through a second door before they both closed and took him from sight.

Minutes passed. Maybe seconds. It felt like an eternity. Too long.

"We need to get in there," I said.

"Go. I can hold her," Gabbi said.

"It takes three of us. What about her arm?"

"I've got it," Gabbi said. "Ricker, get her legs." Then she moved up, straddling Mary across the stomach, using her legs to pin Mary's arms to her sides.

I released my hold on Mary and stood back. I didn't know if I should stay or go. Except we had to help Mary. There had to be something. We couldn't just stay there until the uninfected found us.

I headed after Alden.

"Maibe," Ricker said.

I stopped and looked back.

"Be careful."

The pink lights were hot and made my skin sweat and my eyes swim. The music disappeared. I swore I could hear shouts from outside. We didn't have much time. Either the Vs would find their way in or the uninfected would win and check on the cure.

Alden stood in the middle of this narrow room. There were two rows of seats, like theatre seats, with cushions and arm rests. A sort of window started halfway up the wall that looked down, not to the outside, but to another room.

Alden peered through the glass. "I didn't know this window was here. I thought they could only see me through the camera."

I went to his side. Down below, a full floor below, was a hospital bed with straps. Empty. Everything was cement.

"Is that—"

"Come on."

He grabbed my hand and electricity sparked between us. He didn't seem to notice. He led me down a set of stairs and suddenly we were in the room we had just been watching. Metal rings were attached into the cement. A speaker was mounted in the corner near the ceiling. There was some sort of camera lens next to a vent.

"They hook you to a machine." Alden drew my attention to a door across from the hospital bed. "It's like a dialysis machine. Except, I don't know, different somehow."

Alden shook his head. Actually, it was more like he shivered. "Dr. Ferrad and Dr. Stoven worked on it for months. They said it's the only one like it in the world and that if the world hadn't fallen apart that they'd win an award for it." The way he talked about the doctors and this machine—his voice was full of disgust. "Uninfected blood replaces the infected blood, but it's more complicated than that. It changes the blood somehow."

I headed for the special door. "Then it's the machine we need. We'll take the machine and find something for Mary and—"

He reached out as if to stop me. "No, Maibe."

"You just said—"

He pushed by and his clothes brushed mine. He'd never let himself get close like that before. Now it was like it didn't matter anymore.

"Look." He threw open the door.

Red tubing was coiled like a snake next to this huge sort of boxy machine. Knobs and dials and tubes connected everything together in this complicated system that made my head dizzy.

Alden was right. This looked like it did much more than just clean blood.

My heart sank.

The machine was as tall as me and a little wider. There was no way we could move it, not even if all of us helped.

Something red dripped from one end of the tubing. The light was faint here and I bent over to touch it.

"Stop!" Alden pulled on my shirt.

I resisted.

Something moaned.

I shot up and felt a crack on my skull. Stars burst across my vision and pain lit up the back of my head. I turned and saw Alden rubbing his chin.

And then I saw the bed.

It was just on the other side of the machine. There was someone on the bed and she was uninfected and she was gasping for breath. Tubing snaked into her arm and buried into her flesh as if it had been forgotten there. What dripped from the tubing was her blood.

Alden seemed to float over to the uninfected woman's bedside. "I was in the fevers and I remembered when we sat together on that cliff."

Her breathing became shallow even as I watched.

"You know the one. You got the clue I left you? I was going to get the *memantine* first, for your people, and then I was going here. But they captured me and forced me here themselves— even though I told them I would come willingly."

The world shifted under my feet.

"I thought if things got bad," Alden said. "You'd come looking for me. Over and over again I remembered sitting there on the ledge and the terrible way I acted."

This woman was uninfected. She was dying because they had drained her of too much blood. "This doesn't make any sense." I went to her bedside. Maybe there was still time to save her. We had to try.

Her brown hair curled around her face. Her eyes were closed, her lips pale, her face like ash. She looked almost deflated.

"Where are the doctors? Why did they take so much? If this is how you get cured why would they take so much?" I wanted to rip out the tubing. It looked like this horrifying worm-like tumor growing out of her flesh. But if I took it out, what if she bled more? Why was no one here to take care of her? Had they abandoned her to die because everyone had gone to fight the Vs?

Alden stood there with his hands clasped behind his back. "When you need to be cured, they just hook you up." With the roar in my ears it was like he spoke from miles away. "This was an uninfected that came in with another group not too long ago. It's a life for a life. That's the cure. It doesn't take just a little bit of blood—it takes all of their blood."

The uninfected woman drew a long rattling breath and went silent.

I waited for her to start a new breath. I counted the seconds, long seconds. When I got to thirty—I knew.

She was dead.

I bent over and threw up a stringy film of saliva onto the floor next to the bed. I wiped my mouth and tried to think about what to do. I didn't realize how much I'd come to believe in the cure. I had never counted on it in the first place but then Jane had come along. Ano and Jimmy needed this.

I looked up at Alden in horror. Dr. Ferrad and the other white coats had murdered this poor woman.

Alden's face was open, expressionless. He knew what I was thinking. Someone else had died for him not to be a Feeb anymore.

I wanted to die. I might as well be dead. We might as well all be dead.

This was no cure.

Ano and Jimmy would be trapped for an eternity in that church-turned-hospital.

Gabbi and Ricker would go V and I would go Faint and none of us would ever come back.

A hissing sound came from the other room.

The uninfected woman was so still. The tubing still dripped blood in a pool on the floor. The machine was silent, sitting in judgment.

Alden left the machine room. He just turned his back and walked out. I looked around at all this death. I had always been the bringer of death. When I was born my mother had died. My father had turned from me like Alden had just turned from me. My aunt had taken me in and died of throat cancer. My uncle had sent for me from America and died when I couldn't protect him from the Vs. Those deaths had only been the beginning.

I walked out of the machine room like I was in a funeral march. The vent on the ceiling spewed out steam like a hose. A whitish cloud swirled, expanded, and began to drift down.

"Alden," I said. "What is that?"

"I...I don't know. I though it was for heat. I thought it was broken. We have to get out of here!" He ran for the door, slamming into it with all his weight. I don't remember us having closed it.

The door did not budge.

I didn't move from my spot in the middle of the room. I let the white cloud flow over my head and shoulders. Alden coughed so hard it shook his chest. He banged on the door and screamed in between coughs.

I drew in a deep breath and coughed until I thought it might tear my lungs out. I welcomed that thought. Maybe I could curl up here in a ball. I climbed onto the empty bed. The mattress pad was soft. The sheets were scratchy. If I died here then it could all be over. I wouldn't have to face Ricker and Gabbi and tell them we had all believed in a lie. I wouldn't have to watch the light vanish from their eyes when they realized the cure was murder. When they connected the dots and realized it meant Ano and Jimmy might as well be dead. When they realized we would soon follow in their footsteps.

I pressed my cheek against the sheets and coughed and coughed and watched Alden turn red and collapse in a heap.

ALDEN

It was happening again. The lights, the blood, the fevers.

He kept screaming even though he knew it wouldn't make any difference. He threw himself into the door and felt his shoulder give. They were gassing him and Maibe like animals. That's what the vent must have been used for all along—to put to sleep the chimps they would have hooked to the walls.

He was on his knees.

Maibe was on the bed and she was laying on the bed like it was time for a nap.

His mind began to fuzz and black dots appeared across his vision.

Maibe was still looking at him, at his pathetic body broken on the floor. She was thinking about all the ways he had failed. His lungs hurt so bad. He deserved so much worse. He couldn't bear her looking at him. He couldn't bear that other people had died in order to cure him. He hadn't asked for that. He hadn't known it was like that. He would have never—

A door opened. He heard it but he could not see it. His head was turned away from the door and his cheek was pressed against the cold cement. He thought he was still looking toward the bed Maibe was on, toward the bed they had twice strapped him down to, but he wasn't sure. He couldn't see anything now because the black spots had taken over.

CHAPTER 28

I AWOKE IN THE MIDDLE OF A COUGH. I moved as if on wheels. A deep groove of metal bit into my neck. Something warm pressed against me and it was so hard to breathe. My head pounded. The white cloud had tasted almost sweet, like cotton candy, and the taste was still on my tongue. I tried to sit up but was held in place. My skin scraped against the rough metal.

"Hold it." Ricker's voice, above me. The container I was in tilted as he turned a corner down another dark hallway. The red lights were back on. Something moaned and moved at my feet.

"Keep him quiet, Maibe," Ricker said. "They're not that far behind."

I realized I was in a wheelbarrow, one of those we'd seen beside the chimp cages. Alden was in the wheelbarrow with me, unconscious, moaning, his legs and arms thrown over the sides and his body pressed against mine.

I was not dead. I might as well be dead.

I told Ricker everything. I told him just to stop and give up.

He gritted his teeth and forced the wheelbarrow through a door. The crash almost tossed Alden and me out. The door burst open. An alarm went off and its screeches made me clap my hands over my ears. The brightness blinded me. The smoky smell swamped my lungs and I coughed again. When my eyes finally could see, I wished for the darkness again. We were still inside the perimeter of the facility. There were dead bodies and blood everywhere. More Vs streamed in and the uninfected cut them down with bursts of gunfire from positions on the tops of buildings and from high windows. Anyone on the ground was either dead or a V.

Except for us. We were on the ground and we weren't dead. Yet.

Gabbi appeared. She pushed a second wheelbarrow. Mary was in it, unconscious. Her legs hung over the rim like doll legs. Her mittened hands and masked face were out of something like the movie *Chucky*. Her skin was scratched, bruised, so childlike.

Tabitha followed close behind Gabbi. "Do you have it?" She grabbed at my shirt. "Where's the cure? Do you have it?"

Tabitha must have helped us escape. Dr. Ferrad and Dr. Stoven had tried to gas us and somehow Gabbi, Ricker, and Tabitha had gotten us out.

I couldn't bear to explain about the cure again, not right then, not when any hesitation might get us killed.

"I have it!" I shouted, lying.

Tabitha smiled. She let go of my shirt.

I collapsed back into the wheelbarrow. Ricker grunted from the shift in movement.

Gabbi plunged into a shallow ditch. The wheelbarrow jerked

and almost tossed Mary to the ground. Tabitha pulled it upright. Gabbi pushed on, heading for the downed section of fence, but this took us straight to the Vs and into the uninfected line of fire.

I gripped the sides of the wheelbarrow. "Not that way!"

Gabbi looked over her shoulder at me. The closest group of Vs looked too.

The Vs ran for us. I wanted to shout. I wanted to jump out and run. I wanted to just let them take me.

Gunfire erupted. One V was shot in the head. The blood arced into the air and the V fell to the ground. Tabitha yelled for Gabbi to go left—away from the Vs. Ricker swerved to follow. I snatched at Alden's shirt before he tumbled out.

We raced through the grounds, dodging bodies that lay so still, swerving around other bodies that twitched. The buildings crowded close together. Smoke from the fire made it feel like we ran in the dark.

Large booms sounded. They shook me from the inside out. We crouched as if waiting for something to drop on our heads. My cheek pressed against the metal. My nose filled with its metallic smell. Ricker looked wild-eyed, the whites of his eyes showing. The redness of his last sunburn deepened almost to a purple. His Feeb skin was like an ashy, wrinkled layer that looked like it could be peeled away. The booms continued—far away, but huge, like bombs exploding.

Between the booms, long silences made my ears ring. Gabbi picked up the wheelbarrow again and moved slowly through the smoke and around the buildings. The fighting noises faded.

"It must be Sergeant Bennings," Tabitha said. "The sounds are drawing the Vs away from here."

I knew it was true as soon as she said it. "It's what he did with our town," I said.

All of us were breathing hard. There was a rattle in Gabbi's chest. Dark circles ringed Ricker and Gabbi's eyes, but there was a manic light in them too, like maybe they were channeling the angry energy the virus sometimes gave to push themselves beyond normal limits.

The fence stopped us. The fence was taller than all of us put together. Alden was still unconscious. Mary was awake now. She sat cross-legged in the bowl of the wheelbarrow and watched us with big eyes behind that terrible mask.

On the other side of the fence was a thick row of dead-looking trees that extended in either direction. Through the trees, a hillside of dirt showed. It must lead up to the road. On the other side of the road would be the water from a river the road held back. The fence was chain-link with barbed wire on top. It was too much like the fence at the last camp. I held my breath and waited for the memory-rush to come because it always came.

"How do we get through?" There was such terror in Gabbi's eyes. Tears from the smoke tracked dark lines down her cheeks.

Tabitha loomed over me. "Give me the cure."

I suddenly went cold with fear. Alden was warm against my legs, unconscious, unable to explain. Tabitha looked ready to rip me apart in search for a cure that might as well not exist.

"There's nothing to get." I told them everything I had seen. My voice sounded emotionless even to my own ears. Tabitha cocked her head as if trying to make sense of an insane person's ramblings. I watched as the little bit of hope in Gabbi's eyes extinguished itself. Red covered her hands and dripped onto the dirt.

"Your hands." I said.

Gabbi hid her hands behind her back. "It's nothing."

"Blisters from the wheelbarrow," Tabitha said.

Gabbi turned a burning stare on her.

"Don't hide them," Tabitha said quietly. "Take care of it or they'll get infected."

I tore a strip of cloth from the bottom of my shirt and then tore it again. Another boom sounded. The fence rattled and the metal links shimmered like a snake slithering through the air. There were darker spots of dirt along the fence as if water had seeped through. Gabbi wrapped her hands as best she could.

"Instead of telling me what to do," Gabbi said to Tabitha, "how about sharing some ideas on how to get out of here?"

I waited for someone to react to my news. I waited for the questions, the accusations, the denial, but there was nothing. It was like I hadn't just destroyed all of our hopes of saving Ano or Jimmy or ourselves. It was like I hadn't said anything at all.

"We could search for a gap," Ricker said. "Maybe there's a break in the fence somewhere."

I forced myself to think about the problem in front of us. We had no way to cut the links and no way to climb over it. "We go under," I said because that always seemed to be the answer now. It had been the way into the fairgrounds long ago with Gabbi. It had been the way in and out of the camp when I had lost the Garcia family.

"The dirt's like stone," Tabitha said.

One of the oak trees had fallen and pulled its roots from the ground. One of those roots had grown all the way to the other side of the fence like it had been trying to escape from this place and got the directions wrong. The dirt it had pulled up created a shallow gap. The dirt was darker there too, like the tree had created a safe place for the water to collect.

I shook my head but that only made my headache return. "That root has started the job for us."

I picked up a stick and went to the fence. I struck the dirt. The stick broke into a dozen pieces.

Tabitha let out a breath. "That's exactly—"

"We just need something tougher." I searched the ground until I found a broken piece of cement about the size of my fist.

"What if we're attacked before you're finished?" Tabitha said.

Gabbi picked up another rock. "Help us and we'll make it." She struck the ground and dirt scattered in chunks.

I got on my knees and used the rough cement like a scraper. The dirt crumbled layer by layer. I pushed it out of my way. Dust coated my exposed skin, got into my eyes, my lungs. Gabbi hit away chunks of dirt on one side. I worked on the other. Ricker squeezed between us. Our strikes became the rhythm of a song. I didn't know the words to this song, only that it was a song we all knew, a song we had almost forgotten.

After the top layer had been removed it became easier. The dirt softened and turned to mud. Water seeped up in little pools but it didn't matter, we were clearing the space we needed and making good time.

The exercise sang through my blood. My thoughts seemed to focus, allowing me to ignore my injured wrist and ankle. The smoke was thick around us, suffocating us. The booms that drew the Vs away from the chimps and the buildings and the cure sounded at regular intervals. I had given up and had been living as a stone for a very long time. Long before I'd begun turning Faint. But none of that mattered. None of it touched me as deeply as this—the three of us here, working together in the dirt, scraping and tearing and punching at what stood in our way.

We would keep each other safe at least for the little bit of time we had left. We would find a way.

Alden groaned from his wheelbarrow. Tabitha was nowhere to be found. Every few seconds Gabbi looked over her shoulder to check on Mary. It seemed like tears flowed down Gabbi's cheeks in an endless stream. I thought it wasn't because of the smoke anymore.

Mary was awake and hadn't moved, as if she were afraid of what she might do. The oven mitts hung over the wheelbarrow edge and we could only see the upper half of her face. She was trying to watch us while keeping herself hidden.

Ricker bent into his work as if determined to break the dirt or his hands and whichever broke first didn't much matter to him.

I stood up. "Try going through."

The peace I'd felt before vanished. My hands trembled, not from the work, but from fear. It was happening all over again—the fence, the gap, the escape.

The sound of engines appeared. I ignored them. They were a memory-rush. A side effect. The engines could not be real. They could not so perfectly match what had happened on that hot summer day with the Garcia family and the girl with the crown of braids.

Ricker's eyes locked onto mine. He cocked his head as if he heard something that shouldn't be there.

"No," I whispered.

"Gabbi," Ricker said. "Do you hear that?"

The noise grew until it drowned out the smoke, the heat, the dirt.

I turned around.

At first my eyes saw a truck barreling at us along the edge of the fence line and crossing the open, yellowed field at high speed. People hung off the sides and they had guns. My breathing stopped. I blinked.

The truck vanished.

In its place was a group of people on foot, running at us, weaving in and out of the trees. They could have been uninfected, Vs, or Feebs like us. They were too far away to tell.

"There." Gabbi pointed to where I saw the people, to where the truck had been before my memory had tricked me—unless this now was a trick.

"What do you see?" I said.

"A group of people running," Ricker said.

"Is there a truck?" I couldn't keep out the pleading note in my voice. I swore it took them an eternity to answer.

Finally Gabbi said, "I don't see a truck. But I hear them. Do you hear them? It has to be Vs. They're growling like Vs."

I listened again. The groans overlapped and rose and then fell in volume. If you didn't listen too close, a person might think it was the noise an engine makes.

Tabitha burst through the trees at a fast limp. "Vs are coming." Sweat dripped off her face. Her clothes were torn, like the trees had snagged them. Her eyes were wide and she locked onto the hole we'd carved out from underneath the fence. "I was looking for an opening. They saw me. We have to hurry."

Gabbi and Ricker were already at the wheelbarrows. Mary fought them at first, but then Gabbi crooned something in her ear. This settled her enough to get her to the fence. I crawled through the other side to help pull everyone through. Cold mud seeped into my clothing and it was a welcome relief from the heat and smoke even as it weighed down my clothes and sucked at my skin. Next came Alden's unconscious form. His blond hair was crusted with dirt. His cheek twitched as I hooked my arms under his shoulders. Our faces were inches away when he opened his blue eyes.

A confused expression came over his face. "Maibe?"

He kicked out, hitting Ricker in the jaw with his foot. Ricker moaned and fell back in the dirt. He put his hands to his mouth. When he took them away his teeth were bloody.

"Alden, Alden. It's okay. It's me. We're making you safe—"

The Vs burst through the trees. Gabbi let go and stood up—on the other side of the fence from me. Ricker pushed himself up next to Gabbi.

I shouted but they didn't hear me. Alden was still in the gap. He was blocking the way to my friends.

CHAPTER 29

I USED STRENGTH I DIDN'T KNOW I HAD to pull Alden the rest of the way.

I shouted again and scrambled back under the fence, flinging mud everywhere.

I would not let my friends stand against the Vs without me.

I would throw myself in the way to keep Ricker and Gabbi from getting trapped forever in the fevers.

We would die together.

The three of us stood side by side, holding our digging stones. The first V's hair was long and stringy. His beard made him look more animal than human. He hunched his shoulders so far over it was like he walked on all fours. His eyes were empty, like he wasn't really seeing us, but something else he had once hunted. He sniffed the air.

I shuddered and forced myself to step forward.

"Maibe!" Gabbi hissed.

"I can get bit," I said. "I won't go into the fevers."

"They can still kill you," Gabbi said.

"I know," I said.

The V closed in.

I almost closed my eyes because I didn't want to see it happen. Ricker and Gabbi shouted. The V's eyes widened and locked onto me. I held up my bandaged arm like an offering. If there was any chance of surviving this, I'd force him to damage that one again. He leaned in and sniffed.

Something hit me in my stomach and snatched the rock out of my hand. I was pushed onto the ground, gasping for air. My wrist flared in pain.

I flew back onto my feet, a cry in my heart. Why did they do it? They'd get bit and trapped and—

Tabitha stood there, feet splayed in the dirt, knees bent as if ready to take a tackle. She swung my rock at the V and bashed him on the side of the head. He sunk his fingers and mouth into her shoulder. She screamed. He tore her skin. Blood sprayed into the air.

She shouted for us to get on the other side of the fence. She grunted in pain. She hit at the V with the rock. The other Vs came through the trees.

Ricker grabbed me around the waist and dragged me through the fence. Gabbi slid through and we were all on the other side now except for Tabitha.

Tabitha fought off the first V and dove for the gap in the fence. The links grabbed at her shirt. Her shoulder was useless. She scrabbled halfway through and got stuck. The mud suctioned her to the ground. One V caught her leg and pulled her back. We each grabbed onto her and pulled. My feet slipped in the wetness and I struggled to get my footing back. My injured ankle made my leg give out. The fence shook, but stayed caught on her clothes and dug into her back. Two more Vs were closing in.

Suddenly the V slipped in the mud and fell on his back. He lost his grip and we fell backwards. Tabitha shot under the fence and through the mud like a bullet. Her shoulder was bleeding, her hair was in tangles, there was no time to check her wounds.

The Vs dove into the gap, wiggling through the space.

As they came under, one by one, because that's all the gap would allow—we did what we had to do. It was bloody. It was messy. It stunk, but we couldn't stop until it was done.

The silence after the fighting ended made my ears ring.

Ricker, Gabbi, Alden, even Mary—we were all covered in a sludge made of gore and mud. My chest heaved while trying to take in enough oxygen.

I looked for Tabitha. She had gotten bit by a V. She would be laying down somewhere. She would have fallen into the fevers like her son. Like Ano.

I searched for her, but all I saw were the Vs we had to put down. Then I saw a figure sitting in the dirt, halfway up the slope that would take us to the road. Tabitha. Awake, holding her shoulder, calm—no fevers.

"Come on," Gabbi said. "We have to hurry before more show up."

When we got to the road, we were almost level with the tops of the trees. On one side of the road was the river. On the other side of the river the fields were black and smoking but no longer in flames. The fire had burned to the water but could not jump it. Flames still burned further down along the water's edge. It was moving away from us now, though the smoke would blacken the sky for a long time.

I looked back the way we had come. I saw how the river water must be finding little openings underneath the road to seep through to the other side. Various spots of darker brown mud dotted the edge where the road's mound met the flat ground and led to the fence and the trees and the pile of dead bodies we had just left behind.

Gabbi began to walk the road. Ricker and Alden followed. Mary followed them.

"Where are you going?" I said.

Gabbi didn't turn around. "Home."

CHAPTER 30

"THE CURE IS BACK THERE," Tabitha said. "You can't just leave it with them."

"There is no cure," Alden said, speaking his first words since waking up. His voice sounded hoarse. Dark purple circled his eyes. His blond hair kept falling into his face. Tabitha stared at him like he was a snake that had just slithered onto the path.

"We can't go home," I said.

Alden and Gabbi turned to look at me. Now I felt like the snake. I stepped to the edge of the road. It went for miles in either direction. Below us was the water on one side and the facility on the other. The trees blocked a clear sight line, but the tops of the buildings were still visible. In there was the machine that made the cure possible. In there, Dr. Ferrad took a life for a life.

Gabbi turned away from me. She kicked at a rock that flew off the road and disappeared into the water. "Maybe we just leave and don't come back."

"Gabbi's right," Ricker said. "We run away. That's what we do. That's why we're still alive when everyone else is dead."

"Don't you understand?" I said. "There's no running away from this. We'll be no better than them if—"

"We aren't killing people for no reason," Ricker said, anger flaring in his voice. He stood apart from us. We all stood apart from each other like we couldn't bear being closer. "Don't compare us to them. You know it's nothing close. We have to watch out for ourselves. No one else is going to do it."

"The right thing to do—"

"The right thing to do is survive," Gabbi said.

My thoughts swirled. They didn't understand. I thought at least—

"Alden? You get it, don't you?"

Alden stilled. He was bent over, his hands on his jeans. The fabric had torn at the knees and his skin was bloody underneath. Mud covered his clothes and face and hair, some of it drying into a lighter brown. We were all covered in drying mud. Gray ash covered his blond hair. The Feeb marks on his skin—the veins, the wrinkles, the dry texture—were almost all gone.

"What are you saying?" Tabitha said. "You would destroy any chance—all the research, all the testing? What hope would Kern have? What hope would any of us have?"

"And who would you choose to die so that you could be cured?" I said.

Alden flinched as if my words were meant for him. I wanted to tell him it wasn't the same. He had been forced. He hadn't known what was happening.

"Dr. Ferrad is trying to refine it, I'm sure." Tabitha's face was pale. "It requires a life now, but later—"

"We need to wrap your shoulder," Ricker said quietly.

"Let her bleed!" Gabbi whirled around. Her eyes flashed and her body was rigid.

Tabitha flinched.

"This is your fault," Gabbi said, taking out all her mixed up emotions on Tabitha. "Since the beginning, you've lied, you've planned, you've ruined—"

"They're the ones lying to you." She held her shoulder at an angle like she was in a great deal of pain. Blood soaked through her shirt creating this huge wet patch of red. "We worked in the same building at the beginning. Soldier, doctor, manager. They never thought that highly of me—Dr. Ferrad and Sergeant Bennings. I represented paperwork, regulations, procedures. When my son and I got infected because of THEIR scientific negligence, that's when we finally became interesting to them. They considered exterminating us to cover everything up." Tabitha slumped to the ground. "Except your friend there got infected. Then she infected the rest of your group and they couldn't contain it. So they went to Plan B—the camps."

As Tabitha talked she swayed almost in time to Mary's rocking. Her words became breathy, like she couldn't get her vocal cords to work right. I thought maybe she was about to fall into the fevers after all. She had lost a lot of blood. Even from here I could see the V bite had created a jagged wound that had torn her skin to shreds. It wasn't the fevers we had to worry about with her but the blood loss.

"We need to clean this," Ricker said.

The water was right there, but we had no containers.

I looked at Gabbi so she would know it didn't matter what

she said back to me. "Gabbi, help us move her to the water."

Ricker and I lifted Tabitha to her feet. She swayed in my direction and suddenly her weight was all on me. I stumbled and fell to one knee. My ankle and wrist burned. My muscles ached. I didn't have the strength to get us back up even as Ricker tried to pull her off. I wondered if maybe they were right. Maybe they were all right. We should run as far from this place as we could. We should go to whatever home remained with the time we had left.

Gabbi stepped in and hooked Tabitha's shoulder over her neck. With the weight lifted I was able to stand and help them limp Tabitha down to the water.

"Why did you let yourself get attacked." Gabbi said this like it was an accusation, like Tabitha must have some terrible motive.

I had learned a long time ago that Gabbi did and said things she later regretted. We couldn't unlearn what the fevers revealed about one another, we could only protect it from each other as best we could. I knew Gabbi was trying.

"If I die." Tabitha took a step that twisted her shoulder. Her breath hitched. "If I die, promise me that you will help Kern."

Gabbi didn't respond for the longest time. I thought maybe she wasn't going to. Finally Gabbi nodded. "You know I will."

We stepped down the hill, slipping a few times. This forced out a cry of pain each time from Tabitha. Alden stayed on the road with Mary. There was so much infected blood on Tabitha after all and he was now uninfected.

Ghosts appeared in place of Ricker, Gabbi, Tabitha. I knew they were ghosts this time because they appeared with this faint silver edge, like my eyes couldn't quite bring them into focus.

It was Jane and Corrina and Mark.

Corrina had demanded I hand her a water bottle to help clean Mark's wounds. I'd been uninfected then. We had just lost Dylan, though we didn't know it was to Sergeant Bennings at the time. Mark was already a Feeb and the V bite he had suffered in the fight was throwing him back into the memory-fevers. Though we didn't know any of that either.

I stood at the river's edge and watched the water slowly move by even as Corrina bent to wash Mark's wound. I knew it was the ghost-memories overlapping with the present. Mark had looked so sick, so not right. Corrina and Jane had worked on him like that didn't matter.

I'd been so afraid. That fear struck me again now, making my heart pound so that it drowned out the sounds of water and Tabitha's yelps of pain. I'd been grieving for my uncle. I watched him die under an onslaught of Vs, in the room where we would close the blinds and make popcorn that filled the air with delicious smells of butter and salt, in the room where we watched marathons of apocalypse and zombie movies.

He would hook an arm around my shoulder during the scariest parts and say things like, "I guess our lives aren't so bad. We've still got all our teeth," or, "I give you permission to cut class if you ever see a bucket full of blood," or, shaking his head at a particularly stupid move a character made, "You are so much smarter than them, Maibe. Life is tough, but you're tougher." He'd pop another movie in and we'd start again and whatever was bothering me would fade away for a little while because whatever it was, it wasn't THAT bad, not compared to zombies.

He had died saving me and I hadn't stopped it. I had frozen behind the couch. We'd been watching *Shaun of the Dead* and laughing and laughing and the Vs had burst through. We knew it was coming. We had planned and prepared and been listening to the police scanner. We were leaving the next morning, but it hadn't been soon enough.

He died because I had frozen. He died because I was too scared to do what needed to be done. He had died and I missed him and all I wanted was to eat some popcorn with him again and just sit with him. I wanted to sit next to him on the couch and hear the faint buzz of the DVD player spinning up. My uncle would be alive and I would be taken care of and I would be loved.

This terrible pain gnawed at my heart and made me want to sit cross-legged at the edge of the water and add my tears to the river. I wanted that feeling suddenly, the stone feeling. I wanted to feel like a Faint, just for a moment, if it meant the hurt over my uncle would stop for a little while. I wanted to become like the water that passed by, unconcerned with the fire and death and destruction around it. The water moved over the stones and soil like it always had. The water found ways around and through things like fences and gates. The water would make everything go away.

A tree branch floated by. A section of leaves not touching the water smoldered with orange light.

I did not turn into a stone.

It had always come when I didn't want it, and now that I begged my brain to bring it, there was nothing.

Except.

My uncle always believed I was the hero of my own story. He believed in me even when I hadn't.

I knew, I just knew, what my uncle would want me to do.

Tabitha's shoulder was cleaned as best as we could. Our clothes were soaked now, but it didn't matter. The air was so hot, it would all dry soon enough.

I stood up on the edge of the river. The mud squished under my shoes. The road held back the water. There was another road on the other side of the river, toward the fire, that held the water back from flooding the fields on that side.

"We can't run away anymore. We have to do the right thing, even if it brings the sky crashing down on us. Even if it destroys our only chance forever. Even if it means I do this alone."

I waved my bandaged hand back up the levee road, to the fence and trees.

"I have to destroy that machine."

CHAPTER 31

I FEARED THEY WOULD LEAVE.

I could see the way Ricker and Gabbi looked at each other—this knowing expression that passed between them sometimes. I suspected it was their way of signaling when it was time to run before the cops caught them or worse.

Alden looked out over the water like he wanted to pretend he hadn't heard what I said. Tabitha's eyebrows narrowed but then she masked it with a more neutral expression.

We sat in a circle in the middle of the road.

"What's your plan?" Ricker said finally. His clothes were still soaked from the river water. Hair hung in his face and his eyes looked sunken into his skull. He had always been so thin. I couldn't remember the last time we had eaten something.

"I don't have one yet," I said, but that wasn't completely true.

"What do you expect us to do?" Tabitha said. "This is crazy."

"Maybe Tabitha's right," Alden said.

"Shut up," Gabbi said, always the one who believed in me, even if she could never admit it out loud. "Let her think."

I looked out over that blue water again. We had no guns. We had no vehicles. We were a bunch of kids. We could try to sneak back in, but my mind rejected that idea. We'd barely escaped once. The place was patrolled, the buildings were dark caves of cages and locked doors, people were on high alert after the fighting.

Everything was still now, even the birds. The fire had driven all life away from it and left behind a stillness that only the sound of moving water broke. There was so much power in the water. The levee we stood on was already weak—the seeping mud on the other side was proof of that. The buildings, the cure, the fence, it all sat in a sort of bowl beneath us.

"Ricker," I said.

He bowed his head waiting for my question. Maybe it was the way I said his name, my voice full of an emotion I was too afraid to name. Maybe it was the way I turned and looked at him until he looked back at me. Maybe it was the way we held each other's gaze for an eternity. He couldn't know what my question would be, but all the same, somehow he knew whatever it was would demand a lot from him. Maybe too much.

I couldn't look at him when I finally asked. I stared again at the water, seeing him out of the corner of my eye. "Could an explosion destroy this road enough to free the water?"

Ricker's skin was always pale. I swore it went even paler under the dried mud that coated him.

Gabbi froze, her hands in mid-air, about to scratch her head.

We didn't talk about what anyone confessed during the memory-fevers. No matter what.

I had just broken that pact again.

Ricker's cousin had been a lot older and into bad stuff. His cousin would get these jobs and Ricker would help. The last time, the people who'd hired them had them blow up a factory. Ricker had been fooling around with the leftover explosives. He was just a kid. He had accidentally killed his cousin.

His family couldn't get over what he'd done—what he'd been doing. Neither could he. He ran away to the street and pretended none of it had ever happened.

But the Feeb infection never let you forget.

"Not much," he said slowly. "It's already breeching. That's why water is seeping through."

Alden sucked in a breath.

Ricker walked over to the edge like he was examining the road, except he stared unseeing at the water instead. "We wouldn't need to destroy the whole road. Just get enough to punch a hole and weaken it. The water would do the rest."

"This is ridiculous," Alden said. "Do you even know how to use explosives?"

"He knows," Gabbi said.

Ricker flinched.

"You could kill us all," Alden said. "Even if it works, the water isn't going to stop them. They'll have time to escape."

"We're not murderers," I said.

Alden flinched.

"I'm not calling—" I couldn't finish. "We need to destroy the machine."

"Dr. Ferrad will get out and this will start all over again," Alden said. "Where are you even going to get what you need?"

I felt the boom in my bones and my chest. The low rumble,

the regular pattern of the explosions, the way it had filled the sky with sound to draw away the Vs. It was a memory-flash, different than a ghost-memory, different than the memory-fevers. So many symptoms, so many ways those symptoms tore apart your sanity. But this time, this time the symptoms brought a solution.

I looked at Ricker. He knew what I was feeling and what I was remembering. That's why it hurt so much.

"We steal what we need from Sergeant Bennings."

THE INKY DARKNESS SENT SHIVERS through me. If animals lurked somewhere nearby they could see us but we could not see them.

Ricker walked in front. Alden was behind me. The three of us were out to find Sergeant Bennings and steal the explosives.

Gabbi had stayed behind with Mary and Tabitha.

Tabitha had argued. Her voice had remained steady, almost too calm, as she tried to convince us to sneak in and destroy the machine that way. Night fell, the buildings blazed up. Even from our road, far away from the center of the facility, it was easy to see the patrols. Tabitha stopped arguing.

If we couldn't get the explosives, then we would try to get back inside. That's what I told her, that's what I told all of them. But secretly I swore I would never give Dr. Ferrad another chance to lock me up in the room with the white cloud falling like mist and the dead woman dripping blood on the ground.

Alden breathed heavily behind me. As if even this walk through the field was tough for him. Maybe it was, after the weeks he'd spent locked up.

"How long were you in there?" I whispered.

It was hard to break the silence of the night. It pushed on us from all sides. Not even the insects made noises. We had followed the sound of the explosions into a small town. Its main street was lined with old houses that had front porches and over-grown front lawns. Something smelled like sewer. The smoke from the fire had thickened over the hours. Alden thought it meant the fire was headed this way and we should go back. Ricker said it was probably because each explosion was setting its own separate fire. I agreed with Ricker but didn't want to start an argument between them. It didn't matter which fire it was, only that we needed to be careful.

"Too long," Alden said.

I'd forgotten I had asked a question. It was so strange to have him walk close to me and be without his normal goggles, gloves, and face mask.

There was tension between Alden and Ricker. As if they each pulled a different end of the same rope. I knew some of it had to do with me, my feelings for both of them, how they felt about me, but it was more than that.

Alden represented the uninfected and the choices they made and the way we had needed to live—running from them, dying from them, fighting them.

Someone else had died so that he could be cured. It wasn't his fault, and yet here was Ricker, his very presence an accusation against Alden's clear, uninfected skin.

A metal crashing noise startled us. It sounded like a trash can had fallen over. It was a shock in the stillness of the night. We huddled behind a large oak tree. One heavy branch had broken from the tree and formed an arch that touched the ground. Splinters of the branch were still attached to the main tree but the leaves were dead. There was no one to clean it up. There hadn't been anyone to clean it up in a long time.

The houses felt like tombs. I thought maybe this town would be better off if a fire did blaze through and destroy it. The streets were empty and covered in three years' worth of dirt and leaves. There was no wind. Several parallel lines in the road had depressed the leaves underneath.

My fingers brushed the rough bark of the tree and found Ricker's hands. He radiated warmth and all I wanted to do was press myself into him.

"They've been through here," I whispered.

"I see it," Ricker said.

I shifted position and found the cloth of Alden's shirt. I tugged it to get his attention. "Tire tracks," I whispered in his ear.

At the edge of the horizon, down the long street, there was an orange glow that faded into an ugly brown—the fire, or maybe multiple fires. A shape the size of a football moved across the street from us. Another shape about the same size met the first one in the middle. They chattered at each other. We had no flashlights, we had only the far off firelight to see by. More shapes came to meet each other. What were they doing out here?

"Raccoons," Ricker said.

Naming them did not help. They were acting so strangely. They were acting like humans didn't matter anymore in the daily activities of their lives. Ricker picked a careful path around the animals. Alden and I followed as he led the way down the tire tracks.

The dark of a summer night is different than the dark of

winter, or even spring. The relief from the heat feels like the sun is only holding its breath for a few minutes. The coolness is a luxury, something to welcome. This summer night, covered in a thick layer of smoke, felt like a night where anything could happen, where wild animals took over the streets because there was no one left to make them afraid. We were the intruders now.

The orange glow increased ahead of us. Even though I knew it was because of a fire, I picked up my pace to meet it. Any sort of light would be a relief. Even light that destroyed.

The glow turned into flames. Two houses had been on fire for awhile. Flames flared when they found fresh wood, but otherwise they were two piles of glowing orange coals. Driveways and patios around the houses had formed their own sort of fire break. The little bits of front lawn were piles of overturned soil now. Tire tracks formed large circles and tore off down a different road.

Dark lumps dotted the front yard, smoke trailing off them. They were charred and smelled like barbecue.

Dead Vs.

Ricker kneeled and pulled out a light-colored cloth from beneath a pile of lumber charred to black. The cloth was ragged and torn at the ends, but there were bold, capitalized letters on it. A-N-F. There was a fourth letter, torn off, unreadable.

Ricker dropped the bag and it fluttered to the ground. "I've used this type of explosive before." The shadows the coals threw carved out his eyes and mouth. He walked away from the destroyed house.

We followed the tire tracks. Footprints appeared and crossed over them. They came from every direction, dragging, limping, twisting through the trail. They obliterated the tire tracks but that didn't matter anymore. The trail was clear.

We passed the remains of more explosions, more fires, more bodies. Sometimes the fires cut us off and we hiked into the fields. We linked together, grabbing each other's shoulders or shirts. Without the light of the fires we would lose each other in the dark. When we went away from the light, each step was painful. We didn't know what we were stepping on.

Twice, Ricker cut his hands on something sharp. Three times I tripped and got the breath knocked out of me. Once, Alden yelled out when he stepped in something wet and squishy that threw up a stench so terrible all three of us gagged.

We caught up to the V mob hours later. The sewer stench increased and mixed with the smoke. I lifted my shirt over my nose and mouth but that only helped a little bit. Now I smelled my stink instead of theirs.

The groans, shrieks, and moans alerted us before we got too close. The V mob was here, all in one place.

Trucks and several motorcycles with bright lights bulldozed burning piles of fire toward the V mob. Their bodies churned as they snarled and thrashed against each other. There could have been hundreds and they were all being forced in the same direction.

Sergeant Bennings stood on the hood of one truck, holding onto a rope tied taught through the open windows. He directed the moving piles of fire, shooting bullets at any V that tried to break the ranks. The Vs furthest away from the fire disappeared, like they had fallen off a cliff. I felt sick to my stomach. Everything was flame and shrieks and the stink of blood and decay. Everything was death here.

Alden's face went blank. He'd demanded to come, but worry

hit me. Sergeant Bennings was his father. What if Alden did something to give us away?

Ricker tugged on my arm. He was looking at one of the trucks. It wasn't part of the massacre but held position well back from the other vehicles.

Two people with rifles guarded a pile of bags and a half dozen buckets on the truck bed. The truck latch was open and their feet dangled off the end as they watched the massacre.

"ANFO," Ricker said quietly. "That's what we need. That truck is what we need."

"We can't get it. No way." Panic filled Alden's expression under the firelight. "He'll see us. He'll find us and take us."

"We need that truck." Ricker crept away, everything disappearing for him except for this task I'd set him on.

I looked back and forth. Alden seemed frozen in place. I didn't know what Ricker's plan was, only that I had set all of this in motion. I had used what he confessed during his memory-fevers to bring him here.

There was no decision to make. There had never been a real decision.

I followed Ricker.

The V mob held their attention. The guards wore masks, long sleeves, and gloves, like the uninfected always did to separate themselves from the rest of us.

I felt Alden's presence low on the ground behind me. I hoped the uninfected weren't expecting three kids to jump them from behind. Before I could think, Ricker rushed the truck. His long legs ate up the distance. He didn't make a sound. He jumped on top of the bags and flipped one of the guys off the back.

I jumped in after him and lost sight of Alden. The bags were labeled in these large block letters—ANFO. A bucket tipped over and spilled out liquid. Everything smelled like gas. The second guy turned and all I could see were his eyes behind his mask. They were dark beads filled with hate. I recognized the eyes—Hugh. He didn't even raise his gun. He jumped out, jerked open the driver's door, and blared the horn. The noise cut through the moans and shrieks and shouts. Heads turned—V and uninfected.

Sergeant Bennings fired shots in the air. He pointed in our direction. He shouted Alden's name.

Ricker dove into the cab, forcing Hugh into the passenger seat. The back window was open and without thinking I pulled myself halfway through. The hard edge bit into my waist. I scraped the skin of my arms along it. Hugh's legs blocked me from going further—they were tangled up in the steering wheel. The truck cab smelled like spoiled milk. Ricker jammed the key in and the engine coughed.

I grabbed for Hugh. The truck lurched backward and threw me into the dashboard. My neck and shoulder crunched against the plastic. My legs flailed. I braced myself with my hands and cried out when pain flared in my wrist. Hugh's stink over-whelmed the spoiled milk smell. The truck vibrated my body. I became dizzy and in the darkness lost my sense of which way was up. I had used both hands to break my fall. My wrist burned and felt wet, like the wound had opened.

"Maibe!" Ricker shouted. His mouth felt inches from my ear. I scrambled up, pushing Hugh away from me. I expected him to fight, but he was like a dead lump as I untangled my fingers from his clothing.

I ignored the pain in my wrist even as it traveled up my arm and into my neck. Large rips, like from a knife slash, opened the truck bench to reveal the cushion underneath. When I finally got upright, I realized why Hugh hadn't fought back—Ricker had knocked him unconscious.

The truck moved at a ferocious speed in the dark. Its headlights bounced and matched the bounce of Hugh's head as his skull knocked in rhythm on the window. Ricker kept glancing at the rearview mirror. He looked wild-eyed and white-knuckled at the wheel.

"Where's Alden?" I shouted. I hadn't seen him jump into the truck.

"I'm here, Maibe." Alden's voice was almost lost in the wind.

I looked behind me. The window I had crawled through now framed his face. His eyes were wide and unblinking. There was a grim set to his mouth. He held onto the window's edge with both hands and splayed his body across one of the ANFO bags and a bucket, as if doing his best to pin them down.

Behind him the pile of bags seemed smaller than before. I looked closer. It was hard to see—

There.

A bag slipped away into the darkness.

The truck bed was open.

"We're losing the bags!" I shouted.

"I know!" Ricker yelled back. He made a hard right that threw me into his ribs. He winced as my elbow hit his side. He straightened out the truck and pressed on the pedal until we were going so fast I feared we'd crash.

He looked out the rearview mirror. "They're following us."

Lights, like the shining eyes of an animal, tracked our path. But these lights were too large and bright to be animals. At least six pairs, which meant more vehicles than that if any were motorcycles.

Ricker turned so fast I slammed into Hugh. He grunted, but didn't wake up.

"Lost another bag," Alden said, like he was commenting on the weather.

Ricker cursed. He peered so hard at the road in front of him that his eyes almost bugged out of his face.

I'd never learned how to drive. The world had ended before I could and afterwards there didn't seem much point to it since the noise attracted Vs. But even I knew this was too fast. Even I knew driving like this was going to lose all the explosives and get us killed. We would die for nothing and never see Ano, Jimmy, Dylan, or Corrina again.

"Slow down, Ricker. You have to slow down."

"They'll catch us. They're so close. They're so close and I can't go back. I won't go back. They'll send me to jail and my mother—"

"Ricker!" I shook him by the shoulders. He looked at me but didn't really see me. He held the steering wheel so hard I thought it might break in his hands. He was lost in a memory-rush while driving a truck in the dark.

Fear spiked strength I didn't know I had. I grabbed the gear shift and plunged it to neutral.

Ricker punched his leg down on the pedal again and again, but the truck slowed. He yanked the steering wheel to the left and we glanced off the edge of a car. The impact sent me onto the top of the dashboard, pinched in between it and the glass. Alden was moaning but I couldn't see him. He must have hit the window and fallen onto the bags. Blood poured down Hugh's face from his nose and dribbled into his lap. Our engine noise did not cover up the engines behind us.

Sometimes if you played along with the memory, you could change what happened. I had learned that with my Faints and it had worked with Jimmy.

"Ricker, they'll catch us! You have to turn the lights off. You have to hide us somewhere."

Ricker's cheek twitched. His fingers tightened on the steering wheel. He blinked and a light came back into his eyes. The headlights switched off. The darkness felt complete, almost suffocating, but those other lights were still behind us and growing larger as the growl of their engines grew louder. He was aware enough to shift back into drive. I let him do it. There wasn't anything to do. We couldn't let Sergeant Bennings catch us.

The truck jumped forward then settled in at a slower speed, but now the driving was more dangerous than ever.

Ricker turned left, then left again, and then a right, deeper into a neighborhood, but all we could see were the boxy shadows that loomed out. I didn't know where we were. I could only hope Ricker did.

He pulled us into a church parking lot. He drove to the back of it, parked behind a dumpster, and shut off the engine. The silence rang in my ears. We were quiet now except for our breathing, but our breathing was so heavy I swore it could be heard blocks away.

Engine noise blared, faded, blared again, faded away completely.

"We should keep going," Alden said, his voice quiet.

"We can't," Ricker said, his voice small and strangled. "I don't know how to get back."

CHAPTER 32

IT TOOK US UNTIL DAWN before we found the road we needed. The clouds in the east were this gross brown with edges of pink. The clouds in the other direction were a thick mass of brown that formed a wall. Everything on either side of the road was black and charred beyond recognition.

Hugh was awake. His gun was gone—it had never made it into the truck. While he'd been unconscious, I stripped him of his mask, his gloves, his long sleeve shirt. His face was crusted over in dried blood. His nose was swollen and purple. When he woke, Ricker explained that, as long as he remained calm, we would not infect him.

Hugh saw the bright red blood that had seeped through my wrist bandage. He pressed as far into the passenger door as possible without melting into it.

I didn't need to look behind me to recount. Two bags of the ANFO, a coil of detonator rope, one bucket, and Alden, sore and bloodied, on top of all of it, making sure we didn't lose what was left.

These last few hours had been tense but quiet. It felt like we were between storms. At any moment the relief would end and this time the end would be final.

There were two dots on the gray road ahead. "There, Ricker." I pointed with my good hand. Gabbi and Mary. The oak trees lined the bottom of the road, along the fence. The river rushed by, cool and calm, because none of what we did mattered to it yet.

Ricker slowed the truck and the brakes shrieked. His eyes were bloodshot. His hands shook as he released the steering wheel.

Gabbi rushed to the hood. Dried mud still coated her skin. Her clothes were torn. Long, angry scratches ran through the white scars of names on her arm.

"Tabitha's gone. Mary's flipping out."

Behind Gabbi, Mary rushed up and her hands were in the shape of claws. Her hair was long and tangled around her head. The gloves and duct tape dangled from her wrists like streamers from a bicycle. Her mask was halfway off her face—her mouth was exposed.

I yelled at Ricker to open the door. If Gabbi got bit she'd be gone. We had no hope of a cure to bring her back.

Hugh cried out next to me and pushed at the seat as if he could vanish into it.

Ricker wasn't moving fast enough. He opened the door, but Mary was already there. She pinned Gabbi to the hood. The windshield acted like a horrifying movie screen.

A figure slammed feet first onto the middle of the hood,

denting the metal.

The figure crouched on all fours and then stood.

Alden.

He extended a hand out to Mary. She snapped at it instead of at Gabbi. He snatched back his hand in time and began to speak. Low, soft words. He almost sang them, like a lullaby.

Ricker left the truck. My hands trembled with fear as I followed. Alden stood above us and he looked so much like his father from the night before, when Sergeant Bennings had shouted and fired shots and directed the flames, it made me shiver. I tried to blame it on the cold morning air.

The ground crunched under my shoes. I would throw myself between Mary and Gabbi while Alden distracted her.

Alden held up a hand. "I've been with her everyday for a long time now. She knows me better than anyone at this point. She knows I'll take care of her."

Gabbi's mouth moved, but no words came out. I knew she wanted to deny everything Alden had just said, but she was still pinned to the hood. The manic light in Mary's eyes shut her up.

Alden bent closer. I held my breath. If Mary bit him, we'd have to give him the Feeb infection from our blood to keep him from turning V.

He inched forward on the hood.

Mary tilted her head like a dog listening closely. He never stopped talking, he never stopped crooning—nonsense about sunrises and song lyrics and gardens and friends.

She pushed her head forward and allowed him to reposition the muzzle over her mouth. Next came the gloves. She held her hands up like a little child being dressed for the snow. He slipped the oven mitts back on. He separated the tape as best he could and re-wrapped it around her wrists.

When he was done, Mary relaxed and backed away. She looked at each of us like she could really see us. Tears welled up in her eyes.

"We should put her in the cab," Alden said. "She'll be safe in there."

For a split second Gabbi faced me and I saw the tears that streamed down her cheeks. All I could think was that even Dr. Ferrad hadn't figured out to make Mary better yet.

Ricker bustled Hugh out of the cab. Alden led Mary into it. Gabbi volunteered to watch Hugh because she knew nothing about explosives. I knew it was partly because she couldn't keep herself together and didn't want us to see it.

Alden and I helped Ricker unload the supplies. Two ANFO bags, detonator rope, a bucket of diesel fuel, a lighter sealed up in a plastic bag and tucked into the coil.

Ricker looked it all over and bit his lip, making it bleed. "I don't know if this is going to be enough."

My stomach sank at the thought this all might come to nothing. "It will have to be."

A grinding noise grew in the air until I couldn't ignore it anymore.

I remembered the rest of what Gabbi said.

"Tabitha."

The trucks and motorcycles barreled into view. They came up ahead of us—a dust cloud hundreds of yards away. More appeared from the buildings and drove to the fence.

Ricker tore into the bags and bucket.

Hugh shouted and tackled Gabbi. She fell toward the bumper. I saw it before it happened, how her head would hit the metal, how it would bounce off. My mouth opened in a silent scream. I held out my hands as if to catch her but she was too far away.

Her head hit the bumper. She fell to the ground and lay still.

Hugh ran down the road to the dust storm of approaching vehicles.

I went to Gabbi and knelt next to her on the ground. My heartbeat overwhelmed my hearing, my ability to breath. She had always watched out for me. She had always believed in me. She had always fought for me.

I couldn't tell if she was still breathing. I forced my heartbeat to slow down and my breathing to calm. I leaned over her so that my cheek was barely an inch away from her nose and mouth. I tried to remember what I'd seen in all those movies so long ago about how to give CPR.

How to bring her back.

I waited.

There.

She was breathing.

I drew in a sharp breath of my own. She was still alive.

I touched her hair and my hand came away, wet with blood.

Alden appeared. "Is she alive?"

"Help me with her," I said.

I cradled her bleeding head against my chest and grabbed up her shoulders. Alden held her legs. Every bump, every shift made me want to scream. We dragged her onto the truck bed, laid her out, and closed the bed. I wanted to cry. It hurt so badly to see her helpless like this. "You have to get her and Mary out of here."

"Come with me," Alden said.

I shook my head.

Ricker worked on the explosives. He looked like he was digging a hole. I couldn't leave without him. I would never do that to him.

I pushed Alden into the driver's seat. "Take them away." My bloody hands left bright red marks on his shirt. "If this doesn't work, make sure the machine is destroyed. Promise me, Alden."

His eyes held mine in a way that made me shiver. He placed his hand over my uninjured hand and pulled it to his heart. "I promise."

He opened the driver's door and climbed in.

Mary looked at us, wide-eyed, like nothing more than a scared kid at that moment. My heart ached because I knew Gabbi's own heart was broken over her.

"Take care of them," I said.

He shut the door and drove away. They disappeared and I felt myself go numb.

The dust cloud from the opposite way grew in size. The noise increased. The people behind the fence left the trucks and began to cut at the links. I swore I saw Tabitha with them.

I looked for Dr. Ferrad. Tabitha had run off to Dr. Ferrad because that was better than letting us destroy a cure that murdered people. They all wanted control and power and they were willing to kill for a cure that only brought more death.

I raced to Ricker's side. "How can I help?"

Ricker placed the bucket in the hole and strung out the cord. He shook his head. "Just get back, Maibe."

"Will it work?"

"We'll find out in about a minute."

He bent down to light the fuse. It caught and flared. A shot rang out.

Ricker fell over onto his side. Blood sprayed my face.

I shouted. The world spun but I forced it back into focus. Ricker had been shot. I couldn't let him die like this. Not like this.

A part of me whispered traitorous words to myself. All of us would die soon enough without a cure. Maybe this was a better way to go than to have him become a V.

I pushed those thoughts down into the pit of grief deep inside me. I dragged Ricker away from the spark that crept along the ground and into the bucket. When we reached the road's shoulder, I searched his body for the wound.

"Ricker, wake up! Get up!"

A motorcycle roared by. Next a truck swerved at us. Its side mirror punched me in the shoulder, pushing me into Ricker. We went flying down the slope. The world spun. I hit the water with a splash. The cold soaked me to the bone. I breathed in the brackish water and began coughing. I stumbled out, searching the mud and water for Ricker.

I found him, face up, eyes closed. Something inside me broke. I had always brushed him off, made him take back his words, denied the truth that had sat between us for so long. I had never told him—

The explosion threw me on top of him—a boom that made the earth tremble and the water bounce.

A cloud of orange flame spread into the air above us. Pebbles stung my cheeks. I struggled up from that orange darkness, screaming at myself to get up, get up, don't run. But the very thought of running made my legs take on a life of their own. Instead of my aunt I thought of that family of four and their girl with the braids. The memory hovered on the edge and I untangled it and set it down in the middle of my brain and lived it again. But this time I shaped it to my will.

I began to run.

I ran up the slope. I ran across the road.

I would get Ricker out of this somehow. I would steal one of their trucks and drag him up the slope—a sob caught in my throat. My brain whirled along at light speed trying to think of a way out of this. A way that would keep Ricker safe because he couldn't be dead. He couldn't be.

I ran to a truck that had tipped onto its side, and then ran to the next truck, its front mangled and pushed into the ground. The uninfected groaned inside and tried to pull themselves out. People were trying to help. Others sat on the ground stunned, bloody. Some of them didn't move. I ran to the edge of the blast zone, to the deep crevice that had formed where the bucket had been. It was mud, all mud. It was filling up with water—slowly. Too slow. My ears rang, my shoulder ached, my ankle hurt, my wrist burned. Dirt loosened from the edge and trickled down into the hole.

Something hard poked me in the back of the head.

"I should kill you," Sergeant Bennings said. "I should have killed you in that prison long ago. You want to destroy our one chance at the cure? You're insane."

I turned around. He was geared up again like a normal uninfected—mask, gloves, long sleeves and pants.

Tabitha stood beside him.

They looked at me like I was an annoying insect.

These last days working together meant nothing to him. I should have known that. I was a tool to find his son. I was a tool to get him and Tabitha to the cure.

They were both the kind of people who made sure to dispose of their trash. I was trash now.

I stood tall and didn't say a word. I would not give them the satisfaction. In my mind I told Gabbi I was sorry, I told Ricker things I should have said ages ago, I told Alden to run far away from his father and to take Gabbi and Mary with him. I told Corrina and Jimmy and Ano goodbye.

The ground rumbled underneath our feet. Ricker crawled onto the shoulder and my heart leapt. He was dripping wet. He pushed himself up to standing. Blood darkened one pant leg almost to black. He was alive. He had to be alive. A part of my brain whispered that no, he didn't have to be alive, that maybe he was a ghost-memory.

I didn't care. I decided to believe.

Sergeant Bennings raised the gun and pointed it between my eyes.

His people were still scrambling over the trucks. The ground shook like it was an earthquake. Sergeant Bennings lost his footing.

I slammed into his chest and drove the air out of his lungs. He fell onto his back, gasping, gun still in his hand. A grunt left his mouth. I grabbed for the gun, but he held onto it with an iron grip. I gave up and went for his eyes. I pressed hard even as everything turned into night again and I screamed for Jen Huey to stop and my throat felt like it had collapsed in on itself. He punched me on the side of the head. I fell over, jumped up and stomped on his hand until he let go of the gun. I grabbed it, but then something hit me and I was suddenly flying through the air.

I landed hard on my side. Tabitha wrestled the gun away.

The ground fell from under me. I grabbed at her shirt. The gun tumbled through the air and dropped out of sight. She shouted. My legs dangled in the air and she was the only thing keeping me from falling. The sky behind her was a sick brown. The water beneath me was an even sicker brown.

Tabitha's shirt ripped. My stomach flipped as I fell through the air. Tabitha came with me, her legs twisting her, end over end, like she was doing acrobatics. I hit water and the mucky wetness closed over my head. Water filled my nose, my eyes, my mouth, my ears. I couldn't tell which way was up anymore. I struggled but the muck had caught my shoes. The water pushed at me. Red spots appeared in front of my eyes. I kicked out but it did nothing.

I thought about Gabbi and Ricker and how maybe they were dead. I thought about Ano and Jimmy and how maybe it would be better not to see them waste away and die. Maybe it would be easier if this all ended here. I decided if I died because the water took me on its way to the machine, I would be okay with that. I decided if that was the payment demanded of me, so be it.

There was a deep rumbling like the heart of the earth was opening up. Water pounded into me, dislodging me from the mud. I spun in circles. As if driven by instinct, my body kicked in the direction I thought was up.

I settled on something I could move against.

I dug my hands and feet into the ground and felt brittle stalks between my fingers. I pushed up onto my knees and my head broke through to the surface. I gasped for air. My lungs burned, my brain spun with dizziness. The water flowed strongly around me and threatened to take me under. I crawled diagonally against the current. Every few feet the power I fought against lessened until it disappeared altogether. Here, the water lapped up an inch at a time to cover the bone-dry soil. I looked around and saw I was more than a hundred yards away from the trucks and motorcycles that stood in silhouette on the road.

Ricker's explosion had worked.

Ricker.

I pushed myself to my feet and ran across a dry part of the field, then scrambled up the slope to the road. My shoes squished at each step and felt heavy, so heavy. My legs felt like Jello. A section of road was missing now. There was no getting to the other side. Three trucks were stranded on that side, the people scrambling back from the lip of road that kept crumbling. As I watched, the road took another one of the trucks with it. The remaining people on the other side jumped into the working trucks and drove off.

I ignored the pain that roared in my body. Minutes had gone by, but Ricker was still in the middle of the road, on my side of the gap, sitting up, staring out at the water. I ran to him. The sunlight made his face look ghastly, dangerously white. He pressed both hands over his thigh. Everything there was red, slick with his blood.

I searched the back of the truck left on our side and found rags and rope. I rushed back to Ricker with these tools in my hands.

He closed his eyes when he saw me. "Maibe? I saw you get washed away. Are you a ghost now? Am I seeing you as I would wish to see you?"

I tore the rags into strips. "I'm not a ghost."

"But you would say that even as a ghost." A hint of a smile on his lips. "I can't believe everything I see, you know."

"Believe this, Ricker. I'm not a ghost." I tied the strips around his leg and cinched them tight.

He screamed out in pain.

"See? Not a ghost."

"You must be real. This makes me want to cut off my leg. In my ghost-dreams you always kiss me."

I kissed him. I thought I was going to die. I thought we were all going to die and that it would be my fault because I always got people killed. But he was alive.

When I let go I held my face only a few inches away from his. He cupped his hand around my cheek. I closed my eyes and leaned into his touch.

"Did it work?" He whispered.

I opened my eyes. The water spread across the fields. People raced between the buildings like rats. The road continued to drop into the gap, widening it. There was no one left on this side with us. No Tabitha. No Sergeant Bennings. Only the one truck that looked like it might still run.

"I think so."

I helped Ricker stand. He kept weight off the leg and used my help to hop himself to the truck. When he entered the cab he collapsed. His face flushed and his eyes rolled into the back of his head.

"Ricker!"

I slapped his cheeks because I didn't know what else to do. I needed him to stay with me. I needed him to tell me what to do.

I needed him.

His head lolled on his shoulders. "Maibe, you don't know how to drive."

"Sure I do." I said this like he was being ridiculous and it was no big deal. I stretched his wounded leg out onto the seat bench. The keys were still in the ignition. My hands shook as I turned them. The engine coughed, grated, shuddered.

"Stop. It's already on. They must not have shut it off."

"Right," I said, my voice unsteady.

"Put the gear shift in reverse, you can't turn around here, it's too narrow." Ricker forced his eyes open. "You're going to have to drive out of here backwards."

"Right," I said. Less sure now. I knew what driving was supposed to involve.

Theoretically.

I pressed down on the gas. The truck lurched backward and fishtailed. One tire left the ground and edged over the shoulder into the air.

"Forward, drive it forward."

I changed the gear and slammed on the gas. The tires spun, caught, and flew the truck back up onto the road. I slammed on the brakes. The truck slid to a stop inches from the gap Ricker's explosion had created. The water rushed by like a river. Another foot forward and we would nose-dive into the pit. I imagined the truck going over and the way the cold water would flow into the cab and fill it up. Maybe I could swim out and save myself, but Ricker wouldn't be able to—not with his leg. We would drown in the water together because I would not let him die alone.

I would not let him die.

Not like this.

This moment was all there was. I couldn't let myself think about what would come after. I couldn't think about the future in store for Ano, for Jimmy—for all of us. We had to survive this first. We had to make sure the machine was destroyed.

Ricker held onto his leg with one hand and braced himself against the dashboard with the other. His skin was pale and shined with sweat. He kept blinking like he was trying to hold on to consciousness. I had to get us to a safe enough place to stop Ricker from bleeding to death.

"You can do this, Maibe. Just slow down. Ease into reverse, keep looking backward but keep one hand on the wheel."

Panic made my fingers slippery on the wheel. My soaked wrist bandage dripped pink water all over. Alden and Gabbi and Mary needed us. We had to find them. They would help me save Ricker. I shifted into reverse and pressed my foot down like the pedal was a soft pillow. The truck inched backward at an angle. I adjusted the steering wheel and the truck angled even further in the wrong direction.

"Other way," Ricker said, his voice full of pain.

I turned the wheel, wincing as I did it, fearing I would over-correct and send the truck tumbling off the other side.

The truck straightened out. I pressed my foot down to pick up speed.

It seemed like an eternity, the truck bouncing in reverse, Ricker holding on, but fading, the landscape roiling with smoke and water. We hit an intersection and I used it to flip the truck around so I could drive forward.

"You made it," Ricker said. Blood had puddled on the bench.

He fell unconscious.

ALDEN

Truck lights appeared. The sun was at the horizon. They were outside the truck, hiding against it. He waited next to Mary. Gabbi was on the other side of him. She had a monster of a headache, but he thought her injury couldn't be that bad if she was already awake.

"Do you think it's Dr. Ferrad?" Alden said, speaking to Mary, even though he knew she couldn't answer. It was the wrong direction to be Maibe and Ricker.

"Just be ready," Gabbi said.

She looked at him in that judgmental way of hers that said somehow her time on the streets still counted for more than these last three years of survival ever could. He didn't understand how Maibe could stand her no matter how loyal she was.

"I am," he said. "More than you could know. You have no idea what I've been through these last few months."

"Yeah. You're right. I don't. I've never been captured or held

prisoner...oh wait, yes I have—by your father."

"It's not the same. They tortured me."

"By curing you?"

"They killed people—" he gritted his teeth and told himself to quit it. The truck was coming, the truck needed to be stopped. Dr. Ferrad needed to be ended. All they had was a knife left in the dashboard. A stupid knife.

It would have to be enough. He would make it be enough.

"All right, Alden. I'm sorry. You're right. Just breathe okay?"

He let out an explosive breath he hadn't known he'd been holding. He jumped up and balanced on the balls of his feet.

"Wait, they might have guns," Gabbi said.

The truck slowed at the barricade they'd made out of their vehicle. He had feared exactly this would happen—that in the chaos Dr. Ferrad would escape and it would all start over again.

In the back of the oncoming truck there was something big covered with a tarp and tied down with rope. He just knew Dr. Ferrad had gotten out the machine—that terrible, evil contraption that stole someone's blood and transformed it into something that killed off both infections.

Dr. Ferrad stepped out.

He dashed around even as some part of him heard Gabbi tell him to stop.

Dr. Ferrad saw him. He realized he wanted her to pull out a gun and shoot him. That would be the easiest way to solve everything that had happened.

Fear filled her face and she held up her hands in surrender.

He pulled the knife out from his belt and decided he wasn't going to stop. He was going to keep running and bury the knife in her chest where her heart should have been, if she had ever had a heart.

Something stopped him.

He didn't know how long he stood there, knife out, or how long Dr. Ferrad stayed frozen, her hands up and trying to protect herself.

Sometimes his memory still didn't work right.

He heard his name. He heard Maibe's voice.

"Alden?"

Dr. Ferrad's eyes were bloodshot behind her orange-rimmed glasses. "I know what I've done is not enough. It is only one step closer. I will not stop. I have not stopped my search for a cure that could end this all humanely. Don't think I don't feel the cost." She wiped her forehead with the back of her hand.

Maibe stepped in between Dr. Ferrad and the knife in his hand. Alden's fingers shook. He'd done all of this for her. He had searched for the cure because he'd wanted it for her.

"Why don't I get trapped in the fevers like the others?" Maibe asked. "Why me and not the others?"

Dr. Ferrad squinted at Maibe. She dropped her hands to her side. "The virus and the bacteria are meant to balance each other out but reinfection overwhelms the balance."

"We know this," Maibe said. "People who get attacked by Vs don't come back now."

Dr. Ferrad nodded. "Blood acts as a sterilizing agent for the two infections over time. Saliva and sputum contain heavy enough loads—"

"I don't understand," Maibe said. "Just tell me—"

"This is what I mean," Dr. Ferrad said. "You must let me continue my work. Come with me. Help me. I am so close to another breakthrough. I have discovered so much more about the airborne *qualities of the bacteria—"*

"The bacteria is airborne?" Maibe said.

Dr. Ferrad stepped forward.

Alden raised his knife.

"Please." Dr. Ferrad winced and stepped back. "The bacteria evolved. Or maybe the mutation was always there and they didn't see it. They engineered it, you know, to fight the Lyssa virus, but they didn't realize such a simple mutation would take the Borrelia alucinari airborne. It prefers the lung and brain tissue and spreads like tuberculosis. Not through blood, not through saliva—"

"That's stupid," Gabbi said. "We were all infected through blood—"

"In the beginning, yes," Dr. Ferrad said, "but no longer and never with the bacteria."

"You're crazy!" Gabbi said. "My friends are dying, trapped in the fevers because they got bit by Vs one too many times."

"Exactly," Dr. Ferrad said, sounding triumphant.

"Help me save my friends," Maibe said. "They're trapped in the fevers. They were Feebs and got bit by Vs and now they're trapped."

Dr. Ferrad adjusted her glasses. "I can do that."

Anger flared inside Alden. "She's lying. Look at her. She's lying to you. She doesn't know."

"I know enough," Dr. Ferrad said. "Give me time and I will figure it out."

Maibe looked at me with those dark eyes I'd always lost myself in.

"She'll come with us," Maibe said.

I could forget what she looked like when I was staring at those eyes. I could forget what the disease had done to her when she looked at me like I was all that mattered in the whole universe.

"We'll take her back," Maibe said. "We'll watch her and make sure—we'll destroy the machine."

Dr. Ferrad's eyes widened. "I cannot let you do that."

He snapped to attention. Time sped up. He realized something terrible about himself. He hadn't wanted the cure to save Maibe—not just to save her. He'd wanted the cure because then if she had it, if she looked normal again, maybe they could be together. He couldn't bear to be with her the way she was now. Feeb skin, Feeb memories. He thought maybe he could have loved her except for the disease. He knew this was a terrible flaw inside of him. He wanted to blame his father for this, for helping make him this way, but he knew deep down that maybe he was born this way. Maybe he'd always been a coward.

His hand was still raised, ready to complete the arc. Just another few feet and Dr. Ferrad would be dead and she would deserve it.

"Alden, stop." Maibe's voice pleaded with him.

He flinched under that voice. "She's lying. The information needs to die with her."

Dr. Ferrad moved. Her hand hovered at her waist. Was she reaching for a weapon?

"Don't do this to yourself, Alden. She's not fighting back."

His hand wavered in the air and then steadied. "I'm okay with that." He drove the knife forward. Rays of sunlight bounced into his eyes. This did not prevent him from seeing Dr. Ferrad's eyes widen, how she waited for death, how she didn't fight back, how there was no weapon at her waist.

Gabbi yelled, "Stop!"

There was a blur and suddenly Mary was there and she dove

for Dr. Ferrad's neck and he was driving the knife into her back before he could stop. Her muzzle was off, her gloves were off. The tape trailed from her wrists like a dozen broken leashes.

CHAPTER 33

I CRIED OUT AND RAN for Mary and Alden.

Mary's mouth buried into Dr. Ferrad's neck. Blood spurted and Dr. Ferrad's eyes rolled into the back of her head. Metallic smells filled the air. Dr. Ferrad went limp.

The knife stuck out of Mary's back. She dropped Dr. Ferrad and stumbled to her knees. Her hair was tangled like a huge bird's nest.

Gabbi rushed over. Mary fell onto her face.

Long minutes passed and no one moved except for Gabbi. She rocked Mary like a small child while Mary bled out. We all knew it. Mary was going to be dead soon.

When I couldn't stand it anymore I forced myself onto my feet and checked Dr. Ferrad for a pulse. I didn't need to check— she was a mess and the smell of blood made me gag—but I did it because this was my fault and I had to be sure.

Dr. Ferrad was dead.

With her death had died any chance at bringing back Jimmy and Ano, or keeping Gabbi and Ricker from going V, or me from going Faint.

Ricker helped us take the machine apart. Mostly he sat on the ground, his injured leg extended, as he told me and Alden what to do.

I couldn't look at Alden. When he reached for one of the tubes, I flinched. When we pried open a panel, the metal screeching and leaving indents on my skin, I made sure our fingers didn't accidentally touch. Alden focused on the work, even as a tear dripped down his nose.

I would have tried to comfort him before.

He had killed Mary.

He hadn't killed Dr. Ferrad himself, Mary had done that, but if she hadn't gotten in the way—the knife sticking out of Mary's back said it all.

I didn't know what that made him now, or maybe what that had always made him. Or maybe I did know and didn't want to admit it. I couldn't stop seeing a replay of every time he had shrunk from my infected skin, every time I'd caught a look of disgust on his face, every time he flinched at the ugliness he saw in me.

Each piece of the machine we destroyed became like an unraveling. People had died to make Alden uninfected. Their blood had passed through this thing and transformed into something else that stole away their souls even as Alden regained everything he had lost.

Except that was a lie.

He'd lost his soul in exchange for their lives. He was more like his father than I had ever wanted to admit.

A part of me knew I was being unfair. A part of me knew my anger and my despair at everything we now faced—at going home empty-handed while watching Gabbi and Ricker disappear into the V virus—was unfairly pinning all of this on him.

I didn't care.

We tore apart that machine and we tore apart our friendship along with it.

We finished the work in silence because I had no words left for him.

We tossed everything into the water that filled the bowl of land behind us.

The buildings were destroyed. The uninfected would have been driven out by the flood.

It was finished.

When the machine sunk out of sight, I went and sat next to Ricker. I grabbed his hands and pressed both of them to my cheeks. He smelled like mud and sweat and home. He held me that way for a long time and he didn't say anything even though tears tracked down his cheeks.

Our victories were hollow. We would go home to Ano and Jimmy and Corrina and Dylan with no more than what we had started with.

No, that wasn't true.

We would go home without any hope left.

All this time I'd fooled myself into believing we were dead. It didn't matter if I gave up trying because we were already dead, our bodies just hadn't caught up yet. I'd told myself this lie because I couldn't face all the loss and my own part in it.

Deep down, I had always known the truth but I could only admit it to myself now that we headed toward what felt like a final death.

Alden stood up. He looked at how Ricker touched me and how I needed that comfort from him.

"I'm going to find my father," Alden said.

I did not argue. He had turned into someone I didn't recognize.

"He's probably dead," Ricker said. "I saw him go into the water."

Alden reached out and touched my shoulder as if in farewell.

I flinched.

He smiled a sardonic smile. "I understand."

Alden walked into the sun and disappeared in its light.

I wanted to sit on the road and cry until there was nothing left inside of me. Instead, I helped Ricker over to Mary and Gabbi. Even those steps left him weak. He rested a hand on Gabbi's shoulder. She shook it off.

"Gabbi," he said.

Mary was like a statue.

"We need to go home," Ricker said.

"That's all she wanted, you know." Gabbi wiped her nose on her arm. The arm with the red scratches and the white scars. "She wanted a home for all of us."

I knelt down. "Let's go home then. Let's go home, Gabbi. She'd want us to all be together again."

Gabbi sniffed. Nodded. The light in her eyes hardened.

We spent the next few hours digging. We hiked down the slope on the dry side and dug Dr. Ferrad's grave at the base of the levee road. The ground was soft from the water that flooded the other side. This road wouldn't last much longer, but it would be long enough.

We buried Dr. Ferrad.

There was room for Mary, but I stopped them.

"We should take her with us. I think she would have liked Corrina's garden. We should bury her there."

Ricker gently set Mary's body back on the ground. Gabbi rubbed angry tears from her eyes.

I put a comforting hand on Gabbi's shoulder. She didn't shrug it off. "We'll find a safe place for tonight and then I want you to carve Mary's name into my arm."

CHAPTER 34

GABBI DROVE BECAUSE I wasn't very good at it and Ricker couldn't use his leg.

We stayed the night in a little gas station and filled up the truck's tank. Mary remained in the truck bed, wrapped in layers of bedsheets scavenged from a nearby house.

Gabbi used a bottle of alcohol on a knife before cutting Mary's name into my skin. We howled at the moon for Mary and dared any Vs to attack. None came.

The truck took us home. My arm stung from the fresh scars. My wrist and ankle were inflamed, swollen—infected. Ricker's leg looked an even uglier red. We dumped a bunch of alcohol on our wounds and scrubbed everything out with toothbrushes, but if it helped we couldn't tell.

I sat in the middle of the truck bench. The air conditioning was long broken. The windows were down. All three of us sat in puddles of sweat. The wind helped with the smell, but mostly it gave us an excuse not to talk. Mary's body in the truck bed was a silent accusation.

The Feeb infection had never really changed who we were, not where it mattered most. But I hadn't believed that even though I could see it so clearly now.

Now that we had failed our friends.

Now that we returned with nothing.

Gabbi dealt with constant headaches. She kept rubbing at her eyes even though we'd slept like the dead. The smoke still hung in the air but began to thin. There were wrecked cars, trees that had toppled, buildings that had burned and spread destruction when they'd fallen. We stopped a lot to use the map we'd taken from the gas station. We found ways around all of it.

By late afternoon on the third day, we had made it into the mountains. We watched now for Vs or uninfected or other Feebs, not wanting to draw them along with us.

Gabbi stopped the truck at the obstacle course entrance. The birds sang us a chorus. The trees were green and tall. The weeds grew thick underneath where the sunshine touched them. The air here was fresh and for the first time in days there was blue sky instead of smoke.

These sights and sounds should have filled our hearts with happiness. Instead we walked around the obstacles like it was a funeral march. Gabbi and I slowed our pace to match Ricker's limp. We were careful of the sharp edges and the spiderwebs and the dead ends. We expected to be seen at any moment.

What we didn't expect was silence.

We walked into the center of town. The old Gold Rush-era buildings welcomed us home. The paint was peeling, the sun was hot, the hotel was the tallest building around. Everything was how we'd left it except for the tire tracks. They cut deep grooves into the soil where Sergeant Bennings and his people had been.

The three of us headed for the church-turned-hospital. We didn't need to discuss it.

My wrist throbbed, my arm burned, my ankle ached, but they were nothing next to the pain my heart felt. None of this felt right.

Corrina and Dylan should have been out to see us already. She would have hugged me up into her arms like I was a thirteen year old kid again. She would have gasped at my wrist and sat me down to take care of it. Dylan would have touched the small of her back as she worked and she would have smiled up at him.

We stepped into the church. The floorboards creaked under our steps. The beds were full. Every bed contained a Faint. Corrina's table was cluttered to overflowing with glass containers, piles of books, bundles of herbs, orange pill bottles.

I saw Corrina in one of the beds. Her hair pillowed her head and her hand trailed off the side. An IV hooked into her wrist and a dreamy smile spread across her face.

"No, no, no." The words came out in a cry and I rushed to her bedside. She was breathing, but she was gone, like Jimmy. She'd turned Faint.

A person shuffled out from the back. I looked up, feeling stunned and numb.

His beard was dark and scruffy, almost making him unrecognizable. His eyes were bloodshot. His arms carried bags filled with clear liquid. It was Dylan.

"Maibe?" He dropped the bags and rubbed at his eyes. He bent over like an old man and began picking up the bags. "Stop it, Dylan. You can't lose it now. Get yourself together."

"Dylan?" I stepped toward him. "It's me. It's really me."

He stood up slowly. Most of the bags were still on the floor. He squinted at me and then his eyes hit on something behind me. I turned and saw Ricker and Gabbi at Jimmy's bedside. Alden's mother was in a bed next to Jimmy, a smile plastered to her face too.

"Where's Ano?" Gabbi said. "Where's Kern?"

Dylan blinked. "Is it really you? You're really back? Do you have the cure? Did you find it?" Each question rose in volume and somehow increased the light that shined in his eyes.

I shook my head. The movement drew his attention back to me. "We didn't find it. There isn't one."

My words punched the breath out of him. He bent over again and picked up the remaining bags of fluid. He went to Corrina's bedside. His clothes were wrinkled and he smelled like he hadn't washed in days. I knew I must not smell much better.

"It's just me now." He brushed Corrina's hair back from her sweating face and adjusted the IV that dripped into her arm. "Some of us turned V and we couldn't stop them in time. The uninfected are gone. Some of them turned Faint, others ran when they were only a handful left. We're all Vs or Faints now. I suspect I'll be joining them soon enough."

He motioned to the empty bed next to Corrina. His arm had a white bandage wrapped around it. He half-smiled. "I'm prepared."

"What's that from?" I pointed to his bandage.

"One of the Feebs who went V. She bit me."

"You didn't get trapped in the fevers?"

He shook his head.

My mind began to spin. It was too simple.

I smoothed out Corrina's bedsheet. Sweat glistened on her forehead.

Dylan pointed at my bandaged wrist. It wasn't clean like his. Blood and pus soaked through the layers and my skin was swollen around the bandage. Shaky red lines snaked up my arm.

"That doesn't look good."

I shook my head and bit my lip. "It's from a V, but I didn't get trapped in the fevers."

And I hadn't fallen into a Faint episode in a long time either. I'd been losing hours at a time. The Faint episodes had been crowding so close together and then they had just stopped.

Gabbi and Ricker approached.

"Where are they?" Gabbi demanded.

Dylan motioned us to the back of the church. He shuffled through a set of doors and they followed. I promised myself I would follow soon but my brain buzzed with questions that needed answering. I needed to just stay still for a minute and let it puzzle through all the pieces.

We'd tried blood transfusions before. If someone was turning Faint, give them V blood. If someone was going V, give them Faint blood.

It had never worked.

But maybe just like the virus and bacteria had evolved over time—maybe things worked differently now.

I ran to Corrina's table of medical supplies. I rifled through the glass containers and the bundled herbs. A beaker crashed to the ground. Glass shattered and flew everywhere. I found what I was looking for and snatched it up.

Gabbi and Ricker rushed back into the room.

"What happened?" Gabbi said.

"Are you okay?" Ricker said.

I drew blood from Corrina's arm. I held up the syringe. "Where's Ano?"

I didn't bother letting them answer, but rushed into the back room of the church. My brain was buzzing and my muscles were so tense I thought if I wasn't careful I would jump through the roof.

This was going to work. Somehow this had to work.

The doors had blocked the moans before, but now there was no stopping it from reaching my ears. At least ten people were strapped down to beds in this room. Their arms and legs were tied off, sometimes even their head and chest.

Ano was in the corner, thrashing against the straps. He'd lost so much weight. His collar bone stuck out under his shirt. He'd lost all the flesh and muscle on his arms. His face looked sunken in and revealed the shape of his skull underneath.

I plunged the syringe into his arm.

Ricker, Gabbi, and Dylan crowded around.

We watched Ano breathe in and out, shout in Spanish, strain and grit his teeth and collapse again on the bed and repeat the process. I strained to see a change, any change. I didn't know if he and Corrina were the same blood type, but that shouldn't matter. He wasn't getting a blood transfusion, he was getting a fresh dose of the Faint bacteria. It was supposed to balance out the overload of virus he'd gotten each time he'd been injured by a V. That was what Dr. Ferrad had talked about. That was the point. Balance.

It felt like we held our collective breath for hours.

"How long is this supposed to take?" Dylan said.

"I don't know," I said.

IT WAS LATE EVENING NOW. We had gotten chairs. Dylan brought in some canned peaches and water for our dinner, but otherwise we used the time to help change bedpans and IVs. As the hours ticked by and the moans stayed the same, I thought I might go mad.

"It should have worked by now," Gabbi said. "Right?"

"I don't know how long it's supposed to take," I said.

She looked at me until I looked away.

"But yeah, I think so," I said. "It seemed like it was almost immediate when it happened to me. Each time the V bit me..." I trailed off.

Ricker and Gabbi perked up.

My brain buzzed again. The syringe was next to Ano's bed. But that was wrong.

The bacteria spread like tuberculosis—through the air.

I had begun turning Faint after living with my own Faints—after sharing the same air for months. Dr. Ferrad had said the blood, given enough time, would neutralize the infections. Maybe the lungs kept the bacteria strong, maybe you couldn't get the right dose through the blood, but you could get it through the air. That's why whenever we found Faints it was usually everyone in the house. That's why some of the uninfected in town had turned Faint.

I thought about who else had turned Faint. Corrina. Dylan. They both practically lived in the Faint hospital. Jimmy. I didn't know how much time he'd spent with Faints, only that he had never gotten bit by a V after Mary had infected him.

I explained my ideas about the lungs and everything Dr. Ferrad said before she died. "We have to move all of them into the other room. Put every person who's gone V in between two Faints."

It was as if we were on fire. The four of us dragged the beds into the main church room within the hour. We placed Ano between Jimmy and Corrina. I moved Molly, Freanz, and the twins to the center of the room. They'd been infected longer than most, maybe their breathing contained more bacteria.

We collapsed on a pew pushed up against one of the walls. The beds were packed together with barely any room to walk. Moans and shrieks filled the room. Some of the Faints twitched as if the noises triggered something deep inside their brains.

"Do you really think this is going to work?" Gabbi's eyes strayed to Kern who thrashed around on his bed. "Never mind. Just tell me it's going to work."

I shook my head. My arm pulsed with heat. My ankle had swelled and was leaking pus. Now both of my shoulders and my neck felt stiff and swollen. Something still wasn't right. I was missing a piece of this puzzle. Even if the Faints brought back the Vs, how were we going to get back Jimmy and Corrina?

I considered drawing blood from Ano and giving it to Jimmy but my brain said that wasn't right. It wasn't in the blood. Corrina and Dylan had tried that before. Dr. Ferrad's machine had done all sorts of stuff to the blood before it worked.

My wrist flared as if in answer. Sweat poured down my neck and back. My brain was so fuzzy.

I forced myself to relive the details of each V attack over the last few weeks. Dr. Ferrad's "Exactly!" looped in my brain—

I stood up—

"What?" Ricker said, standing up with me. He felt my forehead. "Are you—"

He pushed a hand out and steadied himself against the wall. He couldn't walk on his leg anymore. It hurt too much. It was too swollen, too infected, just like my wrist.

Except not like my wrist.

At the cave, the V had bitten my ankle. Ricker had slapped me. It didn't trigger the memory-fever that always came. Except not always. Not after that V bite. I hadn't thought about it at the time—we'd been busy trying not to die. But even then, the solution had been right in front of me, I just hadn't seen it for what it was.

Tabitha had been bitten on the shoulder. I'd been bitten on the ankle and wrist. Neither of us had gotten trapped in the memory-fevers.

Bites were what had locked Ano and Kern into the fevers.

The Lyssa virus wasn't in the blood anymore.

It was in the saliva.

The fever kept my thoughts foggy. I didn't know how to get what I needed or put it where I needed it. I hobbled over to Ano's bed and stared down at him. I thought maybe his breathing had calmed over the last few hours, but it could have just been my imagination.

I looked around for something to swab Ano's mouth. I hesitated—Corrina would kill me for what I was thinking. There were so much other bacteria in the mouth. If this didn't work, a different infection would finish off all the Faints.

As best I could, I washed my hands, a knife, and Corrina's skin. She would have wanted me to test this on her instead of Jimmy in case things went wrong.

I used a piece of cloth and stuck it in Ano's mouth until it was soaked, then I opened up a thin cut in Corrina's arm. If I was right, Ano's saliva would be full of active Lyssa virus. Putting it into Corrina's bloodstream would trigger an immune system response or a bacteria response or—I didn't really know. Dr. Ferrad would have known. I could only guess and hope that this time it would work even though everything else we tried had failed.

I rubbed the saliva-soaked cloth into Corrina's cut before wrapping it tight around her arm.

When I finished it was like I had been holding the world on my shoulders and could finally let go. The adrenaline that had kept me moving drained away. All I could smell was the stink of my wrist and the swelling in my leg. My arm felt like it was twice as heavy as the other one. I sat down on the floorboards because the chairs were too far away. My bandage should be changed. I began to unwrap it. The cloth made a sucking noise as it unstuck from the layers of blood and skin. I blacked out.

I WOKE TO A BRIGHT LIGHT. Sun streamed in through the window and hit me in the eyes like a flashlight. I shifted on the bed. The sheets felt cool but in the heat I knew they would soon soak with my sweat. I felt clean at the moment and relished the feeling.

I was awake enough now to remember the last thing I had done before blacking out. My heartbeat increased. I looked at my wrist. It was re-bandaged with thick strips of gauze and the blood hadn't soaked through yet. Instead of the stink of infection, I smelled rosemary, lavender, and other scents I couldn't place. The swelling had gone down in my arm and leg. The red infection lines underneath my harsh Feeb lines had faded.

I tried to sit up.

"Hold on. Take it easy, Maibe."

Corrina's voice.

She sat next to me. Her hair framed her face. There was a grin on her lips. There were dark shadows under her eyes too, but that didn't matter. I didn't even care if she was a ghost-memory. I was so glad to see her. From the beginning, she'd taken me in, cared for me, did her best to protect me. To protect all of us. Tears sprang in my eyes. I used my uninjured hand to wipe them away.

"She's real." Gabbi sat on the other side of the bed. "In case you were wondering. She's not a ghost."

I laughed. The sound surprised me. When was the last time I had laughed?

"Ano? Jimmy? The others?" I held my breath for the answer.

"See for yourself," Corrina said.

Gabbi left my side. I was in a separate room, in a small office away from everyone. Gabbi came back with a wheelchair. The two of them bundled me into it.

"I can walk," I said.

"The infection almost killed you." The smile disappeared from Corrina's face. "You've been in a fever for five days."

I shuddered. I'd been so afraid of getting trapped in the V fevers and instead I'd gotten trapped inside a different kind of fever.

I was glad for their help after all. Moving from the bed to the chair left my muscles weak and shivering.

They wheeled me outside. It was still early morning. The

sunlight had hit the window at just the right angle to wake me. I wanted to ask a million questions, but one look at Corrina and Gabbi and I knew they weren't going to answer them until they were ready. They normally fought like cats and dogs. It was when they got along—that's when you really needed to worry.

Except. Except I wasn't worried. Corrina was awake. Gabbi wasn't scowling.

I felt my face bust into a grin.

Ano's saliva had worked.

Gabbi pushed me along the path to Corrina's garden. The path was overgrown, the weeds wild in their abundance, the colors outrageous in their brightness. We entered through the garden gate.

Along the wooden fence, against the trees, a fresh pile of dirt overlooked the garden beds. Picked flowers and herbs covered it. The dirt mound looked like a grave.

"We haven't made a marker for it yet," Corrina said.

"Ano and I are working on something." Gabbi's words were so quiet I almost didn't make them out.

"I'm glad she's here with us," I said. "I wish I could have known her like you did."

Gabbi gave me a funny smile. "You're too soft, Maibe. She would have forced you to toughen up or eaten you alive."

"Literally?"

Corrina sucked in a breath. Gabbi froze.

I'd spoken without thinking. I was feeling giddy, hopeful. But my joke had been disrespectful. Too soon. Too dark after everything that had happened.

Gabbi looked at Mary's grave.

I opened my mouth to apologize.

Gabbi laughed and there was both joy and darkness in it. Because that was Gabbi. That had always been Gabbi.

She pushed the wheelchair forward. "Forget what I said before. She would have liked you just fine."

I settled back into the chair and released my own shaky laugh. Corrina helped Gabbi push the wheelchair over branches and piles of leaves that made the wheels slip. On the far side, where the evergreen trees threw some shade, people sat together on a picnic blanket. They were talking and laughing and sharing plates of food. My stomach grumbled, but I ignored it. I looked for any sign that somehow this wasn't real. I looked carefully for those silver edges. I found none.

The air smelled sweet and clean. The heat hadn't yet burned off all the moisture from the night. The coolness even lifted goosebumps on my arms. I relished the feeling. The blue sky above us was clear. They took me right up to the blanket. I held my breath as everyone stopped talking.

Ano. Jimmy. Dylan. Even Kern was here.

Gabbi plopped onto the blanket next to Kern. He put an arm around her shoulder and she didn't throw it off. I wondered if she told him about his mother yet but decided now was not the time to ask. Jimmy cracked a joke I didn't quite hear and Dylan laughed next to him. Ano smiled, though the smile didn't quite reach his eyes. He still looked so thin. His eyes glanced at the fresh scar on my bare arm. Mary's name. The haunted look in his eyes told me he knew about all of it.

"Hello, Maibe," Ano said. "Welcome back. And thank you."

I flushed. It meant so much to hear him say that. Jimmy echoed his own thank you. I got embarrassed and looked over the garden.

"The saliva contained the active virus." Corrina shook her head. "The blood didn't. We hadn't thought—"

"I wouldn't have thought of it either," I said. "Except that I couldn't let go of what Dr. Ferrad explained. It was like the last missing piece of the puzzle. She deserves the credit." And my uncle too, for setting me on all those puzzles so long ago. "Not me."

"It wouldn't have mattered to her," Gabbi said. "She wanted a cure. She didn't want something that would make it okay to be a Feeb again. You didn't give up. You figured this out."

"I wonder how many people she killed to get the cure?" Jimmy said. "Don't you wonder?"

"No." Gabbi shook her head. "I really don't."

I looked back over the group. I decided it didn't matter if they thought Dr. Ferrad deserved the credit or not. I would remember how much she had helped, even if she hadn't meant to. My gaze rested on each face for a moment and my heart burst with love for all of them. They were here and alive. They were all here—

I sat up like a shot. I looked around. A roar rose in my ears. "Where's Ricker?"

There was a noise behind me. "Yes, my love? You called?"

Everyone laughed. I felt my cheeks flush.

I turned around in the wheelchair. Ricker had a crutch under one shoulder and limped toward our picnic. He carried something in his other hand, but what drew my attention was the crazy, neon yellow running shorts he wore. His injured thigh was bandaged from the end of the running shorts to his knee. He looked so worn out as he limped over and stood next to my wheelchair.

He fingered the edge of the shorts when he caught my gaze on them. He half-smiled. "It's the only thing that would fit around the bandage."

"Are you really okay?" I said.

"You had it worse," Corrina said, settling herself onto the blanket next to Dylan. "The bullet was still inside his leg, but once we got that out, it ended up being not much more than a torn muscle."

The smile disappeared from Ricker's eyes for a second. "Everyone is waking up because of you and we almost lost you." He grabbed my uninjured hand and squeezed it.

I squeezed back and relaxed into the comfort he offered. I scanned the blanket again, searching for people I knew weren't there. "Does it work on all Faints?"

Corrina shook her head. "Molly and Freanz and the twins aren't getting better."

My happiness deflated. I had hoped—

"But," Corrina continued. "They've been Faints longer than anyone else here. Maybe it'll just take longer. We'll keep trying."

I looked at each of their faces again. I soaked up the sunshine, the trees, the garden, Mary's grave. I had only known the real Mary through her friends, but I thought—I knew—this is what she had dreamed about. Her friends all together like this.

Safe.

As safe as we could ever be in this world.

"No matter what," I said. "We'll keep trying."

ABOUT THE AUTHOR

Jamie Thornton lives in Northern California with her husband, two dogs, a garden, lots of chickens, a viola, and a bicycle. She writes stories that take place halfway around the world, in an apocalyptic future, in a parallel universe—her books don't always stick to one genre, but they always take the reader on a dark adventure.

Join the Adventure through her email list to receive freebies, discounts, and information on more of her dark adventures.

Sign up at

WWW.JAMIETHORNTON.COM

IGNEOUS
BOOKS

OTHER TITLES FROM

LOOSE CHANGELING

A CHANGELING WARS NOVEL

A.G. STEWART

Trade paperback and ebook

Nicole always thought she was regular–issue human...until she turns her husband's mistress into a mouse. The next day, Kailen, Fae-for-hire, shows up on her doorstep and drops this bomb: she's a Changeling, a Fae raised among mortals. Oh, and did he mention that her existence is illegal?

Now she's on the run from Fae factions who want to kill her, while dealing with others who believe she can save the world. And there's the pesky matter of her soon-to-be ex, without whom she can't seem to do any magic at all...

OTHER TITLES FROM

Trade paperback and ebook

Murderers. Madmen. An ancient red–handed spirit named Molly. Patwin County is an unsettled place, full of shadows and secrets.

When Laura Livingstone's mother vanishes, Laura and her husband must find her before evil engulfs the county. As they search the streets of San Augustin, they uncover a terrible secret and fall into a supernatural horror beyond their imagination.

OTHER TITLES FROM

Trade paperback and ebook

When San Francisco is attacked by a giant mechanical spider, three unlikely heroes become humanity's last hope.

Can Dave, the manager of Carlione's Pizza Palace; Dawn, a comic book convention booth babe; and Johnny, a former bodybuilder and infomercial product salesman, come together to battle every diabolical obstacle Mechantula puts in their path?

Probably not.

29599531R00225

Made in the USA
San Bernardino, CA
25 January 2016